The Queen Must Die

Illustrations by Pamela Johnson

W • W • NORTON & COMPANY • NEW YORK • LONDON

WILLIAM LONGGOOD

The Queen Must Die

AND OTHER AFFAIRS OF BEES AND MEN

. . . .

*The text of this book is composed in Janson, with display type set in Zapf
Chancery Lite. Composition and Manufacturing by the Maple-Vail Book
Manufacturing Group.*
Book design by Antonina Krass

First Edition
. . . .

Library of Congress Cataloging in Publication Data

Longgood, William F. (William Frank), 1917–
The queen must die.

1. Honeybee.   2. Bee culture.   I. Title.
SF523.L66   1985   638'.1   84-8153

ISBN 0-393-01896-2

W. W. Norton & Company, Inc.
500 Fifth Avenue, New York, N. Y. 10110
W. W. Norton & Company Ltd.
37 Great Russell Street, London WC1B 3NU

1 2 3 4 5 6 7 8 9 0

This book is about those marvelous and perverse creatures, the bees. In a larger sense it is an appreciation of the daily miracles we dismiss as commonplace or overlook altogether, a minute examination of the small better to understand the larger canvas of life.

Bees are more than a hobby; they are a life study, in many respects a mirror of our own society.

William Longgood

PREFACE

In these pages I have tried to point out certain truths as they appear to me. They are, for the most part, only relative truths; absolute truth, in books as in life, is rare indeed. The most I can hope for is to approximate truth, as I see and comprehend it, to strike as near to it as I dare or can.

In beekeeping, as in most endeavors, there are many ways to accomplish the same tasks and many interpretations of the same facts or data, just as many roads lead to the same destination, although it is equally true that different individuals following the same road can arrive at different destinations. Research sources frequently give conflicting information, based on different observations and interpretations. A writer is often forced to go with that which seems reasonable and is consistent with his or her experience and vision of life.

For all that has been written about bees and their behavior, little is actually known about their more intimate lives, and almost nothing about their motivations and the forces that control them. This is my primary interest, and I have frequently speculated about why bees act as they do, often as perversely as people. There are, I am convinced, mystical qualities in bees, as in the rest of the life community, that elude the most learned and perceptive observers, and often we mistake the illusion of truth for truth itself. I suspect that bees, like other creatures, hear music unknown to human ears, as they march to drums unheard by us.

In presenting this book I will be accused of anthropomorphism, but I do not flinch from this charge. I think we have erred in trying to draw a distinct but arbitrary line between human behavior and that of other creatures. I similarly reject the notion of other life forms as lower orders and the common belief that they were intended only to serve man. We are all different. Each has a unique place and function in nature. Who is to say that one form of life is higher or better than another?

It is true that man dominates all other species. But does dominance necessarily confer superiority? Who is to say what is the great scheme of life? Who can say, with certainty, what each species' contribution is or was intended to be? We have defined the rules all must abide by, but this has changed through the centuries as our relationship to other animals has evolved with new perceptions, insights, and values.

Is it not also true that the life force beats in each of us, expressing itself differently in each? We are different and yet alike. We have similar basic needs that are satisfied in different ways. None is, in my opinion, superior to another. If man does indeed rest atop the biotic pyramid, as he boasts, it is not justification to subdue and exploit those below, but invokes a greater responsibility to better understand, protect, and accord other life forms the dignity, respect, and compassion that we all deserve as fellow transients on this planet that composes such a small part of the universe.

This book is not intended as a work of science or a manual on beekeeping. It is an effort to capture some of the mystery and poetry that I have observed in bees, and to enlarge our conception of the importance, beauty, and universality of all life.

The Queen Must Die

ONE

The bees are flying today and that is not according to the book. Bees usually don't fly unless the air temperature reaches fifty-five degrees Fahrenheit. This is a winter day, in late December, and the temperature is under fifty. The sun must have been shining directly on the hives and driven the temperature up inside, deceiving the bees. It must be a bit of a shock to them to venture outside, expecting benign warmth, and getting a blast of chilling air. It may be that the bees were not deceived but are merely being perverse. Bees almost never follow the rules laid down for them by their tenders. Beekeepers are forever grumbling about "those damned bees." But we have only ourselves to fault because we wrote the book, not the bees. We created our own false expectations.

Apparently, once outside and on the wing, the bees decide to complete the business that made them leave the hives. The snow is soiled with their droppings. It is startling how many brown spots there are; they dapple the snow and white hives as if someone had flicked a wet paintbrush.

Every couple of weeks the bees need a "cleansing flight" in the winter to rid themselves of accumulated wastes or they may come down with a severe bowel disease that, left untreated, can cause a colony to weaken or lead to heavy loss of life. Worker bees are so incredibly clean that they will risk death by flying in cold weather rather than befoul their home. Only the boorish males are guilty of soiling the hive, and there are not likely to be any of them in the winter colony.

When there is a long spell of cold and the bees can't get out to relieve themselves, on the first warm day they fairly explode from the hive; it is not unusual to see the snow splashed almost solid brown for several hundred feet in all directions. Generally bees do not go far from the hive on cleansing flights. This is sensible on their part. If they went any distance and the temperature suddenly dropped, they probably wouldn't make it back.

Bees, unlike humans, have a sound sense of their life mission. They work hard in the spring, summer, and fall, and in the winter they loaf, or take it fairly easy, like retirees at leisure. But that is not an altogether accurate statement. The bees that work so diligently from April through September are probably not the same ones that more or less knock off during the cold months. In the summer the field bees work so hard that their average life is only four to six weeks. Their wings beat about two hundred times a minute, which musicians say is in the key of C sharp below middle C. The fragile wings become ragged and torn, and finally wear out altogether so that they no longer will support flight. An experienced beekeeper can usually tell a bee's approximate age by the condition of her wings.

Hive values are such that when a bee no longer can fly and be an asset to the colony, she will remove herself from the hive rather than be a burden. If she lacks the grace to commit suicide, or to depart of her own will, she will be kicked out of the hive or killed outright by those she served so faithfully while she could. Human societies have no monopoly on ingratitude and treachery.

There is little sentiment in a hive. The motto, indelibly and invisibly etched in bee genes, is "work or die." Every female bee, except the queen, is expected to give full measure in hard labor for her keep, and the queen has her own biological obligations. This is a completely socialistic society, the direct opposite of the competitiveness and spirit of individual advantage that governs most human societies. No goods are owned privately. The collective wealth is the pooled honey in the combs and dedication to a common goal. The individual bee owns

nothing, and owes full allegiance to the colony. In exchange she is provided a place to live and work while she is a productive member of the community.

Many human communes could have used bees as their models, but such experiments seldom come off. Humans rarely are capable of the self-sacrifice and dedication of bees. On the other hand, bees are not wracked and diverted by sexual desire as humans are, and such wholehearted fidelity to ceaseless work may be a questionable virtue: is this drive motivated by pleasure or compulsion? Is it socially useful or only for personal gain?

In a beehive every effort is directed toward the common good. Every individual, except the queen, is expendable, but under certain circumstances even she is eliminated in a dark bee plot euphemistically known as "supersedure," which usually involves the queen's murder by her own daughters, but more about that later. The most ordinary colony is better organized than the most efficient man-made factory. And yet, even these models of nature's organizational efficiency and industry are sometimes less than perfect, beset by such human failings as sloppy workmanship, useless endeavor, and what appears to be poor management or faulty judgment. Bee colonies, like human societies, vary in the standards they set for themselves and in the life-styles they adopt. Some prosper while others barely manage to struggle along, existing on the bee equivalent of welfare provided by their keeper, and some fail altogether, often victims of their own shortcomings.

Worker bees make up almost the entire population of the hive. These are females that lack the ability to produce a fertilized egg necessary to generate a female worker bee like themselves. There is only one queen to a hive, although there have been cases in which a second or even a third have been tolerated, but this is so rare that it suggests some kind of perversion of nature's intentions.

The queen's only function is to lay eggs, as many as two thousand a day. Indeed, she is known as an "egg-laying machine." Completing the makeup of the hive are those comic-tragic, but vital, lusting clowns, the drones. There are relatively few of them in each hive and the number may represent less a necessity than a bee equivalent of conspicuous consumption. Drones are males conceived from unfertilized eggs laid by the queen. Their sole function is to mate with virgin queens, and most live and die without ever fulfilling this mission. The drone lives a life of bullying, nonproductive ease, like the worst free-loading relative, unless summoned to duty, in which case he may sacrifice his life, probably to his own surprise and dismay. For their intemperate ways, the surviving males eventually get their comeuppance in a bloody fall rite known as the "massacre of the drones," a drama that will unfold here in its place.

A worker bee's existence is regulated by a biological time-table, which is one of the profound mysteries that govern a hive. During her brief life, she performs many diverse chores: scavenger, nurse, producer of wax, molder of honeycomb, housekeeper, forager, fanner, water carrier, undertaker, guard, warrior, and, finally, martyr. She passes from one of these roles to another, depending on age and experience. A bee is like a worker in industry who is rewarded for her experience and length of service with successive raises and promotions, until the employee is considered more liability than asset and the employer seeks to unload her and bring in a successor who is young, inexperienced, and inexpensive; success often bears a price tag of diminishing returns.

For the bee, indignity rarely accompanies old age. As noted previously, she either resolves the problem by working herself to death or is dispatched by her younger sisters. The climax role for a worker is that of forager, or field bee, gathering pollen and the nectar that will be converted into honey; but at the same time she is expected to perform other, often menial, hive duties. Efficiency and hive demands and not personal status or job assignment determine her roles throughout life and into death. We know of no prima donnas or egotists in the hive. The function of a bee is always contingent on community need.

Scientists believe that bees, next to humans, have the most elaborate social structure and specialization of labor in the animal kingdom, one far more complex and sophisticated than formerly thought. Only ants and termites approach bees in the intricacy of their societies.

For the multiple, specialized tasks a worker bee performs, she has no training or prior knowledge that we are aware of, but takes to each succeeding role naturally. How does this extraordinary progression come about? Is it genetic transference? Some unidentified dietary substance or secretion that is responsible? Is it due to an abiding animus that dwells secretly in the hive, invisible and indecipherable, and provides this ability, this profound intelligence, that we observe without comprehending?

The mystery is compounded because each phase of a bee's development occurs on a fairly predictable timetable. One thing we know, as observers, is that from the moment of a bee's "birth" she is destined to work until she no longer can do so, but no one has the least notion what dictates this pattern of behavior. The queen and drones are equally condemned by the same invisible forces, although their roles differ. We watch the miracle that unfolds from their various labors with wonder but with little or no understanding of the origins or imperatives.

The colony, as noted, is ruled by one fixed law: those who do not or cannot work cannot remain in the hive and be a drain on its resources. There is no charity, no exception, no compassion. If a bee is born deformed, too weak, or not willing to work, it is ruthlessly killed or thrown out of the hive. The same fate awaits those who become too old or infirm to work. It also applies to victims of mishaps and heroines maimed in combat while guarding the hive against invaders.

There is, for the worker bee, no honorable retirement, no pension, no welfare program or reward for service to the community, no compromising of hive values. The individual bee means nothing. Only the continuing life of the colony counts. This is the first commandment of the hive—a manifestation of that mysterious and dispassionate force that guides all bee life. It is called, with little understanding of what it means, "the spirit of the hive."

The primary rule is inflexible: work or die.

TWO

I have, at this writing, been keeping bees for more than ten years, and in that time have observed and read about them extensively. Like most beekeepers, I understand bees only superficially, and then on the terms they set. Any deeper understanding eludes me. Bees are complex creatures and over the centuries they have worked out many successful strategies that are unique in nature. Much has been learned through observation about what they do but little about why they do it. Like most species, bees tend to protect their secrets from those who would invade their privacy. Only slowly and grudgingly have bees let us learn anything about their private lives, but they reveal nothing about their inner councils; theirs is one of nature's most effective conspiracies of silence and secrecy.

I am not sure how most people get into beekeeping. Interest is kindled in one way or another: possibly they had a friend or relative who kept bees, read an article that interested them, or saw something on television. Bees and men are closely enough related, as fellow members of a life community, that there should be an atavistic interest in some degree, unless this mechanistic human society has smothered such human inclinations as remain to us. Most of us have been trained to ignore or distrust our instincts and feelings unless they can be scientifically substantiated.

My own introduction to beekeeping was accidental. My son, who grew up in the sixties, had left home and was raising his consciousness in a commune-like house in New Jersey. As part of the great experiment in natural living and self-sufficiency, my son and his friends decided to keep bees and bought a beginner's outfit. It consisted primarily of a couple of wooden boxes, without tops or bottoms, generally called "supers," in which bees live and store honey; ten frames with sheets of beeswax, known as "foundation," for the bees to draw out as honeycomb; a bottom board on which to set the supers containing the frames of foundation; an inner cover to place on the top super; and a cover to fit over the inner cover and super. The outfit also included a smoker to subdue the bees, a steel "hive tool" to pry stuck frames and hives apart, a net to cover head and face, and a package of bees with a queen.

Fortunately, I do not know all of the details of the great experiment in raising consciousness, but the bees were hived, more or less successfully, which is probably more a tribute to the bees than to their unskilled would-be keepers. However, the first time the neophyte beekeepers tried to "work" (examine) the hive, the bees took offense and took after the beekeepers, and the beekeepers took to their heels.

The demoralized beekeepers did not return to the hive until the following spring. By then the bees were all dead, apparently starved for want of attention and because of poor timing in introducing them to the hive too late in the season to lay aside a store of honey to feed them through the winter.

I was the beneficiary of this small disaster in self-sufficiency. My son gave me the abandoned equipment. At first I did nothing with it. But gradually the notion grew in me to try my hand at beekeeping. I had a garden. Bees would complement the garden, and it would be interesting to learn more about the creatures. Couldn't I, too, be more self-sufficient?

Since I already had the equipment, why not? Wasn't it a sinful waste not to use that which was already paid for and available? That appealed to what my son calls my "lively sense of thrift."

By coincidence I read in a local paper about a bee school to be held in a town on the opposite end of Cape Cod, where we had recently moved. The course was free, which also appealed to my lively sense of thrift, and I signed up with some forty others of many ages, men and women, for the four sessions. The course was given in a bank's basement meeting room by a couple recently turned beekeepers themselves, the man a retired air force colonel; both man and wife were equally enthusiastic about beekeeping. They brought in area beekeepers as guest lecturers and showed rented or borrowed films. The final session, given at the couple's home in a rural area, was a field demonstration in hiving bees.

The lectures were not well structured, and the volunteer instructors, while generous with their time and information, were not experienced teachers. From the classes I gained only a fragmented, theoretical idea of how to keep bees. At the first session, however, I had committed myself by ordering a package of bees to be delivered after the final session. About half of those attending the course ordered bees. Many of the others never returned after the first class, or subsequently vanished, apparently having decided that beekeeping wasn't for them.

Several were discouraged by the initial cost or were victims of what I have come to think of as the "fantasy curve." Fantasy draws many people to attend classes and attempt new ventures, but when they realize the work and commitment required, the majority tend to fall by the wayside, a kind of social Darwinism that separates the committed from the uncommitted, the interested from the uninterested, the doers from the dreamers. The fantasy curve invariably swoops downward. I conceived it when I taught writing courses in New York, but it applies to most human endeavors.

I was still uncertain about whether I wanted to commit myself to keeping bees until the day of the field demonstration. That made a deep impression on me, cutting through my doubts and uncertainties. As I watched the small army of bees, dumped out of their shipping cage in front of the hive, march up an inclined cardboard ramp into their new home, where the queen awaited them, I felt a sense of awe and wonder about this commonplace biological miracle that I was witnessing. None of it had come through in the lectures or films in class; it had seemed largely a mechanical operation. I have never lost that sense of awe and wonder. Indeed, it increases each year as new miracles unfold.

THREE

My own package of bees arrived a short time after the demonstration. I picked up the package at the home of the couple who had given the course and was sent on my way with cheery cries of "good luck!" It was an odd and moving sight to see the bees, those small creatures I had assumed responsibility for, in the screened wooden shipping cage. They were gathered in a tight cluster, about the size of a small pineapple, huddled around the queen in her miniature individual perforated cage.

The cluster is a natural mechanism to protect the queen, keep the individual bees warm with their collective body heat, offer common security, and serve the colony's sense of unity as social creatures; they are so dependent upon the community that, if isolated, a bee will soon die, even though given the right food and correct temperature. A supreme discipline rules the hive. Bees must be part of a colony in order to survive. Unlike humans, they cannot go it alone.

FOUR

For several months after getting my bees I belonged to an association of amateur beekeepers, one of the few organizations I ever joined. But disenchantment came soon.

Only a small part of each session was devoted to bees. Most of the time was spent in political maneuvering, schemes and coups to overthrow those in office, and endless debates over procedural rules. The meetings were, according to the bylaws, run by *Robert's Rules of Order*, but there was continual debate over what Robert had really had in mind. No one ever consulted the book, if indeed there was one.

Ours was a varied membership, made up primarily of older men with a few women, mostly wives of members, and a scattering of young people. Some of our group were obviously lonely and wanted companionship, others were bored and wanted an audience, and a few seemed genuinely interested in learning more about bees; the latter generally didn't last long.

Some of our members did not keep bees at all but once had kept them, or they knew someone who did, or they hoped to at some future date. The membership was small, held together by a hard core of regulars who juggled the elected offices among themselves and periodically conspired to find some unsuspecting soul to act as corresponding secretary, the one office that had no appeal. I was once solicited as a candidate for this unglamorous post and replied that I preferred being a foot soldier to a general, a comment not held in my favor. Turnover in the association was lively.

The jewel in our crown was the county bee inspector (later defrocked by county budget cuts), who was a charter member. He was usually president, which was fitting because he also kept the most bees. When occasionally voted out of office, after Robert failed to rescue him from some parliamentary pitfall, he would bide his time or boycott meetings until a new election of officers. Occasionally a new member would reveal a power complex coupled with weak organizational skills; failing to win high office, he would drop out and join the competing beekeeping association to seek recognition there. One perennially unsuccessful candidate for vice-president resigned to start a new bee group with himself as president, going off Cape to find a following, as I recall.

I learned that the couple who had given the beekeeping course I attended were defectors from our association and were deeply resented for running the bee school and forming an opposition group. Beekeepers, like bees, are very big on organizational loyalty and almost as gregarious as bees; meetings are their form of clustering.

Our association, after exhausting debate, voted to start our own bee school to compete with the opposition. The members were not deterred by the statistical irrelevancy that there were not enough potential beekeepers on Cape Cod to keep one bee school running continuously, let alone two. There wasn't even enough pasturage on the Cape to support so many hives. It was wonderfully irrational. We could have been warring nations, so intent on destroying the enemy that we forgot we would also destroy ourselves in the process.

The members enjoyed the monthly meetings tremendously, and this, I believe, sets us apart and above the bees, our capacity for pleasure, and not our intelligence, which may or may not be superior to that of bees. For many of our group the meetings must have been a high point of their lives. Each session invariably ended with the president proclaiming, in the finest chauvinistic tradition, "The ladies have provided refreshments." A flurry of female activity was followed by the aroma of brewing coffee, and then cookies and homemade brownies were produced, a plastic cup at the ready for donations.

I joined the association believing the stereotype about beekeepers being kindly little old men who love their bees. There was a chilling letdown when one speaker told about how his bees had betrayed him. He had a super of honey on a hive and when he tried to remove it the bees stung him so that he had to retreat. Later he went back for the honey, but by then the bees had "stolen" every last drop for their own use. "But I got even with them," he said, grinding his teeth. "On the coldest day of the winter I dumped them out on the frozen ground, poured gasoline on them, and set them on fire. . . ." So much for stereotypes about kindly little old beekeepers!

I was further disillusioned when I discovered that periodically there are serious discussions among beekeepers, and in learned bee journals, about whether it is more efficient to leave an adequate supply of honey to winter a colony over so it is strong in the spring, or to take all of the honey in the fall, destroy the bees, and start over the following spring with new bees. Fortunately, people who think like this are exceptions. Most beekeepers are devoted to their bees.

Another misconception I had concerned some of our female members; several were the wives of members and I assumed that they were loyal spouses indulging their mates by accompanying them to the meetings. I had another view of this when one of our foremost members died. His wife had always served coffee, otherwise remaining in the background. But with his death, instead of dropping out, she became an officer in the association.

Gradually I realized that learning about bees was the least important part of our agenda. Bees were more excuse than reason for the meetings. The focus was on parliamentary procedure and finding new members to keep the association alive. The rationale, if any, was to gain political clout (someone is forever trying to banish beehives, license beekeepers, or wipe out both with poisonous sprays) and, subliminally, to destroy the opposition group headed by the colonel and his lady.

I had naively joined to learn about bees, but found myself learning more about beekeepers than bees. To attend meetings I had to make a round trip of more than fifty miles, and didn't reach home until after midnight. Finally I decided to drop out and learn from books, and from the best teachers of all—the bees themselves, who somehow manage their complex organizational affairs with no help from Robert.

In retrospect now I realize that it was chance alone that brought me to beekeeping. I am always fascinated by the role that chance plays in our lives. How many of us would be other than we are were it not for chance, because some small cog slipped in here when it could as easily have gone in there? Would I have risked the time and expense of keeping bees had not some young boys, hundreds of miles away, tried an experiment in self-sufficiency that I would most likely not have attempted on my own? And yet, I would have missed an experience that has enriched my life. Any credit or blame that we take for what befalls us must be shared with the capricious god of chance.

FIVE

One of the curiosities of beekeeping is that bees are sold by the pound. This seems an indignity for the bees and a high-handed way of dealing with another life form, but the human marketplace is less particular about the types of transactions that take place than about their dollar volume. There are about four thousand bees to the pound, so a package usually consists of approximately twelve thousand, almost all of them female workers, with a queen and perhaps a few drones, just about enough to provide the nucleus for a strong colony.

Some affluent beekeepers prefer to buy five pounds of bees, rather than the more common three, assuming that the larger number will make a stronger colony. But it is generally agreed that the extra bees don't make a great deal of difference; in a short time there will be about the same number in either case. Most of the packaged bees die within a few weeks. They are primarily caretakers, their mission being to start raising the young bees that will take over the hive. More important than the number of passengers in the package is having a plucky queen who will lay large numbers of eggs so the colony will build up quickly.

Packaged bees are shipped all over the country, and indeed the world, to new would-be beekeepers and to established apiaries that have lost a colony or wish to add to their number without delay. Anyone who keeps bees can start a new colony by dividing an existing hive, but this takes time; or he or she can hope to find a swarm, which takes luck and imposes certain risks of bringing diseased bees into the apiary. Still another method is to start with a "nuc" (nucleus)—a couple of frames of young bees and a queen from another hive—but for the inexperienced there is no guarantee that the newcomers are disease free, and even the knowledgeable can't be sure that a random queen will measure up.

New colonies are usually started in the spring. It is important that they build up quickly for the first honeyflow, that rich vernal harvest of early nectar, a time when nature herself is drunk with love and ecstasy, a time of alternate warm rains and cloudless skies, of flowering dogwood, locust, iris, shad, and earth. The honeybee, released from winter bondage, revels in the renewed flowering of the earth, humming her own ode to joy. And yet, over this exaltation, this climactic fulfillment of nature, hovers an explicable sadness that seems to have no place amidst such excitement of new life, as if it alone knows how soon all will vanish.

Most packaged bees come from the south, where they are raised in huge apiaries. These bee farms are a picturesque and startling sight: hundreds or thousands of hives, row upon row of stacked white boxes, and millions of bees waiting to be packaged and shipped out, like soldiers in a replacement depot awaiting assignment to permanent units. It is inconceivable that a bee can distinguish her home from all the other identical white boxes, but, possibly, to a bee, all human habitations look alike and all people appear the same, as all bees and their hives look alike to us.

Most packaged bees sold in the spring are replacements for colonies lost due to "winter kill," a wholesale death that covers a multitude of causes, including dampness and fatal chilling (the major killer of bees); starvation, which, as we shall see, can occur even in a hive full of honey because bees are so inflexible in their habits; unusually wretched weather with prolonged cold and lack of insulation to protect the hive; or improper care by the beekeeper. Occasionally a colony brings on its own doom, almost as if it had some kind of built-in death wish, another of nature's more perplexing dilemmas that we shall encounter in its turn.

SIX

Most bees shipped out of the south are young. This is important because they must live long enough to get the new colony established, and older bees would die off too soon. There are also certain hive chores that only young bees can perform, or that we see them routinely performing. But, as in any society, there must be a mix of young and old if the colony is to have proper balance in fulfilling its role in nature; an average hive consists of about one-third young bees and two-thirds foragers.

Bees are clever enough, and unencumbered by sentiment, to have worked out a system so that old age is no problem to the individual or the colony, as they have resolved most of the great social and political problems that still plague human societies. But bees have had millions of years to find their way amidst the perils of evolution, while humans, relative newcomers on earth, are still thrashing about without having developed either an effective philosophy or a long-term strategy for survival. The bees have a track record, as they say, while we're still trying to get the hang of it.

We assume that the so-called lower forms of life are incapable not only of thought but of feeling or pain. In filling orders for bees, the creatures are scooped up and dumped into the oblong shipping cages through a widemouthed funnel. Inside the screened box, and attached to the wooden top, is a tiny perforated cage that holds the queen and a half-dozen attendant worker bees. The queen is almost helpless and must be fed, groomed, and cared for. The shipping cage also contains a can of sugar water inserted in a round hole in the wooden top, secured so it can't pitch about and injure the bees. Tiny holes punched in the bottom of the can permit the sweet syrup to drip out slowly, providing food until they are claimed and hived.

For bees this must be a tremendous shock. Suddenly they are plucked from their colony, with its familiar smells and architecture, and thrust into a barren new prison community. They may be among strangers with alien smells and ways. They probably never met their new caged queen whom they can't even touch. The queen herself, only recently incubated and bred, as suddenly finds herself confined in a tiny cage with, possibly, unfamiliar attendants. All of these strangers, thrust together, have lived in tomblike darkness, and now, abruptly, they are exposed to brilliant southern sunlight with no retreat into the protective darkness of their own hive.

Such is the force of survival that almost at once these alien beings forge a new society of their own, much as a community of strangers banded together in common cause in a small vessel to settle the New World made a covenant even before they touched land. The first thing the caged and disoriented bees do is to cluster around the secured queen cage to protect the being within, who is their vital link in survival, and to provide for mutual warmth and security as a life necessity. Bees are capricious but ever practical. Their covenant is survival.

Can we be sure that they are incapable of the feelings or sentiments that are believed to place them on a lower scale than humans? Do we deny sensitivity to all of the so-called lower orders to blunt, protect, and, ultimately, deny our own? We will see that bees can grieve over the loss of a queen, sound war cries or hum with contentment; they can be angry, docile, ferocious, playful, aggressive, appear happy, or utter pitiful sounds of distress. Are these not emotions akin to ours, merely expressed differently?

To perplex us more, if the hive is violated, or a rough hand thrust within, the bees will attack almost en masse. But an individual bee can have a companion next to her slaughtered or tortured and she will neither assist nor pay attention. What are we to make of this contradiction, this caring and indifference? But if we look deeper at our own kind we see similar conflicting patterns of insensitivity and feeling among different people, and often in different areas within the same individual. Are we, too, more likely to respond to a threat to the nation, but not to a threatened fellow citizen? The bee, like man, is likely to react to that which affects her directly and personally, due not to any want of intelligence or compassion, but, like man, to lack of imagination.

How many of these mysteries and questions could the bees resolve for us if we had the wit and will to interpret their distress, instead of seeing them only as commodities of commerce? Shipping is not only psychologically traumatic for bees but can be physically dangerous, even lethal. In the mails packaged bees get tossed around with other parcels. Some die of injuries, and older bees often succumb from natural causes, age, and the added stress of travel. Shipping cages usually carry the stamped warning: LIVE BEES—RUSH! But the packages may be delayed in the mail or get covered by other packages so that the bees smother or get overheated or too cold, or they are handled roughly and die in large numbers.

An expectant beekeeper is, to his distress, occasionally presented a package of dead bees. Even if he has no feeling for the suffering and loss of life, there is an economic liability. The bees are probably insured and will be replaced without charge, but this puts the replacement colony days or weeks behind schedule in preparing for summer; each day lost is difficult to make up. Bees are on a tight timetable, especially in the spring when the colony is under pressure to build up quickly before the first explosion of flowers.

SEVEN

Insects, including bees, go far back in time. Cockroaches, the scourge of city life, existed some 250 million years ago, and they haven't changed much since then. Other insects followed, adapting and rejecting, imitating and inventing, working things out one way or another with a changing environment. The bee emerged somewhere along the way, made her own compact with the environment, and has stayed more or less the same for several million years, or so fossil evidence indicates.

Insects are the earth's dominant life expression, other than microscopic forms, representing about 80 percent of all known animals. Worldwide, an estimated 686,000 different species have been classified, with more being constantly added to the list; two-fifths of them are beetles. Some 82,500 species of insects have been counted in North America alone.

Only about 10,000 of these species are considered enemies. Insect enemies, or pests, are, in reality, nothing more than small creatures with an appetite or form of which we disapprove or find displeasing, that costs us money, or brings discomfort or inconvenience. Primarily it is a matter of conflicting tastes and interests. Pests among insects, like weeds, are undesirable on man's scale of values, but many may have a role in nature that we do not know about or suspect.

Some scientists believe that eventually up to ten million different kinds of insects alone may be found throughout the world; there are carnivores, vegetarians, and those that eat their mates, children, and relatives. Populations rise and fall, varying from season to season, even minute to minute, depending on weather, soil, plants, and other factors. The ability of insects to hold their own and thrive in competition with literally a million or so other species, in what appears to be a world already overrun with insects, is phenomenal. They are held in bounds and kept in balance only by natural controls, which are often disrupted by man's interference.

A common characteristic among insects is their great reproductive capacity. If all descendants of a single pair of flies born over one summer lived, they would total 191,000,000,000,000,000,000. Aphids, often called plant lice, are even more wildly prolific. A single female cabbage aphid studied in New York averaged 41 young, producing 16 generations between the end of March and the beginning of October. Had all lived, the offspring would have numbered 15,000,000,000,000,000,000,000, which seems to be overdoing it, even for aphids. The melon aphid and cotton aphid are said to bear twice as many young and more generations per female in the south.

A swarm of grasshoppers in the American West in 1951 was an estimated one hundred miles long and three miles wide, rivaling tales of mighty flocks of passenger pigeons that once darkened the skies. Such excesses are usually cut down by enemies who, in their turn, prosper and decline. Nature tends to deal sternly with those who exceed their limits. The last passenger pigeon, named Martha, died in a Cincinnati zoo in 1914. Other once-numerous species are also now extinct. None of us has cause to be too optimistic about our long-term prospects of survival as a species.

The reproductive capacities of bees are more modest, relatively, and their populations more stable. To entomologists, bees are members of a broad grouping called hymenoptera, which includes wasps, hornets, ants, sawflies, and others; in common, they usually have four membraneous wings. Bees are more narrowly classified as *Apis* (carriers) *mellifera* (honey makers). Many races of bees travel under the entomological banner of *Apis mellifera*.

Although not scientifically precise, *Apis mellifera* is generally divided into two major bee groups: dark (blacks and browns) and lights (yellowish). Among the black and brown bees found in North America are Caucasians and Carniolans, but throughout the world, particularly in the United States, yellow bees are considered first in importance.

Most of the bees that we see foraging among flowers are Italians. They have a yellow-tan tone, sometimes compared to the color of mellow shoe leather; Italians usually have three yellow segments or bands edged with black, but both the shade of yellow and the number of bands can vary, as members of the human race have different shadings of complexion and features within their common ethnic background. There is no indication that any race of bees considers itself superior because of its color or is held in higher or lower esteem by other bees.

Historically, beekeeping—at least the stealing of honey from bees—goes back at least to 15,000 B.C., established by a rock painting showing two adventurers, one clinging perilously to a sedge-grass rope while taking honey from a hole in a stone cliff, as bees fly around the intrepid pair of pilferers. I assume that the unprotected "beekeepers" got stung but considered the honey worth the penalty. The ancient Greeks studied bees and some of the great philosophers, including Aristotle, wrote extensively about them. When Greek sailors went on long voyages they took bees along for trade and established apiaries if they were delayed on foreign soil. These bees are believed to have crossed with wild dark bees living in Italy, the race spreading north as civilization advanced across Europe.

Bees are believed to have been brought to America by Irish and Norwegian explorers between A.D. 800 and 900. The colonists brought hives from Europe in the 1600s. Italian bees were introduced into the United States in 1860, and are considered the most beautiful of all breeds, especially prized for their stamina and character. Renowned as hard workers, they are relatively gentle, disease resistant, quiet, do not swarm readily, have a good character, are relatively virtuous, and, generally, are easy to work with. Other bee races have some or several of these characteristics, but Italians are believed to have the most desirable traits.

By now, however, there has been so much cross-breeding that most bees are hybrids, although they may retain the dominant characteristics of one particular race. It is much like Americans saying they are Irish, English, French, German, Russian, or whatever, which may be true enough in an ethnic-origin sense, but essentially they are Americans, shaped more by the culture in which they grew up than by the bloodlines of their forebears.

Bees are too involved in their brief moment of being to concern themselves with ancient history, to seek out their origins, take false pride in their lineage. They are, however, intensely patriotic in the sense of being protectve and loyal to their colony and hive. They proclaim no self-righteous slogans, and do not profess to be created in the image of the Creator or to hold His special favor. They claim no special virtues or privileges for their kind or race. Their motto, judging by the way they live, could be "live and let live." Rarely will they ever sting anyone who doesn't first bother them.

Each individual hive is a city, a state, a world, sufficient unto itself. Each is so isolated and independent that there is no assistance or mutual aid. There is no pity. Often the strong will plunder the weak, taking every drop of stored honey and leaving the conquered to starve, while the raiders' stores are swollen beyond any amount they can consume, a moral shortcoming not limited to their kind.

Bees must recognize intuitively that they, like all creatures on earth, are an accident of "birth" to which they contributed nothing. There is little cause for self-congratulation or to demand special status. They are no more responsible for being yellow than are the Caucasians and Carniolans for being what they are. It probably makes no difference to bees what ethnic legend is stamped on their shipping cage. But for the recipient beekeeper, often a creature of prejudice and irrational values, it may be comforting to know that his bees are descended from a noble breed.

EIGHT

Once a package of bees arrives at a local post office for final delivery, it is likely to cause considerable excitement. The bees are gathered in a fuzzy, throbbing brown ball at the top center of the cage, protectively surrounding their queen, making a soft humming sound, as if trying to keep up their spirits by singing a little hymn.

Everyone who works in the post office is likely to gaze in wonder; although the bees are securely caged, the postal employees tend to keep their distance. The postmaster may be nervous about the possibility of escape—live cargos are unpredictable and unnerving to the bureaucratic mind; he wants the bees claimed and on their way as quickly as possible. This same bureaucratic fear and prudence may be as imprinted in him as is the desire for freedom in the bees.

In the town I formerly lived in, a friendly postal clerk named Tommy would phone me when packaged bees arrived so I could rescue them as quickly as possible, both for the sake of the

U.S. Postal Service and that of the bees. The insects were undoubtedly shaken by their violent uprooting and travels and desperately in need of water and tranquility.

I had prevailed upon Tommy, a kind soul, to give the bees a drink as soon as they arrived; he had learned to place drops of fresh water gently against the screen to avoid injuring the bees' delicate little tongues. It was a source of much amusement in the post office that the bees had tongues. The bees would take water to the queen in her cage before they would drink it themselves. The queen's attendants always quenched their sovereign's thirst before tending their own.

Upon being removed from the post office, packaged bees are not hived at once. They first need to quiet down and recuperate after their traumatic adventure. The cage is left in a cool spot, preferably in shadow in warm weather, until on toward evening, occasionally misted with water or thin sugar water to cool and refresh them. Dusk, or sundown, is the best time to hive bees. This gives them a chance to settle in before dark, with the night ahead to start housekeeping and to take possession of their new home.

NINE

A few technicalities are in order to understand the function of the hive, and as stage setting to appreciate the unique drama that soon will unfold within: the main part of the modern bee hive is a white "box" (without top or bottom, as explained previously); its dimensions are precise: 9½ inches deep, 18½ inches long, and 14⅝ inches wide. These figures have been arrived at after much experimentation based on bee preferences and habits.

The open box is known s a "deep super," "brood chamber," or "hive body." Inside are ten rectangular wooden frames, side by side, like so many slices of bread. The frames have overlapping ends that rest on a little shelf that is inset into each (rabbited) end of the super, so the tops of the frames are just (5/16th of an inch) below the top of the hive body or super, leaving them suspended with the same 5/16th-inch space below. This sounds complicated but, in reality, is simple and can be better understood by viewing an actual hive.

The genius of the arrangement, inventd in 1851 by Lorenzo Langstroth, a Massachusetts clergyman, is that the frames can be removed and the supers stacked onto one another, much like a modern apartment building. The inspiration of movable frames and interchangeable supers revolutionized beekeeping. Before the present standard hive was devised, bees were kept in every conceivable type of hive, from hollow logs and barrels to the most elegant structures, most better reflecting the tastes of beekeepers than of bees.

The most popular hives were skeps, small domed affairs made of twisted straw, still widely used in Europe and some parts of the United States. One technique to remove the bees so their honey could be taken safely was to hold the straw skep over smoke from burning puffballs until the bees were in a stupor and fell senselessly to the ground. Another was to kill the entire colony by holding the hive over burning sulfur, a process known as "brimstoning." Old bee books contain instructionsfor killing bees, and are illustrated with quaint, touching lithographs of colonies being destroyed over a fire billowing deadly sulfur fumes. Early beekeeping was wasteful and often brutal.

Langstroth's masterstroke was the discovery of "bee space," the amount of clearance left by bees between the combs they build and parts of the hive, usually figured at $5/16$th of an inch. He was the first to understand that, if a man-made hive has too much or too little space between the parts, the bees will fill it with comb or a sticky saplike substance caled propolis, or "bee glue," which the bees gather from the buds of trees. This cement can make it almost impossible to remove the frames of honeycomb without damaging or ruining them altogether. There have been improvements and variations on Langstroth's original hive, but all provide the bee space dictated by the bees themselves.

In a modern hive each suspended frame holds a sheet of "foundation," previously referred to. These thin, flat sheets of wax come from used honeycomb, which is melted down and sent to factories where it is processed and embossed with the exquisite hexagons devised by bees in their natural state. Bees "draw out" the foundation with new wax they manufacture, creating the familiar honeycomb that provides thousands of adjoining geometrically perfect cells in which honey and pollen are stored and the queen lays eggs.

The hive body, or brood chamber, rests on a "bottom board," a flat wooden or plastic surface with raised sides and back. The bottom board extends about three inches beyond the front of the hive body, much like a small uncovered front porch, providing bees returning to the hive laden with pollen or nectar a place to land, or sun themselves in rare moments of relaxation. Behind the landing board is the hive entrance, extending the full width of the hive and approximately three-quarters of an inch high.

On top of the hive body is the inner cover, also called the "crown board," exactly the same dimension as the super below, with a shallow rim around the edge and an oblong hole in the middle to provide ventilation for the hive. Fitting snugly over the crown board and the super it rests on is the hive cover, which keeps out rain, and often must be weighted with bricks to keep it from being blown off in storms.

As the season progresses and the colony expands and builds up stores of honey, other supers are stacked on top of the original hive body; supers used only to store surplus honey are shallower than the hive bodies in which bees raise brood, keep honey for their own use, and form their cluster. The crown board and hive cover fit on top of the highest super; as the hive gains height from additional supers, it vaguely resembles an urban high-rise apartment incongruously placed in a rural field.

The bottom board, on which the supers rest, is raised above the ground a few inches to protect the hive from dampness and to keep out mice and other predators; usually it rests on a wooden platorm or cement blocks. The hive should face directly south to get the full warmth of the sun; it should be shielded from the wind by nearby trees or bushes, forming a windbreak, but the trees and bushes should not be so close or high that they interfere with the bees' travels to and from the hive. Almost nothing irritates bees like having an obstacle in their flight path. The hive is tilted slightly forward and pitched to one side so rain will run out.

Nearby should be a source of water, which is essential in raising brood. I use a concrete birdbath, which is aesthetically pleasing, functional, and serves both bees and birds. A shingle rests on the rim, the thin end floating in the water, so the bees can drink without drowning. Usually, however, the bees seem to prefer getting their drinks from the garden, where they are particularly attracted to morning dew glistening on a fat cabbage, perhaps because they feel more safe and it is closer to a natural state.

Bees are not clever about water as they are about most things. If I leave pails of unprotected water in the garden, dead bees will soon be floating in them. The corpses do not deter their comrades from recklessly plunging in to their own deaths; often the bees will bypass the birdbath with its floating shingle for these death traps. I can offer no explanation for this idiosyncrasy. Every species seems to indulge in its own form of irrational destructive behavior, but it may be guided by some deeper rationality beyond our understanding. Who is to say what inner drives, whims and demons propel varous creatures, including humans, to risk almost certain doom or disability in pursuit of their own rainbows, mirages, and fantasies?

Most standard texts on beekeeping call for giving bees plenty of fresh water. But bees do not read the standard texts. At least not my bees. They invariably show a preference for water that is stale, green, and slimy with algae; the more scummy and lethal the water, the better they seem to like it. I have seen bees pass up fresh water to drink dark, festering, sinister brews that would probably paralyze or kill humans. A barrel of manure tea, water with manure immersed in it for fertilizing the garden, sends the bees into a frenzy of excitement and joy. Taste is, after all, a personal preference.

TEN

The final step in hiving bees is to prepare the queen cage and, just before releasing the colony, to douse the entire congregation with a mixture of sugar water. As the bees pour out of the shipping package, suddenly free after long confinement, there is chaos, bodies stuck together, all struggling to wriggle free. This is a crucial moment. The sugar water helps divert them as they lick it off, and the sticky liquid makes flight and escape difficult.

Awaiting, them in the hive is the queen, her cage secured between two frames, at the top of the super, screened side down so the bees can feed her until she is freed. She shares her small prison with a half-dozen attendants, separated from the colony she would serve, prevented from fulfilling her life mission as mother to the hive by a wire screen that must be as formidable to her as the stoutest metal bars in a jail. How strange, how terrifying, this must seem to these prisoners, how baffling not to be able to touch their comrades, to rub antennae, the primary means of communication, not to join in physical contact with the cluster, to embrace its protection and comfort.

Before installing the queen cage, the beekeeper removes the cork plug in one end, exposing a block of sugar. Now the bees can begin work to free their sovereign. This must be one of the great dramas in the life of a colony. The rescuers gnaw unceasingly at the block of candy barring her release, chewing away day and night, tunneling toward one aother from both inside and outside the queen cage, until eventually the two groups meet, like miners digging a shaft toward one another from opposite sides of a mountain. The beekeeper can speed the process, when installing the queen cage, by gently piercing the candy plug with a nail or wire, being careful not to impale the queen.

A hive is not open to prying eyes while the queen is being freed. To disturb the bees at this critical time, after their recent adventures, might further upset them so they would possibly blame the queen for their difficulties and kill her. This poses another dilemma for those who would explain bee behavior: one minute they seek to free their sovereign to ensure the colony's survival, and the next they assassinate her. How do we explain such contradictory acts within this little republic that, now queenless, must almost certainly perish, unless provided with another queen?

Some beekeepers think it unnecessary to have the bees release the queen, considering it a waste of time before she starts to lay. They prefer to free her themselves, at once, placing her among the mass of bees spilled from the shipping cage. Almost all agree, however, that it is prudent first to douse the colony with sugar water. By the time it is cleaned up, the new queen has been accepted.

I have read that an effective technique in introducing a new queen to an existing hive is to kill the old queen by crushing her and rubbing her juices on the substitute queen. The bees, it is claimed, accept the newcomer because of her familiar smell, never suspecting that they have been duped with a bogus mother. This method does not appeal to me, and I wonder if the colony is really so easily deceived, or do the practical bees accept that which cannot be changed and make the best of the situation? Once more we may be mislead by our limited ability to interpret that which we observe, seeing it in our own terms, deceiving ourselves more than observing deception in nature.

I personally prefer to have the bees free their own queen. I like to think they will value her more by having to work for her release, and take greater responsibility for an act voluntarily performed. I probably romanticize the whole thing and ascribe to the bees human motives and values, while they couldn't care less. But if there are none of the psychological advantages I fancy, and the whole process is no more than a mechanical procedure, at least the colony does have time to get used to the queen while she is being released and is more likely to accept her. So far the method has worked well enough for me, although others say the quick-release procedure has worked for them. When possible, I let the bees make their own decisions.

The first time I hived packaged bees, after completing bee

school, I had an unnerving experience. As I prepared the hive, a neighbor dropped over with friends visiting him to watch the excitement. I was already nervous, not knowing what I was doing and not wanting to botch the job. The audience added to my discomfort. As I gingerly thrust a nail through the candy into the queen cage, as I had been taught, one of the men bellowed, "Don't give the queen a hysterectomy."

It was disconcerting. But the queen, the colony, and I survived the ordeal.

ELEVEN

One of the more fascinating sights in nature is watching a colony of bees take possession of its new home. There are many ways to hive bees, but all assume that the bees will cooperate to make the venture successful. Sometimes, however, it doesn't work out this way. The bees may not approve of the new home selected for them, the way they are handled, or the whole procedure might be too high-handed for their tastes and they will take off to find new quarters of their own choosing. The poor beekeeper, looking mournful, is left wondering what he did wrong, if he is of such inclination, or, more likely, grumbling about "those damned bees."

By human logic, bees are maddeningly independent and perverse. They seem to delight in confounding their keepers. There is no accounting for why one colony will remain happily hived and another will take off. This is another of the enigmas we must deal with, accepting that which we can't understand, which may be the beginning of all wisdom.

Almost every beekeeper has his own method of introducing

packaged bees. Some remove a few frames of foundation or drawn honeycomb and dump the entire colony in at once, cold turkey, as it were; the missing frames are slipped back in and that's an end to it. Another technique calls for making space in the hive by removing several frames and placing the shipping cage itself on top of the remaining frames, first having removed the cage's wooden cap and can of sugar water so the bees can escape at their leisure. Other beekeepers have more exotic techniques. Some, like the bees themselves, are secretive and confide in no one. Almost everyone considers his or her way best. Whatever the method, it usually reflects the beekeeper's personal philosophy and attitude toward other life forms.

To plunge bees all at once into a hive is, to my way of thinking, a presumption, if not an outright infringement on their rights. Shouldn't all life have certain rights? Why shouldn't bees have a say about where they are to dwell and who looks after them? Do we necessarily own everything that we pay for? Bees are, from my observations, more temperamental and selective than is commonly suspected.

Another, and possibly the biggest, disadvantage of unceremoniously dumping bees into a hive, without so much as a "by your leave," is the pleasure the beekeeper deprives himself of. Hiving should be approached as a ritual in which the bees, the main participants, share and have a voice. The process is one to be enjoyed by both bees and keeper.

If the packaged bees are gently poured out on a ramp in front of the hive, with a couple of sharp raps on the wooden box to hurry laggards along, they are given a choice: to stay or to leave. If the queen is inside the hive, imprisoned in her cage and awaiting release, almost invariably the colony will enter and begin homemaking and freeing the queen. They are acting through choice, doing what *they* want to do and not that which is forced upon them. This applies to all creatures, but beekeepers were employing the principle long before it was recognized as essential in personnel management. It is, as noted, a stirring sight to watch a colony parade up a ramp in orderly procession, almost in columns, and disappear into the hive, like a conquering army with band and banners, taking possession of a fallen city.

To state that the bees have a choice about whether to enter or depart the hive is to ignore a basic biological urge they have, just as humans are motivated by the need to eat and be paid for work done. Bees almost always go where their queen is. Their inclination is to move upward. A colony can be induced to migrate upward in its hive by a rhythmic pounding on the sides. This is known as "drumming the bees." The cadence must appeal to some ancient impulse or, possibly, it captures an internal vibration of heart or blood, in the same way that a steady beat is picked up by marching men.

A remarkable thing about bees is how quickly they transform chaos into order. When spilled out on the ramp and earth, after being soused with sugar water, they are a squirming, sticky, disorganized mass. Then, out of the confusion a single bee will struggle free and stagger up the ramp, attracted by the smell of the queen and fresh beeswax or honeycomb from the hive, and further drawn upward by natural inclination. She is known as the "lead bee," but whether elected, self-appointed, or fulfilling an impromptu role dictated by instinct is not known. But it must take courage or daring to be first, possibly leading the troops into ambush or some other disaster.

The lead bee, upon reaching the landing board, hesitates briefly, as if reconnoitering or sniffing. Apparently reassured that all is well, she raises her tail, exposing a tiny gland on her rear. She fans her wings vigorously, sending the scent from the gland toward the struggling mass below, signaling that this is their new home. A couple of other bees follow the leader to the landing board; they also raise their tails and fan. This could be an advance guard, calling, "It's okay, gang, come on. Everything's fine!"

The procession starts moving up the ramp, slowly at first, then faster until there is almost a stampede to get inside. Some crowding may take place at the entrance, but never chaos and no display of ill temper, shoving, or unpleasant expressions of "me first." Bees are wonderfully patient little creatures, with no false sense of self-importance.

While this little drama is played out, a beekeeper may sit beside the hive, enjoying the sight with little or no danger of getting stung; for the bees this is a joyful occasion and they are not inclined to sting. They have been through a traumatic experience. Suddenly they are free, taking possession of a new home with a queen. But for the moment they are disoriented. Bees have a strong sense of place. Any movement is upsetting to them. If a hive is shifted only a few feet, a bee will return to the original location and, possibly, perish on that spot, her home within easy reach, forlorn as any world-weary traveler seeking a former habitation that no longer exists.

Bees are delightfully curious but not the least adventurous. They resist any change of routine forced upon them, an inflexibility of habit that often causes their destruction, although it may have helped them survive as a species. Persistence might well be as important in survival as adaptation, for who knows whether new conditions will last or prove to be of short duration?

How many species are extinct because they mistook some environmental aberration on the unmarked evolutionary road for permanent change? Bees, with their programmed consistency, seem to have followed a fairly straight and unerring course through the centuries, but will it continue with man having taken over from nature as the evolutionary force itself?

Once installed in their new quarters, the bees are given combs of honey from other hives or fed sugar water. This provides instant energy to start drawing out comb, making wax, and performing the numerous chores required in building a city. It might also serve a subtle psychological purpose, like the Welcome Wagon, raising spirits and making them feel at home.

When all of the bees have disappeared into the hive, a few handfuls of dry grass are stuffed into the entrance to discourage second thoughts about taking off. Bees despise involuntary confinement, and immediately set to chewing away the grass. By the time they have freed themselves, within twenty-four hours or so, they are settled in. Perhaps they become so engrossed in removing the grass that they forget its purpose; means and ends are often confused. The queen will soon be released from imprisonment and the colony will start fulfilling the role assigned it by nature.

TWELVE

With a bit of luck and reasonably good management, a colony can continue indefinitely. I still have my original hive from ten years ago, although it is true that the line of succession has been disrupted by the introduction of an occasional new queen, after the reigning queen failed, died, or was dispatched by her discontented daughters. The same hive has housed dozens of generations with never a break in occupancy, but none of the present colony is related to the original inhabitants.

It seems remarkable that the physical hive is the only common thread in this chain of continuity. In the wild, colonies have been known to last, uninterrupted, for fifty or sixty years. In such cases there is, presumably, a direct line of descendants and the characteristics of the original colony are passed along through unbroken genetic transmission.

Each new queen that takes over passes along different traits of temperament that soon dominate the hive. If a colony is ugly and stings at the slightest provocation, this can be changed by substituting a queen of more docile disposition; as soon as the old bees die off and are replaced by the offspring of the new queen, the mood of the hive softens. Colonies can also differ in other characteristics, including their industry, tidiness, method of building comb, the amount of honey gathered, and the size of the colony. Many common characteristics exist among all hives, but at the same time there are startling differences from one to another.

In all healthy, normal hives the population ratio is much the same. The colony is composed almost entirely of females. This matriarchal society works with compulsive dedication, and yet, we are forced to believe that for them there is no sense of drudgery or martyrdom. They give more voluntarily than could be demanded of any slave; for them there is no crying out in frustration and despair, no decamping to a better life or easier life-style.

It seems odd that nature imposed on the workers almost the entire burden of running and supporting the hive. A colony may vary from as few as thirty thousand to sixty thousand members, and in excessively successful communities eighty thousand or even a hundred thousand or more, with, generally, no more than a couple of hundred drones at most. Even if nature saw fit not to have a larger number of males, why didn't she make them contribute more to the upkeep of the hive, and when not sexually occupied at least to support themselves? Why this disparity?

Did nature brush drones off, as if saying, "Oh, you know how men are, they just get in the way!" I like to think there is more to the grand design, but females play the dominant role in many species. The drone's sole contribution is his sperm. Could it be that nature considers sex an occupation worthy of all the energy and attention one can give it? Is this, then, why the females, the sustainers of the colony, are all lifelong virgins and spinsters? So they won't be distracted by lust from hive obligations?

Every worker bee is wholly dedicated to the colony, almost like nuns who have taken vows of chastity, poverty, and obedience. However, we assume that nuns choose their path. Bees, unlike humans, can never question the bargain they struck with life, for no bargain is struck; the terms are imposed upon them at birth and, apparently, they accept their lot willingly enough. This must be the major difference between humans and other orders of life: man has choices.

In their unique social organization, bees do not concern themselves with the variables through which humans pile up enormous fortunes. One bee, through greater intelligence, diligence, avarice, or drive cannot exploit the industry or stupidity of another, or lay waste the land that belongs to all for personal gain. All share equally in such resources as exist. Production is geared to need rather than to an artificially created demand. The huge surpluses of honey accumulated through efficient management by beekeepers represent an imposition on bees to exploit their natural drives.

Wily nature takes no chance on defectors rebelling against the rigid hive order. Each member is biologically dependent on the community for life, as we have noted. Honeybees depend not only on physical contact with the colony, but also require its social companionship and support. Isolate a honeybee from her sisters and she will soon die. Few can survive twenty-four hours of separation from the colony, even in warm weather. A bee's dependence on this physical and psychic companionship is as striking in its way as the heroic legends concerning individual men and women who have lived through unbelievable hardships in prolonged isolation, each obeying the laws that separate and unify the species.

THIRTEEN

The honeybee's family tree is, regrettably, not all that it could be. It too has its sour apples, members she would probably as soon forget, along with others that, while respectable enough, have taken a different evolutionary path. Here I digress briefly to examine some of the varieties of bees, to better understand the honeybee, see her in a larger perspective, to look at some of her relatives, how they differ from her, and what they are up to these days.

The outstanding characteristic of honeybees is their social nature: they live together in large communities, store quantities of honey, and care for their young. While honeybees receive the most attention, they are, in fact, a minority in the bee family. Their wild cousins, the solitary bees, are much more abundant. Honeybees also are found in the wild, but most absconded from hives, finding such boxlike quarters too confining and, possibly, domestic life too respectable or stifling; the majority, however, have taken the path of least resistance, living in man-made quarters in exchange for providing honey and service.

In common, all bees provide the same essential service, pollinating plants, but they operate from a different base, often complementing one another. All bees are believed to have developed from hunting wasps, but along the way they followed different stars, experimenting, mimicking, innovating, adopting, and rejecting, the successful living, ever-changing form and style, until we arrived at the diversity we have today.

Solitary bees are, as the name suggests, loners, each going it by herself. Each female builds her own nest, provisions it, and lays eggs. She provides the eggs with a food supply, consisting of a honeycake mixed with pollen, and seals egg and food into a comb of her making. There is no further contact between parent and offspring; this is true of most insects and seems to put honeybees a cut or so above their wild kin and other insect neighbors.

There are said to be at least five thousand species of wild bees in North America alone, but little is known about them. When creatures have little or no commercial value, if they are neither especially harmful nor useful and not strikingly beautiful, fascinating, or bizarre, they are largely ignored to go their own way. This also holds true of most people of little or no distinction.

Solitary bees dwell in a variety of places, usually a hole of some kind in the soil or a convenient cavity of one kind or another. Despite their solitary nature, they are not altogether antisocial; many are quite gregarious, large populations dwelling in ground burrows an inch or two apart. These can cover vast areas and are known as "bee towns." The inhabitants are like recluses who can't quite take the final step of cutting themselves off completely from their own kind. A nesting site studied in Utah contained some two hundred thousand female bees, covering several acres.

We have no way of knowing what honeybees think of this life-style, if they envy the freedom it brings, but scientists believe that wild bees may be in a stage of development on their way to becoming social bees. Groups of individuals occasionally are found nesting together at night on a tree branch; they collect on the same branch every night and disperse during the day, possibly experimenting with a new way of life but still undecided and not wanting the neighbors to catch them at it.

Some female solitaries go a step further by laying their eggs together in a single nest, another step toward communal living. Often a community of solitary bees will stack one on top of another as a single unit. Although some varieties are handicapped by lack of a stinger, they are biters. Stinging bees are said to be more productive as pollinators than biters, indicating a connection between the two.

While solitary bees have not made it socially as yet, they are highly valued as pollinators; they are especially effective in servicing wild plants and out-of-the-way growths, such as forests and ranges, not ordinarily visited by honeybees. Many are specialists, concentrating on various growths which depend on them for their existence. Solitary bees do not store great surpluses of honey, in the manner of honeybees, but gather only as much nectar as they need for their own use. This makes them more efficient, as they do not make repeated trips to a hive to unload, but, on the other hand, they tend to stop working when their needs are met.

Researchers are attempting to colonize one variety, the wild orchard bee, which normally lives in beetle holes or in old lumber and logs. To tempt it to a more domestic life, holes are bored in wood and plastic blocks, a kind of bee condominium. Success has been limited, but a few do move into these homes and others follow, in the best middle-class tradition of social mimicry. The wild orchard bees are driven to orchards, where they do their job, and then are driven to another site. They are, in effect, being turned into migratory workers following the harvest, which wouldn't seem to be exactly what nature had in mind for them.

Another relative of the honeybee that has made its mark as a pollinator is the bumblebee, or humblebee as she is known in England. Bumblebees, almost twice the size of honeybees, are regular visitors to the fields in summer, working alongside honeybees and frequently mistaken for them. Bumblebees are also socially inclined but are considered to be more primitive in development than honeybees. The female is impregnated in the fall and she alone survives the winter, snugged into a hole in the earth, or some protected crevice, occasionally rousing herself to sip from a small pot of honey at her side.

Come spring, the female bumblebee lays eggs in the nest,

and with her offspring forms a working colony. As the young bumblebees develop, they gather nectar while their mother devotes herself full time to laying eggs. Bumblebees pollinate in the same way that honeybees do, pollen clinging to their large hairy bodies. Often they visit the same flowers, but bumblebees have longer tongues and can reach nectar in plants that are inaccessible to honeybees. Bumblebees are especially effective in pollinating red clover; their greater weight enables them to depress the wing petals of the blooms so they can gather the nectar within, at the same time pollinating the plant.

Darwin uses the bumblebee to illustrate one of nature's more complex and unlikely relationships: the amount of red clover produced depends on the number of bumblebees, and the number of bumblebees depends on the number of field mice, who eat the nests and combs of bumblebees; the number of mice, in turn, depends on the number of cats present. Ultimately, the amount of red clover depends on the number of cats. Large crops of red clover were found around English villages because of the number of cats. Most relationships in nature are more subtle, probably unrecognized because cause and effect are so far removed and invisible, but we interfere with natural processes at our own risk, usually to our disadvantage.

The less virtuous members of the bee family, referred to in the opening of this section, are wild bees who have become thieves, living off the labor of others, and parasites. Parasitism, like theft, is prevalent in nature, as it abounds in most human societies. To nature, I suppose, it is just another means of reproducing and, at the same time, a form of "balancing the books" among the species.

Insects, particularly wild bees, have been wonderfully innovative and have displayed wide variations in technique. Some bee parasites spend their days searching out the nests of other bees. They sneak into the nursery, depositing eggs, which the unsuspecting host mother will rear as her own offspring; before departing, the parasite mother may eat a few of the host mother's own eggs. As the parasite larvae develop, they may devour their foster siblings.

Nor does it end there. Parasite bees may lay their eggs in the bodies of other parasite bees, or several species may lay eggs in the same host, all competing to survive on an inadequate food supply, and eventually dining on one another; it is not unusual for a single egg laid by a parasite to divide, with hundreds of individual parasite young fighting it out in the body of the same host.

How these complex relationships evolved is not known, but they are essential in making the whole thing work, and the domesticated honeybee, like her wild cousins, and even the sour apples on the family tree, all presumably have their own place in preserving the delicate balance nature has ordered.

FOURTEEN

*F*or honeybees, the cluster is necessary to their survival. As soon as packaged bees are introduced into a new hive, they gather around the queen cage to keep their sovereign warm and protected while she is being freed; it is of secondary importance that clustering assures their own survival.

Bees are marvelously equipped for this unique acrobatic maneuver; each foot is equipped with two tiny hooks that mesh together and stick like burrs, enabling the entire colony to join in the familiar pear-shaped mass. The hooks have to be extremely sturdy for the bees at the top of the cluster to support the weight of those below; a colony of sixty thousand or eighty thousand bees can weigh fifteen or twenty pounds. Comparable weight for a man, hanging by his knees and trying to support a burden proportionate to his size, would be in the thousands of pounds.

Clustering is probably the most publicized aspect of bee life. Pictures are forever appearing of bees clinging to traffic lights in busy intersections, in telephone booths, or equally unlikely places. A favorite shot is of a beekeeper at a county fair wearing a "bee beard," bees massed from chin to waist, usually the face hidden except for eyes peering out through the thicket of bees.

The trick is performed by hiding a caged queen under the chin or beneath a porous hat, a bee in the bonnet, as it were. The entire colony gathers protectively around the queen, drawn by her scent. The bee beard, or face mask, is easily removed by withdrawing the hidden cage. If the bees are handled gently, there is virtually no danger of being stung. Recently I saw a newspaper photograph of six young college women cheerleaders crouched in a "living pyramid" with what was claimed to be a million bees clustered on them. I wasn't sure what to make of this. Higher education is, I suppose, where it takes you.

FIFTEEN

Once hived and assured that the queen is in no danger, bees begin freeing the queen so she can start laying eggs. It is as essential for the colony to reproduce itself as it is for the individual members to work. Because a bee's life is so short, new generations of young bees must be produced continuously for the colony to survive. A newly introduced colony immediately begins preparing the nursery for its successors. This succession of generations appears to be the only presumption that bees have to immortality.

By the time the queen is freed from her cage, usually in two to four days, the hive is ready for her to begin laying eggs. Should the colony be disturbed too soon, by checking to see if the queen has been released, the workers may kill the queen, probably holding her responsible for this latest disruption. Bees, the evidence suggests, can act as irrationally and self-destructively as human societies.

Killing a queen is a monstrous act for bees. Usually it happens only in moments of great stress, in panic, rage, by accident, or calculation if the colony is dissatisfied with her performance; in the latter instance a successor queen raised by the colony is waiting to replace the failing or rejected sovereign. A queen marked for death, or killed in pique or panic, may be stung fatally by the workers, but this is rare, at best. Some authorities insist it never happens. No individual or "hit squad" apparently wants to take on such a horrendous responsibility as regicide. By this rash act of aggression, comparable to assassinating a president or leader and causing the reshaping of an entire society, a colony may destroy not only its queen but its means of existence.

Queens are sometimes killed accidentally when the entire colony, if threatened, forms a solid protective mass around her and inadvertently smothers or crushes her. For the luckless queen, the usual life-sustaining cluster becomes a death trap.

A queen marked for execution is usually assassinated by the entire colony in a formalized death ritual known as "balling the queen." Her only offense, probably, is that she no longer is able to lay enough eggs to satisfy her daughters, now turned executioners. All members of the colony participate. They form a solid ball around their mother, pressing harder and harder. The ball becomes progressively smaller as it squeezes in, until the queen is crushed, suffocated, or starved.

This is an ingenious political solution. No single executioner can be blamed. No culprits are fingered and punished as enemies of the state. There can be no individual blame or accountability in a collective act of homicide. There is no cover-up to expose.

It is, in effect, like a mob lynching. But we have no idea whether the "mob" is set into motion by judicial decision or triggered by an enraged individual gone berserk, whose own excitement inflamed murderous passions in others. Some authorities believe the lethal mob is set in motion by one or two ringleaders or bees that panicked, which is common to mobs. But whether by judicial fiat or spontaneous madness, the queen must die.

SIXTEEN

I have a neighbor who loves flowers with the passion of the bees themselves. We were discussing the bees from my hives who visit his yard. How is it, he asked, that, if bees are smart enough to fly miles for honey and find their way home, when they get trapped inside the house they stay against a windowpane instead of having sense enough to go out an open window?

He thought this indicated a lack of intelligence in bees. I pointed out that bees always fly toward the light. In nature there is no equivalent of glass. Their behavior suggests not a want of intelligence but a lack of experience. Light, to a bee, represents warmth and life; it must be akin to the sun itself. What other brilliant light exists in nature? Moving toward sunlight is, for a bee, instinctive and logical.

Maurice Maeterlinck, in his classic, *The Life of the Bee*, cited an experiment in which a fly was able to escape from a bottle in which it was placed more readily than did a bee, the experimenter concluding that the fly was therefore more intelligent than the bee. Maeterlinck challenged the conclusion, stating:

> Turn the transparent sphere [bottle] twenty times, if you will, holding now the base, now the neck, to the window, and you will find that the bees will turn twenty times with it, so as always to face the light. It is their love of light, it is their very intelligence, that is their undoing in this experiment. . . . They evidently imagine that the issue from every prison must be there where the light shines clearest; and they act in accordance, and persist in too logical action. To them glass is a supernatural mystery they never have met with in nature; they have had no experience of this suddenly impenetrable atmosphere; and the greater their intelligence, the more inadmissible, more incomprehensible, will the strange obstacle appear. Whereas the feather-brained flies, careless of logic as of the enigma of crystal, disregarding the call of the light, flutter wildly hither and thither, and, meeting here the good fortune that often waits on the simple, who find salvation there where the wiser will perish, necessarily end by discovering the friendly opening that restores their liberty to them.

He observes that the bee "was intended to live in the midst of an indifferent and unconscious nature, and not by the side of an extraordinary being who is forever disturbing the most constant laws, and producing grandiose and inexplicable phenomena."

It is these grandiose and inexplicable phenomena that we shall encounter frequently in these pages.

SEVENTEEN

In recent years scientists have been taking a new look at the intelligence of other creatures, pursuing it so avidly that they have introduced a new scientific discipline known as cogitative ethology, the study of the conscious thoughts and feelings of nonhuman animals. The basic question ethologists are asking is whether animals are capable of reasoning the way humans do. The ultimate object, I suppose, is that by learning more about animals and their mode of thought, if it exists, we learn more about ourselves.

Maeterlinck speculated at length on the intelligence of bees, comparing our inferences on bee behavior with what an inhabitant of Venus or Mars might conclude as he contemplated us from the height of a mountain, "watching the little black specks we form in space, as we come and go in the streets and squares of our towns":

> Would the mere sight of our movements, our buildings, machines and canals, convey to him any precise idea of our morality, intellect, our manner of thinking, and loving, and hoping—in a word, of our real and intimate self? All he could do, like ourselves when we gaze at the hive, would be to take note of some facts that seem very surprising; and from these facts to deduce conclusions probably no less erroneous, no less uncertain, than those that we choose to form concerning the bee.
>
> This much at least is certain; our "little black specks" would not reveal the vast moral direction, the wonderful unity, that are so apparent in the hive. "Whether do they tend, and what is it they do?" he would ask, after years and centuries of patient watching. "What is the aim of their life, or its pivot? Do they obey some God? I can see nothing that governs their actions. The little things that one day they appear to collect and build up, the next they destroy and scatter. They come and go, they meet and disperse, but one knows not what it is they seek. In numberless cases the spectacle they present is altogether inexplicable."

Would not Maeterlinck's mythical observer be even more perplexed today, as he observed our frantic haste and the magnificent inventions that we often debase in their usage? To better understand us, he would have to know something of our more recent history, the traditions we have drawn from and rejected, and our laws, customs, aspirations, dreams, fears, superstitions, prejudices, and frustrations. This being from space might be impressed and admire our mighty achievements: our soaring cities, the vast connecting network of great highways and airports, huge factories and social institutions, universities and museums, the physical conveniences and comforts with which we surround ourselves, and the advanced technology of electronic communications, computers, satellites, and space flights. Could he help but marvel at the intelligence and cleverness these feats represent in human thought and accomplishment?

But would he not, at the same time, be confounded by our violence toward one another, our devastating wars, the accelerating degredation of the earth's sustaining waters, air, and soil, our rampant crime, vandalism, commercial exploitation, make-work, the cornucopia of useless and inferior goods, labor unrest, ill health, ethnic hostility and paranoid suspicion among nations, political deceptions, whole populations imprisoned by totalitarian governments, wholesale torture and suffering, social dislocation, racial ferment, economic inequity and instability, the accelerating imbalance between rich and poor, between hunger and waste?

Would he not be perplexed watching us scurrying from here to there over those imposing highways and airways, restless, discontented, driving ourselves in endless competitions and compulsive work, wasting the earth's resources and despoiling our habitat, our endless pursuit of trivia and diversion?

How would the observer from space explain or account for our technical success and social failure, our wealth of goods and poverty of spirit? Would he not wonder if our intelligence does not preclude reason, compassion, some sense of equity or morality? Would he not question whether we professed a diety, some guiding philosophy or ethic, or if our purpose was not one of insane, ultimate self-destruction? How could he even begin to make sense of us? And yet, do we not take pride in calling ourselves rational, intelligent beings?

Maeterlinck observed that the being from space would see a few of our number living in great opulence:

> They occupy buildings ten or twenty times larger than ordinary dwellings, and richer, and more ingeniously fashioned. Every day they spend many hours at their meals, which sometimes indeed are prolonged far into the night. They appear to be held in extraordinary honor by those who approach them; men come from the neighboring houses, bringing provisions, and even from the depths of the country, laden with presents. One can only assume that these persons must be indispensable to the race, to which they render essential service, although our means of investigation have not yet enabled us to discover what the precise nature of this service may be. There are others, again, who are incessantly engaged in the most wearisome labor, whether it be in great sheds full of wheels that forever turn round and round, or close by the shipping, or in obscure hovels, or on small plots of earth that from sunrise to sunset they are constantly delving and digging. We are led to believe that this labor must be an offense, and punishable. For the persons guilty of it are housed in filthy, ruinous, squalid cabins. They are clothed in some colorless hide. So great does their ardor appear for this noxious, or at any rate useless activity, that they scarcely allow themselves time to eat or to sleep. In numbers they are to the others as a thousand to one. It is remarkable that the species should have been able to survive to this day under conditions so unfavorable to its development. It should be mentioned, however, that apart from this characteristic devotion to their wearisome toil, they appear inoffensive and docile; and satisfied with the leavings of those who evidently are the guardians, if not the saviors of the race.

Do we recognize ourselves in this description? Could it apply to us today, taking into account that more than a half-century has passed, in which we have been propelled from the horse and buggy into space? Has our social behavior changed in this time to keep pace with the changes in the conditions of our lives? How different are we today, with all of our modern trappings, than we were a half-century ago?

And what of the bees, whose lives have similarly been modernized with technological changes in the hive? Bee literature from the last century suggests that there has been no noticeable variation in their social habits. Bees, unlike humans, apparently are able to accept altered circumstances in their lives without touching the context itself. But we have no way of knowing, in the case of bees or men, whether standing still in time represents advance or retrogression. It is an odd sensation to be zipping through space and not know whether you are going forward or backward, whether you are being clever or stupid.

Like Maeterlinck's being from space looking down upon us and misinterpreting our actions and motives, so do we look down upon the bees with our own ignorance, blindness, and distortions. Dare we say that the bees are not at least the equal of man in the ordering of their lives within the framework of their existence? They have found the answers to their problems while we are still struggling to ask the right questions to define ours. In looking down at the hive we do not see the great disparities and unrest that disrupt human societies. In place of competition they have cooperation, and organizational harmony rather than chaotic imbalances and inequity.

Maeterlinck pointed out that the aim of nature is manifestly the improvement of the race, and this can be accomplished only at the cost of liberty, the rights, and the happiness of the individual: "In proportion as a society organizes itself, and rises in the scale, so does a shrinkage enter the private life of each one of its members. Where there is progress, it is the result only of a more and more complete sacrifice of the individual to the general interest."

While it is not possible to apply all of the rules that nature lays down for other species to man, it is evident that the bees have accepted this principle of individual sacrifice for social progress, just as it has been stoutly resisted in most human societies, in some almost to the point of deifying personal freedom to the detriment of the common good.

We do not see or understand the cause of the sacrifice, unity, and organizational genius of the bee, but we admire the result and are awed by the universal dedication to the common good. Man, with his capacity to think and reason, is, generally, unable to achieve this. We assume that intellectualizing is limited to humans and does not preoccupy other orders. Whether bees conduct their lives and affairs and build and manage their magnificent cities through individual or group intelligence, or as part of nature's grand design, dictated by the indefinable "spirit of the hive," is irrelevant to the result. With only about one milligram of brain matter, less than four ten-thousandths of one ounce, bees can perform feats of communication and navigation and solve orientation and organizational problems. Often this is attributed to instinct, but many scientists who have studied bees closely agree that it alone does not account for these extraordinary achievements.

T. D. A. Cockerell, an authority on bees, said that, although the dominance of instinct has been observed in the affairs of these insects, "it must be admitted that ordinary memory and what we must call intelligence have a part." A similar sentiment comes from entomologist E. O. Essig, who posed and answered the question: Do insects display intelligence? "Although entomologists and biologists disagree on the point, it is important to remember that such a phenomenon as instinct, bordering on intelligence, exists among insects and must exert a considerable influence upon their attainment of their present conspicuous status in the life of the world."

Whatever the bee's intelligence, its source or limitations, recognition or denial, it serves her well within the scheme of her life.

EIGHTEEN

*B*ees are, above all, creatures of the future. For them there is no past, no "good old days." They are not like man, so preoccupied with not being engulfed by today or entrapped by yesterday that he rarely prepares for tomorrow. The bee's today is made up of anticipating tomorrow, like the pharaohs of ancient Egypt who devoted their lives to building great tombs and seaworthy galleons for the journey into eternity. The focus of the entire colony is on the future.

The queen spends her days and nights laying eggs that will form the next generation and generations to follow; the drone stands by, stoking his lust with honey that he had no part in producing, ready to fertilize new queens to perpetuate the race; worker bees tend the young, perform hive chores, and forage for food that will not be consumed until after they have perished. For all, the present exists only as a time to prepare for the future. The vital link in the chain of unbroken time is the nursery.

Before eggs can be laid by the queen, there must be honeycomb to deposit them in. If no comb exists, it must be made. If old comb is already in place, left by former inhabitants, it must be cleaned or repaired. Honeycomb is the material of which the city is built; it is used not only to receive the queen's precious eggs, but also to provide storage space for honey and pollen used as food for embryo bees.

If only flat sheets of foundation fill the frames, suspended in the supers, the foundation must be drawn out into honeycomb. The bees, ingenious acrobats that they are, form an inverted cone over the face of the vertical walls of foundation by locking the hooks on their feet together, generating heat as they do when clustering, making possible the formation and molding of wax. Some bees reach the foundation by building "ladders," small pillars of wax, from the hive bottom.

Usually only young bees are capable of making wax, but, when necessary, older bees can turn the trick, in the same way a retired craftsman can, in an emergency, recapture a former skill. After eighteen to twenty-four hours of clinging together, the temperature climbs to about eighty degrees Fahrenheit and a strange thing happens—tiny wax flakes appear on eight small, pocket-like glands on the abdomens of young bees. The bee scrapes off the wax with her forelegs and kneads and chews the secretion in powerful jaws until it is a soft, pliable ball.

She frees herself from the clinging mass and deposits the wax at the base of the sheet of foundation with its hexagon imprints. Quickly she moves away, and another bee takes over, perhaps a celebrated artist or architect, who pushes and tugs at the soft wax, drawing it out in the hexagon shape. Then she, in turn, steps aside and still another craftsman comes along to draw the cell out farther, each a specialist, it seems, in a different phase of cell building.

We watch with wonder as the honeycomb takes shape, awed not only by the artistry but by the organizational efficiency. Other crews are, simultaneously, building comb on other frames. This labor is carried out in darkness, the wax makers and artists hanging upside down by their heels, clinging to a partner above. How do these artists, guided only by touch and by such limited light as penetrates their multifaceted eyes, produce such an exquisite product under such adverse conditions: How does nature herself produce a design of such functional eloquence? Who is in charge? Who runs the show? Who or what power coordinates this activity? Are we to believe that the decisions were made millions of years ago and are now being automatically retrieved from some repository called instinct?

It is not only the city being built but the plan behind it that stirs wonder and respect for these architects and artisans. Every plan represents some kind of intelligence or order; the more complex the plan, generally, the greater the intelligence or the higher the order. By looking at the plan it is usually possible to tell much about those who conceived and executed it. A city built by bees is an indication of their intelligence or, at least, the order imposed upon them and which they obey. The hive, provided by man and furnished by bees, with its interchangeable supers and removable frames, its storage vats and passageways, nursery and nest, is an almost perfect representation of the architectural dictum that form follows function. It is perfect of its kind, accommodating both man and bees.

The work continues until thousands and thousands of the contiguous six-sided wax combs are completed. More astonishing, both sides of the sheets of foundation are drawn out at once by crews working independently of one another on opposite sides of the frames. Somehow the workers are in constant communication through a solid barrier of wax, as the base of each cell lies precisely at the point where the three sides of the cells on the opposite side meet to give greater strength. How do we explain this fact of engineering, this mystery of communication?

Few of nature's creations are more acclaimed than new honeycomb, the creamy hexagon cells exuding their fragrance of flowers and honey; this unique material, with its rich incense, is the essence of life in the hive, formed of the juices of the bees themselves, combining beauty, great strength, and efficiency.

NINETEEN

The hexagon cells of beeswax, like the substance they are made of, have been studied, analyzed, and measured, but these calculations fail to capture the genius of the bee. Each cell is about a half-inch deep, but can be made deeper. All are not uniform in size, if inspected closely; larger cribs are built for drone brood than for the smaller workers, and still larger ones for queens. To compensate for the discrepancy in size, bees build so-called transition cells to make the finished comb come out even. These odd-shaped accommodation cells are used only to store honey or pollen and are not for rearing brood.

Comb always looks the same, but there are minute variations from cell to cell, comb to comb, and hive to hive. Nature's universal rule in all things is diversity within uniformity. She could be saying, "I will give you the design, but you must figure out how to achieve it." Thus, we have likeness but not sameness, infinite variety of execution within conformity of design.

When sheets of foundation are drawn out, there is normally just enough space between the adjoining frames for two bees to pass, the "bee space" I previously wrote about. Later, alleys and passageways will be chewed in the combs so the workers can move quickly to and from the cradles and great storage vaults of honey; these thoroughfares differ from one hive to another, depending on how the architects or planners conceive their city, or the workers take it upon themselves to alter it, taking shortcuts or improvising new routes.

Allowances apparently are made for local differences and creative impulses among colonies. Impromptu cuts in comb sometimes seem to be based on whimsy alone, serving no real purpose to the observer and seeming to contradict the meaningful industry that we expect. I have seen corners chewed out of honeycomb far from the scene of action. Why this odd and unnecessary passageway? I speculated. Later it occurred to me that this was not intended as a passageway at all—the bees had needed wax for a quick patch or repair and this was a convenient source that could be replaced when the crisis had passed, or left if not needed.

If there are damaged or incomplete combs in the hive when

it is occupied, the bees will reconstruct them rather than start afresh. These efficient engineers know the work goes faster restoring, enlarging, or completing old or damaged comb rather than building new. By the same logic, they prefer drawing out foundation, with its embossed designs, to starting from scratch.

The science of modern beekeeping is based largely on that one simple truth: bees will draw out foundation before they will build from nothing. This alone makes possible the movable frames and interchangeable hive bodies which enable beekeepers to rob their charges without killing them. Beekeeping is, in essence, taking advantage of the bee's instinct to produce in the most efficient way. She is betrayed by her instinct, as man may be the victim of his own intelligence and loss of instinct.

TWENTY

It is not by chance alone that bees decided upon the delicate hexagon shape for their honeycomb. Mathematicians consider it the most efficient form possible, providing a cask that holds a maximum of honey with a minimum of wax. The walls are so incredibly thin that it would take two thousand to three thousand laid on top of one another to equal a single inch. At the same time, the shape and substance of which it is made have such amazing tensile strength that one pound of beeswax will form thirty-three thousand cells holding twenty-two pounds of honey. A single hive body filled with honey weighs about eighty pounds, making backache a common ailment among beekeepers.

Beeswax is as mysterious as it is remarkable. Although the major ingredients are known, it has never been duplicated in the laboratory. It has an antiseptic quality that allows it to last for centuries; beeswax was found in the tombs of the pharaohs, still pliable, and it has been rescued from the sea after years of immersion with no damage. Beeswax is widely used in industry, with more than a million pounds used annually in cosmetics alone, but a shortcoming that limits its usefulness is the wide variation in quality, depending on the comb from which it is rendered.

For many years scientists disagreed over whether bees purposely designed and used the hexagon because of its efficiency, or it evolved as a result of natural forces. Those supporting the latter thesis argued that if numerous round cylinders or objects are pressed together they will be forced into a six-sided figure, and they proved it by experiments with peas and other substances and mathematical calculations. Their theory, sound as it appeared, was discredited in other experiments using bees. Forced to build single figures, the bees formed a six-sided base and maintained the hexagon while drawing it out. The figures were not as perfect as in comb but there was no denying their intention. Bees also have their own clever mathematicians, engineers, and architects.

In the wild, honeybees build the same hexagon-shaped combs, but not in the orderly arrangement provided by foundation. Foundation is well named. It is the basis of hive order. When bees make comb on their own, not guided by foundation, it may take on the most fantastic shapes, with greater irregularity in the sizes of the individual cells, as the artists and architects, having no matrix to inhibit them, are free to give vent to their own creativity or rash impulses. But invariably, regardless of design, the bee mathematicians insist upon the same six-sided cells, even in combs twisted in wild pretzel-like configurations. Bees are beholden to the hexagon imperative while free to choose their own art form.

Even in man-made hives, bees frequently ignore or violate the factory discipline thrust upon them by orderly frames of foundation. Colonies often build, "burr," or "brace" comb, which has no place in a tidy, well-managed hive. The names are often used interchangeably, but brace comb joins two parts of the hive together, while burr comb is built on comb or on a part of the hive and is not attached to anything else.

Brace comb does have its logic, providing extra room to store honey or raise brood, if a beekeeper is negligent in providing extra space when needed. But burr comb appears to be busy work, serving the compulsive need of bees to keep occupied when they have no other hive chores. Some colonies build more burr or brace comb than others, often turning the neglected hive into an almost solid block of wax with only narrow passageways for the bees to move about. A beekeeper trying to pull such a comb-locked hive apart invariably causes extensive damage and loss of life.

While bees are content to go their own way, as they have for millions of years, researchers are more inclined to want to improve on nature. They have conducted some odd experiments with bees and comb. It has long been known that the size of a bee is largely determined by the size of the cell in which it is raised. The investigators decided that by building larger cells they could produce larger bees that would be more efficient, producing larger amounts of honey at a lower cost in time and effort expended. Larger cells, it was reasonably concluded, could also hold more honey, further increasing efficiency. The theory was tempting. People can rarely resist the temptation to reform or instruct nature rather than learn from her.

There is, I am convinced, a law of the Perverse Nature of Theories, and this experiment followed that law. Larger bees were produced, according to plan, and they had longer tongues that enabled them to gather more honey quicker. But, as so often happens when man meddles with nature, he did not foresee all of the consequences. The larger bees required so much more honey to sustain their bulk that they were not more but less efficient than the smaller bees.

There was another unexpected result: the larger bees could not squeeze into small flowers to gather nectar, like normal bees, and were not able to pollinate them. Nature, in her wisdom, created flowers and their pollinators of a size to serve one another. In any case, the researchers put aside their flawed calculations and accepted nature's own dimensions evolved through trial and error in the laboratory of time. Foundation is now standardized to suit worker bees of normal size, providing precisely 4.83 cells to the linear inch, in keeping with the harmonies of the great design.

TWENTY-ONE

One of the joys of beekeeping is watching bees bring pollen into the hive. They light heavily on the landing board, laden with what looks like brightly colored saddlebags attached to their hindlegs, and waddle through the hive entrance. Pollen, as most people know, comes from flowers and some trees and shrubs. As every elementary botany text teaches, the male element is produced in a small sac in a flower's anthers and transferred to the female stigma to complete fertilization. This method, with a bewildering number of variations, innovations, technical and biological inspirations, and breakthroughs, is the basis for almost all reproduction throughout the plant and animal kingdoms. Man, perhaps, has been the most active and agile in sexual experiments, but despite the most heroic efforts has not yet succeeded in improving on the basic idea.

Pollen can be almost any color, depending on its source. Individual grains differ in size, but most are no bigger than specks of dust. It would take a single bee six hundred hours to collect one teaspoonful of the tiny grains, according to those who calculate such things. One industrious bee usually requires only about a half-hour to gather as much pollen as she can carry in flight. In adverse weather she may have to visit a hundred or more flowers and take up to two hours to collect a full load; rarely will she return to the hive with her baskets less than full.

The task may be made more difficult because flowers can be temperamental and open only at certain hours of the day, remaining open for varying lengths of time; some demand the right weather conditions before they will produce pollen and make it available, a problem in receptivity encountered by other species in their sexual adventures. Some plants adjust their flowering period to the emergence of the insects that pollinate them.

The honeybee, sexually disfranchised herself, is one of nature's primary pollinating agents, along with rainfall, gravity, the winds, birds, and other insects, as well as mammals, including humans. Bees pollinate about 80 percent of all plants, some one hundred thousand species of plants in all, making the bees invaluable in agriculture. Because of their size, compared to most other insects, bees are especially useful in transferring grains of pollen that are too heavy to be borne on the wind. They are the principal pollinators of plants bearing flowers with colors. A bee's normal visual color range is blue, yellow, green, and ultraviolet. Beekeepers often paint their hives these colors to help homecoming bees identify them. In addition to colors, bees recognize certain flowers by the number of petals and their arrangement.

The honeybee's role in fertilizing plants is inadvertent. As she makes her rounds gathering nectar, scurrying from flower to flower, grains of pollen dust cling to tiny hairs on her body and antennae and are transferred from male to female organ in one of the symbiotic economies in nature: the bee is drawn to the blossom by its seductive fragrance, color, and secretions, and while gathering nectar or pollen for her own sustenance and the reproduction of her kind she makes possible the host plant's survival.

The marvel is not only what takes place but the efficiency and grace with which it is accomplished, almost like a ballet movement. On a bee's upper hindlegs are small hollows ringed by stiff bristle-like hairs; these are aptly named pollen baskets and, as their name suggests, are used for the collection of pollen. While tripping among the flowers, a worker gathers grains of pollen with her mouthparts; simultaneously she adroitly removes pollen which adheres to her antennae with tiny splines, for just that purpose, on her front legs.

In a single effortless motion, while in flight, her mouthparts and all six legs work in unison. She chews pollen grains to dampen them, using forelegs and middle legs to relay the moist ball to her baskets. The compacted pollen resembles small loaves of colored bread, and indeed pollen mixed with honey is known as "bee bread."

Bees generally gather pollen from only one kind of flower at a time, which was long assumed to be nature's way of trying to prevent the cross-pollination of plants and preserve integrity among species. Thus, pollen brought into the hive is usually pure in context and uniform in color, although the same flower may produce pollen of more than one shade.

How nature imposed her will on bees so they tend to collect a single variety of pollen we do not know. But alas for the assumption! More recent research has revealed that bees bring in mixed pollen more often than was formerly believed; in fact, up to 40 percent of the pollen samples brought into a hive under study were variegated. Bumblebees are even less constant than honeybees in sticking to one kind of blossom, and it seems reasonable to assume that other insects and pollinators are at least equally faithless and indifferent to the integrity of plants in serving their own needs and convenience.

Bees are, however, above all, practical. They prefer pollen from a single type of blossom when it is available, but if it isn't, or if there is a shortage or they tire and one type of blossom is exhausted, they simply switch to another. This may be the root of infidelity among all species: if the object of commitment is not convenient, will not another at hand do just as well?

Nature, always amoral in sex, seems to be at least agreeable to the cross-pollination of plants, occasionally using the method to produce beautiful and useful new varieties. This may be evolution in operation, or nature's way of being experimental and permissive, but she doesn't want to overdo it, so it happens only now and then.

TWENTY-TWO

Pollen is to bee larvae what bread is to humans—the staff of life; mixed with honey and stored in combs, it is well named bee bread, providing not only the sustenance of bee life but having a breadlike taste. Pollen is a source of protein, while honey gives energy for growth and warmth. Nutritionally pollen is a complete food, consisting of a high percentage of nitrogen, sulfur, phosphorus, carbohydrates, oil, and sugars; it has at least ten vitamins and a dozen minerals; an average colony consumes about seventy pounds annually for its own use, representing a staggering number of bee flights and industry.

Gathering the tiny grains of pollen must be a tedious business at best, going all day from flower to flower, taking a speck here, a speck there. But is it any more tiresome or boring than squandering one's days and life juices performing any of the infinite repetitive tasks most humans must do in order to live?

Bees, unlike many humans, seem content enough to earn their beebread by the "sweat of their brow."

To a beekeeper, seeing bees return bearing pollen is a reassuring sight. That and the hum of contentment within tell him that the queen is laying brood and all is well. On a summer day, pollen-laden bees return to the hive in a procession, baskets loaded, bumping down on the landing board and scurrying inside with their treasure.

Inside the hive, the pollen bearer scurries up a frame of honeycomb, which probably holds hundreds of eggs and larvae. She selects a cell that is empty or only partly full of pollen, usually near the upper edge of the frame where the substance is deposited close to the brood. Thrusting her rear legs with the pollen baskets into the cell, supporting her abdomen on the edge and clinging with her forelegs, she uses the brushes on her middle legs to kick free the pollen from her baskets. These brushes have many uses, including that of a handkerchief to wipe pollen dust from her eyes. A bee is really quite well equipped for almost any emergency encountered in line of duty.

Pollen is not used at once, in the way that the devilish propolis is. The honeybee leaves her load where it falls and hurries off in search of more. Her attitude suggests that she considers her time too brief and valuable to squander it on a chore that a less-skilled hive member can handle.

Later a young house bee, not yet ready for field duty, will pack the pollen into the cell, or she may move it elsewhere and combine it with deposits left by other workers. Pollen is then capped with a mixture of honey and beeswax that will preserve it indefinitely.

In recent years pollen has become another article of commerce provided by bees. Ingenious traps have been devised to rob them of the substance for human use. Bees are forced to pass through contraptions made of fine wires, which scrape the pollen off their bodies and it falls through wire mesh into collecting pits; an unbelievable amount of pollen is collected in this way, but the more that is taken, the harder the guileless bees work to gather new supplies. The harder she works, the more she is exploited. Should we pity her or exalt her labor? The bee is not the slave of man but of her own instinct.

Pollen taken from bees is sold as a wonder food by health stores. Athletes, and especially runners, are major users, claiming that it gives them stamina and energy. Aside from pollen's inherent food values, researchers have been unable to substantiate the glories attributed to it. But those who buy and sell this life force of flowering plants and embryo bees insist that it contains mysterious and marvelous powers that elude the test tube, a testimonial that the bees themselves undoubtedly would endorse.

TWENTY-THREE

In visiting the fields for pollen and nectar and performing hive tasks, it is not to the future alone that the bee pays tribute, but to ancient memories that speak in silent voices heard across millions of years. One of these voices tells her to gather propolis, that sticky, resinous material with which she seals her hive against the elements.

The word propolis is of Greek derivation, *pro* meaning before and *polis* city, a reference to its use by wild bees to close off their cities, which were little more than an exposed cavity in a tree or the face of a cliff. Propolis is no longer necessary in today's man-made hives, but is lavishly used just the same, as if the nest were still exposed and had to be protected against the weather.

Propolis itself is as sticky when the weather is hot as it is brittle when cold. Often it is described as sap, but it is of a different chemical composition. It comes primarily from trees and is very sticky, which is why it is known as "bee glue." Once it gets on the fingers it is virtually impossible to remove without the use of mineral spirits, or rubbing the fingers vigorously in the dirt, removing propolis and skin together.

Bees go almost berserk in its use, as if trying to keep out the elements and all intruders as well. They not only seal each crevice, but may lock together every movable part of the hive until it is a solid unit and must be pried apart with the steel hive tool; sometimes old wood splits before the propolized parts separate.

The longer propolis sets, the harder it gets. In cold weather it shatters like ice. It has certain protective or antiseptic qualities, and bees spread it thinly in cells of honeycomb as a seal, like varnish or shellac, to protect the surface from drying out. Otherwise it is a nuisance to beekeepers and must be scraped off the hives when they are examined. To the bees this must seem a wanton act of vandalism, undoing all of their trouble gathering it.

Bees gather propolis much as they collect pollen, but even for them it is a problem. When the days are warm enough for the stuff to be soft and pliable, a honeybee lights on a juicy bud and uses her mouthparts to tear out a chunk of the material, careful not to let the clinging filaments entangle her. She removes it carefully from her mandibles with the claws on her rear legs and stuffs it into her pollen baskets where it is kneaded into a ball-like shape, a wonderfully adroit maneuver performed while she is flying to another bud for more.

When both baskets are full, containing about a drop of propolis in all, she returns to the hive. What follows has its comic aspects, but to the bee it must be irksome and hard on her dignity. Unable to remove the gooey stuff herself, she clings desperately to the hive, while other bees tear off the propolis with their mandibles. Often the carrier is pulled loose from her moorings and there appears to be ill temper and recriminations on both sides.

Bees often return from gathering propolis late in the day and by then the stuff has set so hard that it cannot be removed until the temperature rises again. The carrier is almost immobile, and walks as if she has a cast on her leg. In the morning she doesn't go directly to the fields but suns herself until the substance softens and can be removed.

Propolis, unlike pollen, is not stored until needed but is used at once, perhaps smeared on an inner cover, a wall, or used to bond frames to their supporting edges, often serving no apparent purpose and wasteful of time and effort, or so it seems, although it is possible that there is a purpose that eludes us.

How does a propolis-gatherer feel about this? Is it considered hazardous duty or punishment? Is it an honor, requiring strength and agility and entailing risk? Does she ever look about her and see the propolis she gathered with such difficulty being smeared senselessly about and grumble to herself, "Why am I doing this?"

Or do we assume that the force of instinct is so powerful that she obeys without question? Will evolution ever relent and free our modern bee of this ancient burden that no longer seems to have meaning? Or is she destined forever to respond to the same voices that spoke to her wild ancestors?

TWENTY-FOUR

Nature both gives and takes life with a lavish hand. As her first law is multiplication, her second is decimation. Thus we have the great cycle of life begetting death and death begetting life, two mighty forces as divergent and yet complementary as the mature Atlantic salmon swimming from the vast sea up an obscure stream to spawn in the pond where it was conceived, great armies of lemmings periodically marching toward the sea in what is, in effect, a suicidal migration, or huge herds of pilot whales inexplicably beaching themselves to die.

I have already noted the prolific reproduction of flies, aphids, and some other creatures. A single oyster can discharge 125 million eggs, or spat as it is called. But even this prodigious output is topped by a termite queen that was clocked laying one egg every second, eighty thousand a day, or more than twenty-eight million a year, and capable of continuing at that brisk pace for up to fifty years, which must be some kind of record even among insects. Such fecundity makes the queen honeybee's two thousand eggs a day seem small potatoes indeed.

The most primitive and elementary form of all life is probably an egg, possibly nature's most ingenious creation. An egg may produce a single individual, divide and produce two, or keep dividing and produce many. In some insect species a single egg may result in fifteen hundred to twenty-five hundred individuals. Nearly three thousand small parasitic wasps were counted emerging from a caterpillar in which not more than a dozen eggs had been laid.

Bees do not go in for this sort of thing, really a kind of reproductive exhibitionism. One bee per egg! That is the rule. Within each egg is the matrix of the bee's life, millions of years of experience condensed in one tiny fragment of protoplasm, the intelligence or programming called instinct, the destiny she will fulfill. Each egg is so small that it would take 240,000 to weigh one ounce. Imagine! The white, cylinder-shaped egg, hardly bigger than the tip of a needle and almost invisible to old eyes, is deposited in its cradle by the queen mother, standing on end, held upright by a dab of adhesive. After three days it begins to tilt over on its side, preparatory to hatching, the declining angle indicating its age. What unknown sensors rule the unfolding drama in this speck of living matter?

The egg is the locus of our universe, the origin of life, which not even the greatest minds among us can define, let alone explain or duplicate. An egg forms spontaneously inside of a body. It is fertilized by sperm from another body. Out of this union arises a third and new being, like the pair that generated it, yet different, a unique individual with characteristics of its parents and still a personality and character of its own. Is this beginning of a new life not miracle enough for anyone?

TWENTY-FIVE

$\mathcal{F}$or the first three days after the egg hatches all bee larvae are fed nothing but royal jelly, one of the wonder foods of nature; it is a pasty, creamy white substance with a strong odor and a somewhat bitter taste, known to be rich in vitamins and containing sugar, proteins, and some organic acids. But there are also mysterious properties that escape the chemist's scrutiny and defy his ingenuity. Royal jelly, like life itself, cannot be synthesized or duplicated in the laboratory. For all of the genius of modern science, nature is still able to withhold her most profound secrets, something like the wily cook who gives away her favorite recipe but omits a key ingredient.

Royal jelly has also become a popular and expensive health food, with miraculous powers attributed to it, but it appears to have a more profound effect on embryo bees than on humans searching for the elusive fountain of youth. Royal jelly is produced only by young nurse bees from glands in their heads. After a few days they are no longer capable of secreting the substance and move along to other tasks.

The most amazing property of royal jelly is that any bee larva from a fertilized egg fed nothing but the substance will become a queen. Other embryos, taken off the substance after three days, become workers; they are then fed a less exotic diet of pollen mixed with saliva and its unknowns from nurse bees, so-called worker jelly, that is mixed with honey. Oddly enough, worker jelly alone will not support continued larval development as royal jelly does, although it has a higher protein content. Drone larvae, after three days on a diet of royal jelly, are fed a more coarse mixture of undigested pollen and honey.

How these various dietary elements or their absence cause such profound physiological and morphological differences is not known. It is another riddle of nature, like an unfolding flower revealing its beauty but withholding its secrets. But the bees could properly say, "You are what you eat."

TWENTY-SIX

*A*n egg, or a newly hatched larva, is a beautiful and welcome sight to a beekeeper. It means the queen is present and working. There is no need to search her out, as the eggs and larvae are proof enough that she is on the job.

The larva, or grub, is pearly white and lies curled in the bottom of the cell in a crescent shape, moving occasionally to some unknown command to keep in contact with the food supply. Nurse bees start supplying the egg with royal jelly even before it hatches; the emerging larva virtually floats in a pool of the secretion, absorbing it through an almost-transparent skin. Royal jelly, along with its other mysterious qualities, is so thoroughly utilized by the crib occupant that there are no bodily wastes to be disposed of, a remarkable biological feat in itself. The secretion is also believed to help eggs hatch.

From the time an egg is deposited in a cell, nurse bees keep visiting it. No other species is known to lavish such attention on their newborn. Most insects deposit their eggs in a waiting food supply, often in someone's garden, and that's an end to it between parent and progeny. The young must fend for themselves while their mother is off having new affairs and laying more eggs.

The nursery in a beehive is incredibly busy during the brood season. Nurse bees visit each cradle to look in on or feed the inhabitant on an average of three hundred visits or feedings in a twenty-four-hour period, a total of ten thousand during the growth stage; and yet, despite all of this coming and going, there never appears to be any confusion, but only purposeful activity. The nurse bees, it will be remembered, are only hours or days out of the crib themselves, and are already performing their first hive chore automatically, as they will their subsequent tasks.

There must be some kind of system or schedule to regulate the feedings, other than a hit-or-miss operation with passing nurse bees popping a bit of food into a waiting "mouth" each time she passes. If no one knew what anyone else was doing, it would seem that some embryos would be overfed while others would starve. This doesn't happen, to my knowledge, but who does keep track of who has and who hasn't been fed among their multitude of cradles and formless bodies without known voices to complain or summon help?

The amount of food given at each feeding is infinitesimal. A popular saying among beekeepers is that it takes one cell of honey to produce one bee, a frame of honey for a frame of bees. But that hoary expression may be incorrect; research now indicates that embryo bees may require less food than was formerly believed, and one cell of honey provides food for as many as five grubs. Nature is more efficient than given credit for.

An average colony uses about one and a half pounds of honey a day in rearing brood during the peak season. Since it takes four pounds of nectar to produce a single pound of honey, the support system for the young takes most of a colony's energies.

The average colony requires about four hundred to five hundred pounds of honey annually for its own use; that means almost two thousand pounds of nectar must be gathered by each hive. The stronger a colony is, the harder it must work to maintain itself, and the more complex its logistics.

The constant feeding of larvae causes exceedingly fast growth. Upon emerging from an egg, a grub weighs only a tenth of a milligram, and after five days on a steady diet of honey and pollen the average weight soars to 150 milligrams. If the same held true for a baby, I once read, an infant weighing six pounds at birth would, within a few days, weigh four tons if it were fed and responded like a bee.

As the wormlike figure curled in the bottom of the cell out-grows its horizontal position after a few days, it wriggles about so it stands upright, the head facing the light, in obedience to a command that regulates its growth.

For six days it remains in the grub stage, continuing to be fed steadily, while taking on a more definitive outline. Then nurse bees cover the cell with a cap made of wax, pollen, or a combination of the two. Each nurse seems to have some lati-tude in her choice of materials, but her creativity must stop there; the cap is slightly raised, or convex, to permit growth, and is porous to admit air for breathing.

A single hive can contain up to twenty thousand cells of brood, the occupants in various stages of development. The eggs and tiny unformed bodies are in an oval shape, like a foot-ball, and ringed with pollen on the upper corners. I never remove a frame of brood from a hive without being stirred by the exquisite artistry in the creation of new life. The bees do not seem to resent this intrusion during periodic inspections, if it occurs during fine weather, almost as if they are pleased to have their handiwork admired.

O nce the cell is capped, another miracle takes place as the occupant within completes her development. Honeybees, as members of the insect order hymenoptera, undergo a complete metamorphosis, changing from one form to another.

These growth stages are common among insects undergoing metamorphosis, some having as many as seventeen separate transformations; at each stage the change may be so radical that they appear to be different types of individuals. Other insects undergo only partial metamorphosis, like that garden terrorist the squash bug, which increases in size through a series of molts while remaining active and recognizable in form. A third group, which includes the speedy silverfish, hatches from eggs as perfect miniature replicas of their parents, growing to adulthood in a process of direct development, much as a human infant reaches maturity.

The initial growth stages of the bee are as egg and then as larva. In the larval or grub stage she is largely formless, little more than a worm, somewhat thick in the middle and tapered at each end, the head slightly larger than the tail with only a suggestion of facial features. She admittedly isn't much to look at in this stage.

The third stage of development takes place after the cell is capped. The grub, again obeying some internal command, spins a cocoon of fine hair around itself, like a silken shroud, and pupates, or rests. This is the first time the embryo bee takes a hand in her own development, previously leaving everything to the nurses. It is here, out of sight, that nature works her miracle, transforming this shapeless living matter into highly specialized organs in a new and more complex form of life.

Do we here have a speeded-up process of evolution, radical changes that once required millions of years now taking place in days? What did the original bee look like as it descended from its Carboniferous ancestor 250 million years or so back, when the first six-legged creatures appeared and the earth labored in converting carbon dioxide into coal?

Our little contemporary worker bee presumably does not concern herself with such idle speculation. After spending three days as an egg and six in the larval stage, she pupates in her cocoon for twelve days, a total of twenty-one days in all, compared to sixteen for her queen mother and twenty-four for her drone brother. The honeybee, so far as is known, has not deviated from her schedule and incipient life-style for millions of years, while other forms were experimenting and changing around her, as if she decided long ago that she had a good thing going and would stay with it, and evolution could go hang.

TWENTY-EIGHT

*F*rom the time a worker bee crawls unsteadily out of her crib, all golden, downy, all innocence and new life itself, she is ready to embark on her work. She has reached her fourth and last stage of development, perfect of her kind, structurally suited to the tasks she must perform. The first day is spent gaining strength and, it seems reasonable to assume, trying to comprehend the strange situation into which she has suddenly been thrust.

Anatomically, she is made up of three parts, with a head, thorax, and abdomen, and covered with a hard outside skeleton, or exoskeleton, made of chitin, a hard, horny substance found throughout nature. Chitin serves as a kind of cast or armor to protect the soft inner tissues, the opposite of a human's inner skeleton and soft outer body.

In her head are the mouthparts, set vertically in the face, with powerful mandibles, or jaws, that chew sideways instead of up and down like a person. Her tongue is a strawlike sucking tube used to extract nectar from the most delicate flowers; the length of the tongue, or tube, in sucking insects determines which flowers they can gather nectar from and pollinate; there is considerable specialization among them.

On each side of her head are two huge compound eyes, each having sixty-three hundred facets, in effect like so many individual eyes pointing in different directions, the tiny immovable lenses providing a wide area of fixed vision. There are, in addition, three simple eyes grouped together on top of a worker's head, the two sets of eyes enabling her to see near and far objects and to distinguish among the colors within her visual range, but researchers do not agree on which set of eyes performs which task, information that is probably more important to investigators than to bees.

The drone has two enormous bulging compound eyes on top of his head, giving him a somewhat comical, leering expression; each eye has an extraordinary thirteen thousand fixed lenses, presumably to help him track the queen during the mating flight, and possibly to keep a few thousand eyes on competing drones in the mating chase to see how he is faring.

The queen, who lives out her days in almost perpetual darkness within the hive, has three compound eyes, but each has only thirty-nine hundred lenses, as if nature were reluctant to waste unnecessary equipment on her. This is another example of nature's efficiency in doling out equipment; each functioning part of a colony is provided the degree of sight necessary to fulfill its role.

In the center of her head are two antennae, commonly called feelers, used not only for feeling but also for communication, hearing, smelling, and probably other undetermined functions. With her antennae she probes the darkness of the hive, measures danger, distinguishes friend from foe, and sniffs out pollen and nectar. A bee's antennae may be the primary equipment that puts her in touch with forces that elude researchers who try to cross that fine and invisible line between scie·ce and the unknown powers she is tapped into.

A drone has 37,800 nostril-like olfactory centers in each antenna, compared to only 500 in a worker, again, probably, to aid him in the nuptial flight; at the same time it indicates how nature favors reproductive capacity over the search for food.

The acute sensory organs in an antenna not only enable a worker to fulfill her complex duties in the darkness of the hive and to sniff out fruit trees or fields of clover in bloom a mile away, but it may have another and more sophisticated role, helping bees and other insects to transmit and receive electromagnetic signals, much as humans use electronic equipment for broadcasting and receiving. If confirmed, this could explain a long-standing mystery of how insects invite their friends and relatives to enjoy the bounty of lush gardens they discover.

Completing the organs found in a bee's head are the glands that help produce the secretions with which she feeds the young, and that possibly regulate the performing of various hive functions.

Joined to the head is the thorax, or upper body, and attached to it are two pair of silvery, veined wings and three pairs of legs. On the front legs are small brushes used to wipe pollen and dust from the eyes; there are also small grooves for cleaning the antennae of pollen. Workers are forever cleaning their antennae, almost like a vain young girl combing her hair. Two hooks on the terminal ends of each foot make possible clustering, and between the hooks is a sticky pad that enables a bee to walk on slick surfaces and vertical planes.

A bee's two pairs of wings make her a powerful flyer, able

to buck raindrops almost as large as she is, fly against strong headwinds, and carry loads of nectar equal to her own weight. Her wings are stubby, but beat so rapidly that she is able to fly an estimated fifteen to twenty-five miles per hour. The double set of wings hook together in flight, providing power; when not flying they lie flat on the back, making it possible for her to crawl into the small cells of the hive to care for eggs and larvae. For her weight and size, a honeybee is said to fly faster and farther than any other winged creature. She is the opposite of her cousin, the cumbersome bumblebee who, according to aeronautical flight criteria, has been proved incapable of flight:

> I like the joke on the bumblebee;
> His wings are too small to hold him.
> He really can't fly, professors agree
> But nobody ever told him.
>
> —Anon.

A honeybee's wings, as noted previously, beat 160 to 220 times per minute, according to the authoritative United States Department of Agriculture 1952 Yearbook, *Insects*, producing the note C sharp below middle C. The publication states that insect wings vary from 350 strokes a second (21,000 per minute) to as few as 6 per minute for the yellow swallowtail butterflies, which seem to float as much as they fly.

The bumblebee manages about 130 beats per minute (D above middle C); June bugs, 46 (F sharp, three octaves below middle C); dragonflies, 20 (E, four octaves below middle C); and the cabbage butterfly, another garden predator, 12, producing a sound inaudible to human ears. A housefly's wings beat only 190 times a minute (G flat below middle C), but with such rapidity that she can travel up to 50 miles per hour. A fly's speed and agility are her primary means of defense, while a bee's power enables her to fly long distances with heavy loads of honey, which seems fair enough.

The third segment of a bee's body is her abdomen, separated from the thorax by a narrow waist. In a bee's abdomen are her honey sac, stomach, and intestines. Many believe that a bee's honey sac and her real stomach are one and the same; the crude and uninformed have called honey "bee vomit," but this is a libel. The honey sac lies directly on top of the stomach proper, separated by a shutoff valve so there is no mixing of the contents of the two. If a bee needs a quick pickup in flight, she has only to open the valve and let a bit of nectar or honey trickle into her stomach. When nectar is regurgitated from the honey sac, it contains enzymes that give honey its unique properties.

At the base of the abdomen, like a tiny tail, is the stinger, which will be dealt with later. On the abdomen are also the wax glands, previously referred to. Recent research has revealed that in the abdomen are cells containing iron, with nerves leading to these cells; they are believed to act as a navigational aid, enabling bees to sense the earth's magnetic field. If verified, this could help explain how bees return unerringly to their hives from distant fields. It has long been known that bees use the earth's magnetic field to sense direction, but it was not understood how it was done. It could also, possibly, yield insights into how birds, butterflies, turtles, and other migrating creatures and wanderers navigate over long distances.

A bee does not breathe like a person, taking in oxygen through the lungs, the blood transporting it throughout the body; rather, bees have tiny openings, like open portholes, along the length of the thorax and abdomen, and attached air-conducting ducts convey oxygen to nearly every nerve. Since hemoglobin is not needed to carry oxygen, a bee's blood is not red. This arrangement is satisfactory enough for most purposes, but nature obviously didn't count on insecticides. When poisons enter the breathing holes bees die of suffocation or destruction of the central nervous system; millions of bees, even whole apiaries, are wiped out every year by great toxic storms, particularly around orchards. It is often claimed that insects do not suffer when poisoned, but anyone who has watched them die, twitching, writhing, and finally paralyzed, would have trouble accepting this claim.

After an embryo bee is sealed into the cell, spinning her web and pupating, the various organs and vital processes are formed—heart, nervous system, muscles, alimentary canal, and bloodstream. Some great intelligence directs the show and the bee, in her shroud, follows its commands. On the twenty-first day after the egg was laid, the new worker chews away the wax capping to emerge from her cell and join the colony, playing her small role in the great design.

Here I have described the worker bee, her structure and components, and yet, it is more inventory, or laundry list, than description. I have told little about what a bee is really like. Essence and spirit are not qualities easily captured on paper; it is, at best, a bookkeeper's view of life.

TWENTY-NINE

The honeybee, we assume, is what nature intended her to be. She filled an existing need, or found a response to her need. We do not know if the bee adapted to the flower or the flower to the bee, but these two mighty instincts worked out a mutual accommodation. Bees, unlike man, know their role. Untold generations have carried on the same traditions and practices; long, long ago they decided where they were going and held true to course.

In pursuing the adventures of the bee, there is one profound mystery that, above all, intrigues and eludes philosopher and scientist alike. During her brief life, a worker, as we have seen, performs many diverse chores. She assumes these roles without training or prior knowledge that we are aware of. A British writer, Herbert Mace, who pondered the dilemma I refer to, noted that the worker is descended from parents who have never performed the chores expected of her, neither having the organs nor the requisite intelligence for what is required of their offspring. How then, he asks, is this complex instinct transmitted?

By special food the ovaries of the embryo queen are developed, he observes, "but it is quite another matter to understand how the withholding of such food can produce, for instance, the pollen basket of the worker, which both the queen and drone are destitute of. In a word, how are the working qualities of neuters transmitted to an offspring they have no part in the production of?"

Is it genetic transference? Some unidentified dietary element or secretion passed along? A more complex governing biological mechanism of which we have no knowledge? Is it some abiding animus that dwells secretly in the hive conferring this ability, this biological sleight of hand?

The mystery becomes increasingly complex. The queen is a mother in a biological sense only. She has no maternal instincts or abilities. She does not care for her young. After depositing an egg, she is completely through with it, like the most wanton of insects; giving birth is an end in itself. Her daughters, the workers, who cannot themselves generate a fertile egg in their atrophied ovaries, are left to care for their younger sisters and drone brothers. It is these incomplete females who provide the "mother's milk" and nurturing for the offspring they cannot normally produce.

The irony is compounded because, with a secretion from their glands, they can produce queens like their mother, but cannot themselves become queens. Their lifelong role, from birth, is limited to being surrogate mothers and servants of the hive, an odd arrangement, even among insects, as if nature purposely contrived a special plan to make bees completely and inextricably interdependent.

THIRTY

C ooperation is programmed into a bee's genes. Each colony functions less like a group of integrated individuals than a multitude of cells making up a single organism. This interlocking structure is the most distinguishing characteristic of social bees, just as competitiveness dominates most other forms of life. Almost from the moment she emerges from her crib, a bee plays a community role.

Because life is so brief, with so much to do, little time can be wasted becoming acclimated. After spending the first day gaining strength and learning her way around the hive, she goes immediately to work. Her life is divided roughly into two phases, first as house bee, and then, in maturity, at about the halfway mark, as forager. She will continue to work the fields into her dotage and until early death.

On the second day of life, now stronger and her orientation completed, she dips eagerly into the stored honey for her first meal and begins her first job, as if trained for it. For a couple of days she performs menial tasks, cleaning and polishing empty brood cells, "sweeping the floor," and so on. She then becomes a nurse, making the numerous trips to feed newly hatched larvae, alert to provide the proper formulas to embryo workers, drones, and queens. The frequent feedings in tiny amounts are necessary to keep the food from drying out so it can be absorbed through the grubs' transparent skins.

After about a week as a nurse, our young worker makes way for new nurse bees and starts performing more demanding hive chores, among them receiving and storing nectar brought in by field bees, fanning honey, attending to the queen, capping cells, or anything else that needs doing. During the second week of life she is able to produce tiny wax flakes on her abdomen, providing the material of which honeycomb is made, functioning as architect, builder, and artist. As the glands that produced royal jelly dry up, the wax glands become active.

By the end of the second week she has matured and lost that soft, downy appearance. She is now an adult bee approaching her prime, ready to assume greater responsibilities. She begins taking her turn as a guard at the hive entrance, charged with repelling invaders or sounding the alarm in case of attack, ready to give up her life in defense of the hive. At this time she also prepares for the second phase of her life, as a fielder, joining in the "play flights" in front of the hive, making short excursions to get acquainted with the area and developing those powerful wings for the demanding and hazardous job ahead; she is a journeyman in every sense of the word.

The transition from house bee to forager marks a time to begin her life's work. Now those valiant wings come into use, so quickly to wear out. The job of a fielder is the most strenuous and dangerous in the hive; she must travel long distances for provender, up to nine miles if necessary but rarely more than two or three. She and her kind are prey for birds and other predators; they may be ambushed by enemies lurking in flowers, or killed or injured by storms, mishaps, or insecticides.

Most field bees die outside the hive, with their boots on, as it were. The worker must fly low to avoid winds, burdened by her heavy load of nectar or pollen. The powerful but fragile wings are torn while dodging through shrubs and brambles and worn by constant friction entering and backing out of the flowers she raids and the constant beating in flight and fanning at the hive entrance at night to evaporate moisture from honey.

There we have the chronology of the bee. I have seen her

job schedule broken down into the specific number of days spent on each succeeding task. But the progression from job to job is not so precise or straightforward as it was once believed to be. Studies at Cornell University have revealed that unforeseen factors may influence or interrupt the job progression that once seemed to proceed so unwaveringly for all; it is now recognized that there is more job specialization than was formerly believed, more individualism and flexibility within the framework of conformity. Once more nature has surprises for us, a greater diversity than we assumed.

THIRTY-ONE

"There seem to be castes of bees that do different tasks, but most of the jobs are temporary, though a bee can stay on a job for a fairly long time," says P. K. Visscher, a Cornell professor. Dr. Visscher paid particular attention to "undertaker bees" who remove the dead from the hive, concluding that the small corps of morticians may refuse to do other jobs and others may refuse to do theirs. He found that about 1 percent of a colony's population takes care of the dead. About an hour after a bee dies, an undertaker bee picks up the body and carries it away, flying up to four hundred feet from the hive before dropping it. He finds it remarkable that a bee can carry a body equal to her own weight such a distance. "Bees," he says, "realize that keeping a dead body around threatens the health of the other bees by carrying disease or attracting predators."

Dr. Visscher and other researchers are no longer so sure that bees are born genetically prepackaged to perform their multiple tasks on an inflexible biological timetable. Now they are asking how bees fall heir to certain jobs. What determines which individuals will perform given tasks? Are they assigned by older bees? Is the division of labor dictated by chemical or other unknown cues? What causes an individual to stay on one particular job for a while before switching to another?

"It's a mystery," says Dr. Visscher. He and other scientists offer several theories to answer the questions they raise. One holds that a bee performs a job, becomes adept at it, and is resistant to take on other tasks with which she is less familiar. "A bee that gets good results by visiting a certain type of plant will become an expert in gathering nectar from its flower and will continue that job," he says. Another theory is that the size and weight of a bee, which can vary according to the size cell she was born in and the amount of food received as a larva, may determine the job performed, just as a human's physical build may predispose him or her to certain jobs and exclude others. A longer, heavier bee, for example, may wind up as a hive guard.

Another theory advanced upsets many existing notions about the uniform characteristics of colonies. It contends that since the queen has several mates on her nuptial flight—it was long believed that she had only one—her offspring will be a genetically mixed bag; some might have a predisposition to a particular type of job by reason of genes inherited from one father, while others might incline toward other tasks because of different characteristics passed along by another sire.

This is a revolutionary way of looking at bees, seeing them not only as an integrated unit but as individuals with personalities and eccentricities or abilities of their own. It also provides new insights into bee intelligence and personality; their job specialization and division of labor suggest that there may be more similarities between bees and human societies than was formerly thought. We may be subject to many of the same laws as bees, and that which we think is free will or choice may, in fact, be dictated by a higher power that we fail to recognize. Do we, like bees, live by chance or design?

But is not something missing here in this account of bee specialization of labor? Are there not laggards, shirkers, renegades, misfits, and malcontents among them, and how are such deviates and nonconformists among the industrious dealt with? Perhaps the answer is to come. Dr. Roger A. Morse, also of Cornell and an authority on bees, says, "What we are learning is that the division of labor among honeybees is more finite and precisely defined than we had thought. There is still much to be learned."

One surprise that has turned up is that bees may not always be as industrious as once was believed. Most sources have held that foragers are rarely in the hive for more than five minutes between trps to the field. But one researcher now claims that bees have their own form of loafing or resting; after a foraging trip, he says, a field bee crawls into an empty cell and snugs in for a half-hour siesta; she is quiet but it is not known if she is asleep in the sense we know or merely resting. Upon arousing herself, apparently refreshed, she again takes off for the fields, like Mediterranean people returning to work after a midday rest.

A more startling revelation appeared in the newsletter of the Northeastern Kansas Beekeepers Association, *The Bee Buzzer*, which I subscribe to. Editor Maynard D. Curtis coolly disclosed that a USDA laboratory found that in 178 hours of consecutive study a bee spent 73 percent of her time "doing nothing," a figure that I am unable to accept with the equanimity of Editor Curtis.

Wherein does truth lie? In the legend or the lab? I like to think it is, in this case, in the lab; I can better identify with the honeybee if she does knock off now and then and isn't quite so compulsively industrious; excessive virtue is somewhat intimidating.

"Busy as a bee!" Indeed!

THIRTY-TWO

Play flights are well named, characterized by what appear to be wild confusion and jubilation; there is much buzzing and daredevil aerobatics as the young aerialists circle and dart in daring swoops and dives, exulting in their vigor and release from the confinement of the hive and its tasks, testing their courage and measuring their strength. They have discovered the sunshine after the gloom and darkness of the hive; for the first time they are able to come and go on their own, free as they will ever be. New beekeepers, seeing their first play flight, often think something is amiss, that their bees have gone berserk.

It is, in a sense, a rite of passage, a kind of graduation exercise without the solemnity of diplomas, "Pomp and Circumstance," or a speaker proclaiming that the world is their oyster, or honeyflow, as it were. They first take short flights around the hive to taste freedom, become familiar with the terrain and memorize landmarks. Gradually they increase range and awareness, learning to orient their flight to the sun, that constant reference point that will guide them to and from distant fields of booty.

What urgency within tells the bee that she is ready for this final step from hive bee to fielder? Is she aware that already her life is half spent? Soon the wild exuberance of the play flight is gone. Almost at once, in the compression of time, she is responsible, sober, industrious, bent on fulfilling her duties, the moment of ecstasy gone, the sweetness of fleeting youth forever lost. What happens to bees, puppies, kittens, and children who so soon lose their capacity for play and joy? What abiding sadness is woven into the tapestry of life itself?

THIRTY-THREE

For a new fielder, the great adventure begins the first time she leaves the hive to forage and must find her way back. Is she nervous during this initial excursion? Does she keep repeating to herself various landmarks she can identify? Or does she depend on some kind of homing instinct, a route committed to memory or a navigational system known only to her? Whatever the method, it is almost eerie the way she can go two or three miles distant and fly directly to her own hive. The feat is more remarkable because of the manner in which large apiaries or beeyards are usually laid out.

Beehives are generally placed next to one another in row after identical row, sometimes in pairs but often without even this small distinction. In large commercial operations there may be hundreds or even thousands of hives, all indistinguishable to the human eye, so many identical wooden boxes on some kind of platform, gleaming in the sun. And yet, in some unknown way, our initiate fielder, new to the game and loaded with nectar or pollen, is able to tell her own hive from all the others.

Occasionally a worker bee does mistakenly enter a strange hive, possibly due to a mental lapse or navigational error. This is known as "drifting"—is it due to daydreaming? If she arrives empty-handed, she is almost sure to be challenged by a sentry guarding the entrance and promptly thrown out. If she tries to bull her way into the hive, unable to accept her own error, she most likely will be mauled by the outraged inhabitants and lucky to escape with her life. A worker arriving at the wrong address with a load of nectar or pollen, however, may be permitted to enter without challenge, as a person with full purse is rarely denied entry into a bank, even if unknown and with no account number; an appearance of prosperity almost universally confers respectability and assures a welcome, a truth that seems to cut across all class lines among all species.

A drone who enters a strange hive by mistake is usually permitted to enter without challenge, which occurs frequently with drones, perhaps because of their limited intelligence. They pose no threat to steal the hive's wealth, and bees are too hospitable to begrudge giving a stranger a handout. Is this another example of sex discrimination, the male, as usual, coming out ahead? Do the female workers make allowances for male stupidity, or just like "having another male about the place"? Is there a bit of the coquette in these incomplete females? Who is to say?

Often a drone, mindlessly blundering into a strange hive, does not bother to go home but simply moves in as an adopted member of the community. A drone's primary loyalty seems to be to his stomach, apart from his fatal lust. He seems to feel that one set of "women" looking out for him is as good as another; the drone is a virtual fountainhead of rampant male chauvinism.

Worker bees are less adaptable to changing hives or locations than the absent-minded or stupid drones. Generally bees are thoroughly oriented to one tiny spot on this earth that is home. Move the hive only a few feet from its customary place and they will return to the original site. If a hive is to be moved from one spot to another, even in the same apiary, beekeepers first take it at least two miles to disorient the bees, and then transfer it to the new location. If, in moving a hive, the entrance is not completely blocked, the bees will escape and try to return to their former abode. Home is a compelling concept for most species, a refuge of safety in an often perilous world.

Curiously enough, among bees, the homing instinct varies from one race to another. Italian bees are especially prone to return to the hive's original location, even if it is moved only a few feet away. Other strains, particularly the darker races of bees, are more adaptable to being moved. They tend to seek out their home hive if it has been moved nearby. How do we explain this difference between one strain of bee and another? It is not worth the trouble to speculate whether it is genetic transference of an acquired characteristic or some mystical force beyond us. A beekeeper in Maine, attending a conference of beekeepers there, expressed the enigma nicely, saying, "It is the fascination we have with the bees, the elusiveness of them that forms our attraction. Bees are one of the phenomenons of nature that God put on this earth that we can't understand but we attempt to manage."

THIRTY-FOUR

As a field bee gets old and her wings begin to fray and wear out, when she is no longer able to fly great distances and carry heavy loads, she may be permitted to work inside the hive again, as she did in her youth, helping to care for brood or guard the entrance—light duty, as it were. This is probably the closest bees ever come to any expression of sentiment or gratitude for services rendered, but it probably represents less compassion than squeezing out the last semblance of usefulness she has to offer.

Even on the rare occasion when such charity is shown, a failing bee's days are numbered. When no longer useful to the community, she is gotten rid of, as an aging or infirm human worker may be fired or forced out of his job. Is this an arbitrary decision by some ruling authority? Or is it hive policy based on some criteria of efficiency that the aging can no longer measure up to, some inflexible scale that objectively determines job performance with no consideration of past contributions?

An infirm bee is not fired, in any sense we know, and left to try to find employment or safe harbor in her dotage. There is no farewell dinner, no symbolic presentation of a watch, no hypocritical speeches or mawkish sentiments inscribed on a silver tray enumerating her contributions and the esteem in which she is held. Instead, one of the young fielders may suddenly pounce on the unsuspecting superannuated member and drag her out of the hive to drop her unceremoniously over the landing board. And that is it.

Since the victim can no longer crawl or fly back with her ravaged wings, she must starve or be eaten by enemies, a form of dispatch which may or may not be more merciful than its human counterpart of unloading the unwanted aged or ill worker no longer capable of productive labor.

Should the ousted bee manage to make her way back to the hive, a younger worker may grab her and fly a half-mile or so away to drop her to make sure there will be no second return, a disposal method gangsters may have borrowed from the bees, with cultural refinements.

If even then the unwanted bee somehow manages to return again, no further time is wasted impressing on her the message that she is no longer welcome. Some bees, a "death squad" in effect, sting her to death or tear her to pieces and then go about their business, unmindful and uncaring, it seems, of her contributions to the community before she grew old and infirm from overwork and service to the colony. Her only real offense, like that of the aged human employee, was that she had nothing more left to give. This may be why socialism works in the hive but not in the competitive human marketplace. There is no place for heart or sentiment in the "perfect society."

I wonder, in passing, about this so-called death squad. Are its members volunteers? Assigned? Chosen by lot? Are they, too, specialists in their own way in the hive's division of labor as "undertaker bees" are specialists?

Generally, such Draconian measures are not necessary. Bees incapicated by age or injury and no longer able to work may remove themselves voluntarily by "committing suicide." The old or sick bee, at a time of her own choosing, simply crawls or drags her way painfully to the landing board and quietly topples over the edge, to perish in the tall grass or weeds below so she won't be a burden to the colony, a final sacrifice for the collective good of the community to which she devoted her life and energies, and I do not know whether she is to be pitied or exalted.

THIRTY-FIVE

$\mathcal{I}$n paying tribute to the division of labor in the hive, we are likely to make the error of comparing it to a factory where workers are trained to perform a particular job and are limited to that one operation or task, repeating it endlessly, and that is all that is expected of them; if their function is changed or eliminated, the person must be retrained for another job or let go. That is not the way a beehive functions. There is a division of labor, as we have seen, but it is based less on individual preference than on the convenience of the colony. Certain bees may be specialists but they have probably had a turn at most jobs and are able to perform them in an emergency; even older workers whose time of secreting wax is past can, if need be, reactivate their wax glands. In a crisis each individual ceases whatever she is doing to pitch in and do whatever is necessary for the common good. Individual sacrifice for the good of all! That is the cachet of hive life; it is an immutable law.

Let us now observe the bees in a crisis situation, our focus on the indomitable water carriers. They are primarily in charge of regulating the hive temperature during the summer. It is an essential role, demanding expertise. If the queen is to lay eggs, a temperature of about ninety-four degrees Fahrenheit is necessary, and the hive must remain in the range of ninety-two to ninety-eight degrees for metamorphosis to occur. But if the hive gets too hot, the wax combs will melt and the delicate brood can bake; if it becomes too cool, the brood will chill and die.

Maintaining this critical level of heat requires almost constant vigilance and temperature control. In the cold months heat is produced by clustering, but since most brood is raised in the summer, air conditioning is essential. Should overheating threaten from the sun beating on the closed, boxlike hive and all of the activity within, an emergency call is sent for water. Bees have an internal biological thermostat that triggers an alarm signal that is immediately relayed throughout the colony.

Field bees who are between trips drop whatever they are doing to rush to the nearest water source and scurry back with a mouthful of water. There, waiting house bees called from their regular jobs take the liquid from the fielders and spread it on the frames of honeycomb. All bees in the hive cease whatever they are doing to beat their wings vigorously, in unison. The fanners have been described as sitting like little living ventilators over the cells, driving the air toward each other and pushing it out through the entrance. Their fanning sets up a draft that evaporates the water, a primitive form of air conditioning that lowers the temperature, cooling the hive.

It is an ingenious system, much like one used in the Midwest before the advent of mechanical air conditioners; sweltering families would rig up a bale of straw at an open window, let water from a hose trickle through it and a fan inside would circulate the cooled air, lowering the temperature. But the bees developed their own method millions of years ago and incorporated it into their genetic pattern.

How do such things happen? Does one bee figure it out,

then tell another, and she, in turn, passes it along until all are doing it? Then how does it get incorporated into the gene pattern and passed down from generation to generation, practiced by different races of bees all over the world? How did the first bee make the connection between water and temperature control? Who can explain the quantum leap from idea to practice, and then to the genetic transference of information echoing down through the ages? It is too much for me!

During a heat crisis, each bee seems to know her role, as if she had been drilled, as in civil defense or fire drills. It would be stretching things a bit to call our whimsical but vital water carriers specialists. They do not sit around waiting for a heat crisis. But there is no confusion or hesitation. The alarm is sounded. Individuals drop whatever they are up to for this new priority, scurrying to their stations, just like small-town volunteer firemen quitting their jobs to answer a fire alarm.

Here we have what appears to be a spontaneous new division of labor. How do the individual bees know what they are supposed to do, what is expected of them? Who carries water and who fans? Are we to believe this is all neatly packaged in some little gene marked "heat crisis, instructions therein"?

During a heat crisis, field bees may make a hundred trips or more gathering water. Each can carry only a tiny amount at a time, and after transferring it to a hive bee they zip away for more. It must be a time of high drama; you can sense the urgency as the fielders shuttle back and forth from water source to hive, and hive bees race to and fro smearing the dabs of water on the combs. No military operation could be better synchronized.

There is, for all of the drama, a comic side, all of this running back and forth. Eventually the hive is cooled down. The crisis is over. The hive bees return to their regular tasks, but no one, it seems, bothers to tell the field bees the emergency is over. They keep appearing with their mouths full of water, looking desperately for someone to take it from them. The busy hive bees ignore them. It is, apparently, a breakdown in communications. Nature, or evolution, it would seem, could have taken the next logical step and had someone inform the foragers that they could return to the fields. Would that have taken so much more space in the gene package? Or does nature, at times, enjoy mocking her own, playing small jokes, some of them amusing, some grisly and horrible.

The division of labor is never quite so coordinated and unified as when all hands fan together. This is a vital function in curing honey. Nectar, when brought into the hive, contains about 80 percent water, and most of the moisture must be reduced to approximately 18 percent to produce thick honey. At night, after the runny nectar has been deposited in open wax vats, like so many miniature barrels stacked row upon row on their sides, the comb cells tilted slightly upward so their contents won't spill out, the colony gathers at the hive entrance to evaporate the water by fanning.

Half of the colony is on one side, beating their wings in unison to blow air into the hive, while the other half fans on the opposite side, creating a breeze that carries water vapor from the nectar out of the hive. How do the bees decide who is to blow in and who is to blow out? The draft produced is so strong that if a lighted match is held at the hive entrance, the flame will bend in the direction of air being forced in or out. The method is so effective that puddles of water often are found on the inner cover after a night of fanning.

During a honeyflow, nectar must be processed immediately so the honey can be capped in preparation for the next day's collection. In the summer bees often work around the clock, field bees bringing in nectar for twelve straight hours and then fanning for the next twelve, rapidly wearing out those wings, which have only so many beats in them. There is no division of labor now, other than those who blow in and those who blow out. There are no individuals; there is only the common good to be served.

THIRTY-SIX

*I*n the hive's division of labor, no member is as specialized or vital as the queen. She alone is indispensible, her fate tied to that of the colony. A corps of workers attends her, caring for her every need, but we do not know whether this is a position of honor, or merely another job assumed or assigned by the unconscious hive logic called instinct or local authority. It is likely that no task performed by young bees is considered more important than caring for the queen.

Nonetheless, we are aware of no special privileges or prerogatives accorded members of her retinue. Indeed they function more as servants than as ladies in waiting, cleaning up her wastes, feeding, grooming, caressing and bathing her, licking her with their tongues, as she works almost without pause in her mechanical egg laying.

Much has been made of the circle of a dozen or so attendants surrounding the queen as she lays eggs. New beekeepers are told that the way to find the elusive queen is by first locating her circle of attendants. The attendants, it is claimed, never turn their backs on the queen, as befits a royal presence, ever encouraging her to greater efforts as she moves from cell to cell, comb to comb, endlessly laying eggs around the clock during the busy season, even as she "sleeps," or does what passes for sleep.

Later I learned that the circle, as usually described, is more romantic myth than fact. Less fanciful accounts point out that the attendants gather around the queen only when she is being fed. This makes sense; the colony always controls how often and how much the queen is fed, as this regulates her egg laying. Too, if the attendants never broke ranks, it would represent many lost bee hours of work, contrary to hive principles.

Because of the enormous physical drain of laying so many eggs, the queen must eat frequently. The circle forms. An attendant opens her mouth, exuding a tidbit of honey. The queen flicks in her tongue for a snack, hardly breaking stride in her unremitting egg laying, a hive version of eating on the job. Another attendant also thrusts in her tongue for a quick pickup. There seems to be no objection to this sharing of the royal repast, so it must be fair game, a part of the job. Drones often take their food in the same manner, too lazy to go to the honey stores to feed themselves, a practice tolerated by their sisters, who may mark it up as another score to be settled in the fall.

The queen progresses from cell to cell, comb to comb, pausing only to inspect each crib to make sure that it meets her standards before depositing an egg, or perhaps to make sure she isn't confusing a drone cell for a worker crib so she will lay the proper egg. Royalty is notoriously absent-minded and it does take a bit of concentration to avoid mistakes. Occasionally a crib does not measure up, and the queen moves along to the next cell without leaving an egg behind. Her entourage follows, the committee members apparently satisfied with the queen's decision, and she continues to lay eggs, driven by the invisible and indefinable force that gives her no rest.

THIRTY-SEVEN

People unfamiliar with bees often think the queen rules the hive. Long ago it was believed that she was actually the king, with all of a sovereign's authority. This misconception was probably due to her being the largest mem-

ber of the colony, size being equated with power, and it probably says more about those who made the error than it does
about the bees.

The ancients, not understanding the queen's role, had some
odd notions about bees and their origins. The *ABC and XYZ of
Bee Culture*, an invaluable reference book published by the A.
I. Root Company, and known as "the Bible of Beekeepers,"
states that it was not until 1609 that an English beekeeper named
Butler affirmed that the "Kingbee" was really a queen, because
he had seen her deposit eggs.

Before that, the ancient Greeks believed that bees came from
dead oxen and could be raised by killing an ox and leaving it
in a sealed room for thirty-two days; the belief persisted for
hundreds of years, and directions for producing bees in this
way were published as late as 1842, the last time they appeared.

The *ABC and XYZ of Bee Culture* states that Virgil wrote that
bees collected their embryos from leaves and sweet plants. The
Greek historian Xenophonon compared the work of the queen
with that of a housewife and considered her the guiding brain
of the hive. The Dutchman Swammerdam thought that queens
were fertilized by a seminal exhalation of "odoriferous effluvia"
produced from a large number of drones. The Roman scholar
Varo thought that diarrhea in bees could be cured by giving
them urine to drink and that bees gathered wax from flowers.
Pliny the Elder wrote that echoes kill bees. It was widely
believed that the sound of clashing symbols causes bees to
swarm, a long-disproven idea that still persists.

Aristotle was the first to study bees scientifically. He was
the first to drop the notion that bees come from dead oxen, and
gradually scholars better understood the nature of bees and the
queen's true role in the hive.

The queen is more servant to the hive than sovereign with
little, if any, control over her life or destiny, living at the convenience and tolerance of the colony. She cannot perform the
simplest survival tasks for herself, even depending on her worker

daughters to make possible the conditions that enable her to lay eggs. Because she will not sting any bee except another queen, she is virtually defenseless against those who control her with their hive machinations and the threat of their lethal prison or death chamber.

If the queen were smarter, she would probably be hopelessly neurotic. As is, she is shy and skittish, possibly because she never leaves the hive but spends her days confined in darkness, a kind of eternal night, perpetually in labor, experiencing no life other than that which she generates in her own body. When the hive is opened, suddenly dissolving the darkness with blinding sunlight, she is likely to take to her heels, hiding in far corners and making it difficult to find or identify her, risking death or injury as the frames are manipulated.

Her position in the hive is ambiguous at best. Despite her own dependency and perilous position, the colony is dependent upon her for its existence. She is indispensible and yet subject to being killed in panic or by whim, or replaced in what amounts to star chamber proceedings against her. Any figurative crown she wears must rest uneasily on her head. Her true role is less that of queen than mother of the hive, a title often accorded her. And yet, this is something of a mockery because of her lack of maternal instincts or the ability to care for her young. She is, more than anything else, an automated egg-laying machine, a derogatory but descriptive name she must bear.

In appearance, she is a striking insect, larger than her daughters, more slender and longer; if of Italian extraction, she has a tawny, golden hue with the characteristic black bands of her race. She has a regal air and is properly named queen for that alone. With exquisitely tapered wings folded back over her elongated body, she is the picture of insect grace as she glides from cell to cell depositing eggs in mindless dedication to her life's work.

Nature, always expeditious in matters of reproduction, has

a queen emerge and mature in less time than is required for a worker or drone. We have already noted the physical differences between the queen and her daughters. She has neither their ardor nor their equipment to harvest the fields; her tongue is only about half as long as that of a worker, and even if she visited the blooming meadow she probably could not extract the nectar with her stub of a sucking-tube tongue.

Except for her brief mating flight, she spends her days in the darkness of the hive, a stranger to sunshine and flowers. Her eyesight is only about half that of the workers. A queen can live up to seven years, compared to the brief four- to six-week span of her daughters of summer, but she is usually worn out, her fertility exhausted, after a year or two.

While the queen's wings are short, they are extremely powerful. She can fly faster and higher than her daughters; only the most powerful and swift-flying drones can catch her in mating. Her stinger, although used only on other queens, is a deadly rapier-like instrument that she could easily sink into flesh, administering a painful wound or death to insects like herself, without damage to herself; but she will die rather than sting to defend herself.

The queen's true uniqueness and indispensibility reside not in the external organs she has or lacks, but in the two large ovaries in her abdomen for the production of eggs, up to two thousand a day, as I have noted, an oviduct for their passage into the cell crib, and a spermatheca for the storage of sperm which enables her to lay fertilized eggs that become the workers who provide the nuturing qualities in which she is deficient, and unfertilized eggs that produce drones who will mate with future queens.

Everything about her is a contradiction. If queen she is, she is a queen with servants but no subjects. We assume that she is privy to nature's complex strategies only as a blind slave to her own needs. Would she accept her oppressed role if she had greater intelligence to comprehend it? Is it completely accidental that she is endowed with less brain power than her dim-witted sons or domineering daughters? Why is nature so par-simonious in doling out intelligence to those she exploits the most? Is it to spare them or to serve her own needs?

THIRTY-EIGHT

*B*ecause of her own biological complexity and built-in obsolescence, queens are subject to endless manip-ulation and frequent replacement. If bees decide that a queen is failing, they will replace her with a new queen of their own making in the process called "supersedure," a nice euphemism for the premeditated murder of the old queen who will be sup-planted by one of her own daughters.

In literary terms we have here the ingredients for a first-class Shakespearean drama: the reigning queen witlessly bringing about her own ruination by providing her successor, a secret privy council plotting against the throne and selecting from among candidates in the nursery the one to become the new regent, keeping the reigning sovereign in the dark so she will continue to serve until convenient to oust her in a coup d'etat, palace intrigues among the conspirators, the double bloody deeds of regicide and matricide by an assassin chosen by lot. We may further garnish our fanciful plot with a bit of sexual titillation: the handsome young prince who will win the beautiful prin-cess, but only at cost of his own life, etc.

Bees do not share the human need for fantasies, romance, and contrived plots to divert them from the realities of life and its agitations, but there is little exaggeration in the scenario presented; the parts that apply are played out without dra-matic embellishments as the bees go about their business of promoting the common good, quietly, efficiently, and resolutely.

An existing colony can get a new queen by two primary means: supersedure and requeening. They are, in effect, the same, in that a new queen is introduced. In requeening, the beekeeper provides a new queen, one he has raised himself or, more likely, one bought from an apiary in the south. In supersedure the bees produce their own queen. Most beekeepers prefer to provide a queen of their choice before the bees can take over to assure greater quality control. Often there is a conflict between what the bees and their keepers desire: man usually seeks uniformity in the same way that nature prefers diversity.

It is understandable that most queens use up their supply of sperm within a year or two. Every twenty-four hours a queen lays eggs equal to her own weight. When her sperm is largely spent, she starts laying at a reduced rate; when it is completely exhausted she can lay nothing but unfertilized drone eggs or none at all.

Bees almost never supersede a queen if she is producing brood satisfactorily, but the prevailing wisdom among beekeepers is that queens should be replaced routinely every year, two at most, *before* they fail. Commercial operations rarely keep a queen more than one year. Requeening usually means killing the old queen, an unpleasant business that I flinch from, preferring to let the bees work it out among themselves. To the old queen who must be replaced, I suppose, it makes little difference whether she is dispatched by her own from within, or by the beekeeper from without. In either case the queen must die.

The best queens come from eggs only a few hours old, the fresher the better. The bees may select a newly laid egg and build a queen cell around it, or move it to a waiting royal crib. Both methods require preparation and planning, so supersedure cannot be an impetuous act, but represents a sober judgment by the colony's ruling councils. Supersedure cells, unlike swarm cells, are usually found high up on the frames of honeycomb, near the center of the hive, probably so the young princesses can be protected from the old queen's jealousy and wrath.

Supersedure cells are about three times the size of worker cells and double that of drone cells, sticking out from the comb they're attached to like the nose of a bullet, with a corrugated peanut-like texture. Once supersedure cells appear, the old queen's days are numbered, but business in the hive goes on as usual, the failing queen laying as best she can. It would be rash on the part of the colony to dispatch her before a successor is ready to take her place. Treachery has its own logic.

THIRTY-NINE

Supersedure must, of necessity, be a surreptitious undertaking. Otherwise it probably couldn't come off. Why would the queen, dim-witted as she is, cooperate in providing her own successor? And yet, to confound us a bit more, queens have been seen actually depositing eggs in supersedure cells. But this is so rare that we are left wondering whether it is an absent-minded act, unnoticed by the queen in laying thousands of eggs, a breakdown of instinct, senility, a flaw in her programming, or done under duress.

The fact tht any fertile egg is a potential queen suggests a perfect biological democracy within the hive, each egg being the equal of all others, assuming that an egg selected to become a queen is chosen at random. But that may be a romantic notion with no basis in fact, and bees have an elitist or selective criterion unknown to us. Certainly they have the highest standards for their young. Any worker or drone born with the slightest imperfection is destroyed at once. However, in their perversity, colonies do occasionally tolerate a queen who is inferior in the quality of her laying and the bees seem to honor and care for her as they would for a more robust or fertile mother. Does this mean that special criteria apply or allowances are made for queens that do not apply to others?

Because any fertilized egg can be made into a new queen, the old sovereign makes possible her own succession and death at the whim or convenience of the colony. Is she aware of her vulnerability? Does she know or suspect that treachery is afoot? It would seem that when a new queen cell appears she would know the game is up for her and she would balk or go on strike, but instead she goes about her business as if nothing unusual were taking place.

How do we interpret this? Do the bees in some way try to deceive or placate her? Is she privy to the skulduggery but unable to do anything about it? Are the bees putting her on notice that she isn't measuring up and had better improve her performance or it's all up with her? Is she too stupid to recognize the significance of what is taking place? Or must we ask more profound questions in the hope of getting more profound answers to understand this unfolding dilemma?

FORTY

Bees usually do not raise just one supersedure queen at a time, but two, three, or four. The cells generally are built on a staggered schedule so the new princesses will not all emerge at the same time, providing a backup candidate if the first born fails in her mating flight or doesn't return.

The first out frees herself by chewing a perfect circle in the wax cap that imprisons her, or she may be aided by the bees who eagerly await her. Her first act is to utter a high-pitched cry that sounds something like "Zeep . . . zeep . . . zeep!" She is, in effect, proclaiming, "I'm taking over here." Another virgin queen in a nearby cell, restrained from getting out by guards, replies with a kind of muffled "quahking" sound, as if it were coming from deep within a manhole; this seems to mean, "We'll see about that."

Oddly enough, queens make the same "quahking" sound when they are grabbed or balled by the colony. More curious still, the same sound made by a reigning queen, if endangered or alarmed, will bring bees gathering around to protect her. Place two queens in nearby separate cages and they will call back and forth, challenging one another to mortal combat. Queens, so passive in their egg-laying role and domination by the workers, are murderously aggressive with one another.

If the first virgin princess freed is not restrained, she will rush immediately to the nearby queen cells, furiously tear them to pieces, and sting the rival princesses inside to death. The workers may stand by and watch her fury, or even help the enraged queen in her deadly assault. Generally, however, guards prevent the freed princess from attacking her imprisoned sisters, or spare at least one, until the first has mated and is ready to take over as the queen mother. Those held on standby status poke tiny proboscises through the thin wax cover to be fed by nurse bees or their guards.

If the newborn queen is successful in her mating flight, she will challenge the old queen to a fight to the death. Almost always the vigorous new queen wins. Should she lose, another virgin is freed to try her luck. Eventually the old queen is defeated and replaced, and the new hive mother wipes out any remaining virgins in their cells. This time she is not restrained.

The principle of one queen to a hive is powerful among bees. Occasionally, however, two queens will be found laying side by side. But this is as infrequent as it is inexplicable. It may represent some unusual accommodation between the two queens, or a negotiated truce or decree laid down by a weak colony to speed up brood production for the good of the hive. Even such an inbred tradition as queen rivalry must yield to the common welfare.

The arrangement, whatever is behind it, does not last long. One day the older queen simply disappears; I surmise that the bees, at a time of their own choosing, for reasons known only to them, have done away with their old mother, or she died of natural causes, which led the colony to build supersedure cells in the first place.

FORTY-ONE

After killing her rivals, or being prevented from doing so, the new princess spends the first few days of life preparing for her great moment: the mating flight. If successful, she will kill the reigning queen, her mother, and herself take over as mother to the hive. First, however, she wanders aimlessly over the combs; the colony pays little attention to her before she has proved herself. The virgin princess tends to race about the hive giddily and aimlessly. During this period she must feed herself from the stores of honey, but after the mating flight she will never have to do this again. She pauses occasionally to peer out the hive entrance, as if contemplating what lies ahead.

On a warm sunny day, she ventures outside on the landing board, at first hesitant, dazed by the brilliant sunshine after the darkness of the hive. She pauses briefly, getting used to the outdoor world which she will forsake immediately upon taking over her new role.

Suddenly she tucks her long, slender legs under her body

and gracefully takes to the air. This princess is a strong flier from the beginning, but at first she takes only short flights to develop her wings and learn to find her way back to the hive. Upon gaining strength and confidence, her flights become progressively longer and she ventures farther from the hive.

Even these prenuptial flights are not without risk. She may be eaten by birds, killed by other bees, fall victim to mishaps due to abrupt changes in weather, or encounter unforeseen foes. The longer she is away and the farther the flight, the greater the risk.

After the fourth day, the virgin princess is ready to mate, but this must occur before the twentieth day or she cannot become fertile, one of nature's built-in timetables that demand that certain events must happen at a given time or they can never take place in a normal manner.

The crucial mating flight of our virgin princess usually takes place four to ten days after she emerges from her cell; the average is about the ninth day. If bad weather or adverse happenstances delay the mating flight beyond the critical twenty-day limit, she has violated nature's inflexible timetable. The bees must send forth another queen or be provided with one. Time has passed this princess by. The rule is irrevocable.

FORTY-TWO

It is a perfect day in late spring or early summer; the weather is warm, sunny, and windless, probably early afternoon. The princess hesitates briefly on the landing board. Suddenly she springs into the air. Today there is new determination about her, a sense of mission. There is no circling about the hive or indecision. This is, for her, the supreme moment.

She flies swift and high, soon joined by hundreds or even thousands of drones. Their own built-in sensing system tells them the virgin queen is ready for mating. Now the drone's special tracking equipment serves him well, the powerful wings, the wide range of sight, the keen sense of smell, the mighty instinct to mate. Nature mobilizes all forces in this drama of reproduction.

The virgin queen is pursued not only by drones from her own hive, her brothers, but also by those from neighboring hives, all drawn by her scent and signals. Often the drones gather in a common congregating area, spending their days in idleness, like so many loafers in a neighborhood park or pool-hall, perhaps boasting of their prowess, but certainly not of past conquests. They engage in daily reconnaissance flights, a kind of cruising, to sniff out receptive females.

The queen passes over this sexual staging area, alerting the lusting drones. The diversity of males helps prevent inbreeding, but the fastest and fittest will prevail. Today the drone is no longer a greedy buffoon. He is all grace, power, and determination, fired by his own ardor and life's mission.

The virgin queen usually goes on her mating flight alone, although she may be accompanied by a few bridesmaids from her hive. If she comes from a weak hive, and possibly is the only princess, the sole hope for a marginal community, the entire colony may accompany her.

Quickly the virgin queen and her suitors outdistance any escorts or bodyguards. She and the drones fly faster and higher than the workers. Nature has given the queen powerful wings and a streamlined body to outdistance all but the swiftest drones.

Before her mating flight, the virgin princess passed among the drones in the hive without causing the least excitement or arousing passion. Until the mating flight there can be no union of drone and queen. Copulation can take place only in the air.

The mating flight is brief, usually lasting less than twenty minutes and averaging about thirteen. No facet of a bee's life is private; her most intimate secrets have been documented and timed.

Queen and drones fly higher and faster. Soon only the most stalwart suitors are left; the feeble, sick, old, malnourished, and uninterested and those from inactive or impoverished hives have given up the pursuit. Finally one remains. Because of the intricacies of his anatomy, the drone can mate only when the rush of air forces open the lower part of his abdomen, freeing his genitals to enter the queen's open vulva.

His organ enters the queen, ejecting his sperm. There is a pop, resembling an explosion or cracking sound. The successful drone pays dearly for victory over his less fit rivals. In the instant of copulation his genitals are torn from him, his abdomen ruptured; he falls to earth paralyzed, to die, his male organ left behind dangling from the queen like a trophy. This seems a rather high price for success, even by nature's standards, a cruel and lethal jest. Is it altogether chance that the mating pair outraces the other drones, who do not see what befalls the victor?

We know the mechanics of this sex act but nothing of its emotional state. I like to think there is an instant of pleasure or rapture for these pawns of nature before the drone is struck down. Is the queen briefly a voluptuary, taking pleasure in her body and its fulfillment, or only mechanically obeying a biological drive with no sensual satisfaction?

In any case, there you have the sex life of the bees, a rather grim ending for the lecherous drone who gives his all for survival of the fittest, his fit progeny surviving as he perishes. How did bees ever become equated with sex? They do not live a riotous sex life themselves, and are mere agents in pollinating plants. A hive suggests the cloister more than the bordello. All but the queen and the condemned drones who mate are chaste from beginning to end.

It was long thought that a queen mated but once. Now it is known that she may have many partners, seventeen in one study, but usually considerably fewer. She continues to mate until she has stored sperm enough to last her lifetime. Queens have been found with up to 7.5 million sperm, averaging about 5.5 million.

The triumphant male's organ still dangling from her, the now-fertile queen returns to the hive, a true femme fatale widowed in the conjugal act. Some researchers say she is received with wild excitement and joy, the exuberant workers eagerly removing the drone genitals and grooming her with their tongues. Others claim this is so much romantic nonsense and she is greeted with no unusual show of emotion. I do not know. I have never witnessed a nuptial homecoming.

Which version are we to believe? We must accept that which appeals to our own nature. The reception may vary from hive to hive, depending on how vital the mating flight is to the future of the hive. It seems reasonable enough to believe that a weak colony, dependent on the queen's successful return, would display a certain jubilation. In her now-fertile body is their future as a colony. For stronger colonies, with reserve princesses in waiting, who is to say what raptures they may express or suppress?

But what of the drones, defeated in the chase and now returned home? What do they think when they see the newly fertile queen return with her bizarre trophy? Will they push quite so hard to catch the next virgin who entices them? And what of the presiding hive mother? For her this moment of triumph can have only one ending. What, if anything, does she think?

FORTY-THREE

The mating flight does more than transform the princess into a queen. She takes on a new personality, no longer a flighty virgin running aimlessly about, almost unnoticed; she has matured physically, now lighter in color, suddenly grown longer, and assumes a stately quality, suggesting a sense of self or pride in her new role. The colony responds to this change and pays her homage as befits her new status and responsibility. Our giddy princess is now a queen in both name and fact.

If there is an old queen in the hive, or rival princesses, the new queen quickly disposes of them, making her the sole mother of the hive. In her spermatheca are the millions of sperm, and from her ovaries will come the outpouring of eggs. About forty-eight hours after mating she can start laying. At first, lacking experience and techique, she may deposit two or more eggs in a single cell, lay in an irregular pattern, or deposit drone eggs in worker cells or worker eggs in drone cells, with somewhat odd results, but soon she has the hang of it.

If she laid all of the eggs theoretically possible, about 2,000 in a twenty-four-hour period, it would amount to one very 43.2 seconds. If all eggs developed, in a week there would be 14,000 new bees, in three weeks 42,000, and in five weeks 70,000. Fortunately these figures are only theoretical or soon the world would be awash in bees. The queen, in fact, does not lay steadily at such a rapid rate, each queen developing her own pace and rhythm. Some eggs never hatch, and old bees keep dying off. The mathematics of calculator and laboratory are seldom those of nature. Bee colonies rarely exceed 80,000 or 100,000, at most.

Even discounting the number of eggs laid, it is still a torrent of fecundity. As eggs are released through the tubelike oviduct, the queen can, by relaxing or contracting certain muscles, control whether sperm brushes the egg or is withheld, the choice determined by the size of the crib in which the egg is laid. The queen is able to use her front legs, like tiny callipers, to measure the size of the cell in the darkness.

As previously pointed out, an egg fertilized with male sperm becomes a female worker, while those not touched with sperm become drones. Thus, female qualities are provided by the male element, and male qualities by the female, a curious reversal found commonly in nature. A worker bee has a mother and father, while a drone has a mother and no father, making him not subject to the same double-parent genetic influences as his sisters.

All of this is quite complicated, and the process of bee reproduction was misunderstood for many years, despite a correct explanation as early as 1845 by an astute German beekeeper, the Reverend John Dzierzon, whose theory laid the foundation for the scientific study of bees. For another half-century it was commonly believed that the sex of a bee was determined by the size of the cell in which the egg was deposited, rather than vice versa, a conclusion based on the fact that the queen almost invariably laid worker eggs in smaller cells and drone eggs in the larger cribs.

The theory supporting this false conclusion was that the smaller cells pressed upon the queen's oviduct, forcing out sperm that fertilized the egg, and since no pressure was exerted by a larger drone cell she was therefore able to deposit egg unfertilized by sperm. "I see, therefore I believe!"—a problem Galileo ran into on a more cosmic scale. Humans have always had a talent for believing what they want to believe.

In a series of experiments in 1895 it was proved that the queen controls the sex of her offspring in the manner described, although some diehards still held that the sex was determined

by secretions of worker bees. Finally, however, Rev. Dzierzon's theory prevailed, and it was recognized that the queen is
merely an order taker, depositing fertilized or unfertilized eggs
according to cell size, as dictated by the higher authority that
rules such matters.

FORTY-FOUR

The queen strides regally over the honeycomb, picks
a cell, inspects it briefly, and backs herself over it
to deposit a single egg in the bottom. The pose would seem
awkward, less than majestic, but she performs it with grace
and dignity. She goes about her work methodically, inspecting
each cradle and laying an egg or passing by those cells that do
not measure up, hurrying on to the next. This, at least, is what
we perceive.

Beyond that we have no insight into the level of insect consciousness, if it exists. There is no evidence that the queen
takes pleasure in her work, or that she looks upon it as a necessary task and makes the best of her lot. She goes about her
business as diligently as any housewife doing domestic chores.
The process appears to be completely mechanical. But can we
not believe that at least one part of her small brain is making
small decisions as she inspects the individual cells, laying an
egg or rejecting the crib as unfit?

One wonders. Is this the whole of it for her? Is there no
other dimension for this mechanized, driven little creature? Is
she, like most inhabitants of the earth, merely performing an
imposed task with no comprehension of the grand scheme? Does
man alone ponder the unfathomable riddle of existence?

Why do we dismiss other creatures with such cavalier indifference? Can we be sure they have no voice simply because we cannot hear? Can we assume they do not have yearnings of their own because we cannot penetrate their consciousness? Does the loathsome squash bug want to be a splendid butterfly? The lowly worm become the bird that pursues it? Does the oxen not tire of the yoke and long for a saddle? Would the hare not wish to be a hound, the hound a horse, and the horse to have the wings of Pegasus? Does the sparrow crave to be a hawk or eagle, the crow to sing like a mockingbird? Does the queen bee covet the majestic power of her name rather than being a parody of her royal title?

My heart goes out to the little queen, living out her days in darkness, laying all those eggs, the only one of her kind in the hive with no peer to confide in and, in the end, fertility exhausted, to be ruthlessly dispatched. The queen business isn't all it's cracked up to be. It is true that she has attendants who look after her needs, but it sounds like a public relations scam to extract the last egg out of her. I wonder if, along the way in her cheerless life, anyone ever takes her aside, pats her on the back and says, "You're doing a great job!"

FORTY-FIVE

The queen's misadventures are not confined to natural processes. Disaster can also come from other sources. The scene is the beeyard in late afternoon after school is out. There is bedlam. Rocks bounce off the hive. The frantic bees search for the enemy who attacks them from ambush. A long pole emerges. The hive is knocked over. The vandals flee. Bedlam turns into panic. What cataclysm has ruptured the colony's secure existence? What madness? Why this sudden upheaval? Who is to blame for this catastrophe?

The overturned hive is in ruins, lying on its side, the frames of honeycomb scrambled like so many jackstraws. The brood is exposed. Honey drips from uncapped and smashed cells. What maniac would commit such an act? Most of the bees are flying, raging in wild gyrations. Those left on the exposed combs race blindly about, bumping into one another, disorganized and distraught. Other bees may appear to steal the unguarded honey, or the crazed bees, for want of a visible enemy to punish, may begin fighting among themselves. They roll and tumble about in combat, friend mistaken for foe. The entire colony has gone insane.

The queen dashes frantically over the combs. Incongruously she straddles an empty cell and begins laying an egg, as if this routine act will restore normalcy to her chaotic world. She is disoriented by the tumult within and blinded by the sunlight that has banished the safe darkness of the hive. A berserk worker suddenly attacks the queen, spinning her off her feet. Another joins the charge. Then another, and others. A scapegoat has been found. Guilt or innocence matter not. Revenge alone counts.

The queen squeals her high-pitched cry of terror. But the bees have forgotten that she is their mother, their salvation. They form a ball around her. This time it is not for her protection but a death sentence. Now, at last, they have united in a single purpose. They tear at the queen's wings and legs, suffocating her, focusing their own terror and frustration on the central figure in their lives. This could be a primitive tribe trying to appease angry gods with a living sacrifice. The queen's shrill cries of terror are unheeded. The ball of bees squeezes tighter and tighter. The cries become more faint. For the queen there is no mercy, no reprieve.

The dead queen is dropped over the landing board, her spent body resting between two blades of grass. The bees, as if purged of the violence against them by violence of their own, try to resume a normal life. But the combs are lashed by rain and winds, subjected to sun and snow. The brood are dead. The violated hive is doomed. Without a queen or brood there can be no future.

Usually cause and effect are not so clearly established when a queen vanishes from a hive; her end is not so dramatic or definitive. But once her ovaries are worn out or her reservoir of sperm depleted, the end is near. The anonymous lethal ball of bees is her executioner.

In death she is shown no more respect or honor than any other felled member of the community. All distinctions end in the abyss beyond the landing board.

FORTY-SIX

If there is no mishap and all goes well with queen and colony, and the outpouring of eggs brings a buildup of bee population and crowding, nature intervenes with a mysterious and wondrous solution: the bees prepare to swarm. This is their way of preserving the species and increasing their numbers, the most powerful drive in all of nature. The earliest bees must have responded to the same silent summons millions of years ago.

Before a swarm can issue, it first must provide for a new queen to be left behind, as the old queen accompanies the departing bees to get them established in ther new home. The process of producing a new queen to stay behind is much the same as that in supersedure, but the technique and circumstances differ.

While supersedure cells are attached high up on the side of the comb, jutting straight out, swarm cells are built on the bottom, drooping down below the frame, resembling a peanut hanging from one end. No one knows why bees employ different techniques of placement and construction for supersedure and swarm cells; it could be a signal to the community, or convey a message to the occupant of what her role would be. Again, it could put the queen mother on notice that this newcomer is not a threat to her as a supersedure queen would be and not to bother the princess within.

In any case, supersedure and swarm queen larvae alike are fed nothing but royal jelly. While the circumstances of birth differ, both have the same destiny: to replace the reigning queen, each responsible for the continuity of the colony.

A swarm usually departs on a sunny day in late spring or early summer, most likely in May or June, between the hours of ten in the morning and three in the afternoon. From half to two-thirds of the colony may take off, accompanied by the old queen, to establish a new home elsewhere. Behind they leave enough brood, young bees, queen cells, and food for the parent colony to build itself up again.

Until the new queen goes on her mating flight and starts laying eggs, the parent colony suffers a severe setback. A colony may be so weakened that it has a hard time recovering; the swarm impulse is felt not only by strong colonies, but often by those that can ill afford to lose numbers. If the new queen fails in her mating flight or doesn't return home, and there is no replacement for her, the hive may die out altogether. Swarming can decimate as well as increase.

Once bees start building swarm cells, they have made up their minds to leave. Swarms may take off any time after these cells are capped. Most swarms issue eight or nine days after placing an egg inside of a queen cell, an act of optimism, considering all that can go amiss.

Since most swarms issue at the peak of the spring honeyflow, it represents a grievous loss for the beekeeper, but it makes sense for the bees, giving both the departing swarm and the parent colony time to recover before cold weather sets in. People logic and bee logic are often at odds.

Bees occasionally violate the rules by swarming in late summer when there is not time enough to collect sufficient honey to see them through the coming winter. This is no more easily explained than those individuals, considered so steady and responsible, who suddenly take off, leaving behind all that once meant so much to them, and who knows what was really in their hearts and minds all the while they were taken for granted?

Such perverse behavior cannot be explained in man or bee. Is it as irrational as it appears, or is there a logic unknown to us, as observers? Are bees, like people, also subject to whim? Is there some flaw in the original programming, or are there circumstances about which we have neither knowledge nor control?

Bees, whatever their idiosyncrasies, never swarm without giving notice. One, two, up to a dozen swarm cells suddenly appear. Once a colony commits itself to swarming, it is difficult to get the bees to change their minds. But the decision is not irrevocable, and chance may play a role. If the weather turns chilly, or rain and cold persist for several days, the swarm may delay its departure; in such cases, the parent hive keeps the virgin princesses captive in their sealed prisons and the rest of the colony bides its time.

On the first sunny day after the weather clears, the swarm will take off. However, for no apparent reason, the colony may tear down the swarm cells, killing the princesses within, and go about its business as usual. But this is rare. Most colonies, having decided to swarm, are determined to go; the voice they hear is not easily resisted.

We assume that the decision to swarm is made in the hive councils. In the final minutes before departure there is a sense of expectancy. The buzzing in the hive becomes louder, almost ominous. Large numbers cluster on the front of the hive. Others gather on the landing board, facing the entrance, among them drones making a raucous sound; the noisy drones are believed to stimulate the swarming impulse, like drummers charging up patriotic sentiment. The old queen has ceased laying eggs several days earlier to lose weight so she can fly. All of the bees appear larger than usual, abdomens extended with honey to get the new city under way.

As if at a signal, the great moment is at hand. . . .

FORTY-SEVEN

J am working in the garden when I notice unusual agitation and excitement in the adjacent beeyard. I am still new to beekeeping, so I attach no importance to it and continue weeding. The noise becomes louder, more insistent. I go to the fence to see what is going on. Bees are flying all over. At first I think one of the hives is being robbed. But the problem is more serious.

The buzzing gains in volume. It becomes a roar. More bees are now swirling about in wild, swinging patterns. Suddenly there is a mass exodus from the hive. I have never seen so many bees at one time. They make an alarming sound, flying wilder patterns, as if gone berserk. And yet, they do not appear angry or menacing.

I am not alone witnessing this drama. On the adjoining lot a new house is under construction and today the well is being dug. The carpenters and well-diggers have heard the bees and stop work to watch. Mouths hang open. The carpenters stand far back, ready to take flight if the bees attack. But the well-digger joins me in the midst of the tumult, leaving his crew. He and I went to bee school together and he also keeps a hive of bees.

He is laughing. "What the hell kind of beekeeper are you, letting your bees swarm?" he says. Then he admits that his hive also "threw a swarm" the previous week. "I've been too busy to look after them," he explains, almost apologetically.

"I checked the hive last week and there were no swarm cells," I reply, and I detect the same note of apology in my voice.

We both know the bees are full of honey and euphoria and not likely to sting, so we sit under a nearby pine tree and watch the spectacle together.

FORTY-EIGHT

Before a swarm can issue, elaborate preparations must be made. Queen cells are capped and pupating princesses await within. Even before building these swarm cells, the bees raise drones so the virgin princesses will have mates. As soon as large numbers of drone cells appear, the colony has probably decided to swarm. Sexual logistics dictate this order, when it is recalled that a drone takes twenty-one days to form, compared to only sixteen for a queen, and twenty days more for a drone to become sexually functional, against only forty-eight hours for a queen. The decision to swarm is probably made at least a month before the actual departure.

Members of the swarm, just before leaving, fill themselves with honey; an average swarm carries with it about a pound and a half, enough to last several days and provide energy to build comb so the old queen can start laying brood at once. A hive without sufficient stores to spare will almost never throw a swarm.

On the day of departure all activity slows down. Bees that ordinarily would go to the fields hang around the hive, one of the few times they will be seen loafing. Others cluster in a thick mat on the front of the hive; there is no room inside with so many bees at "home" and it is hot and uncomfortable. Only workers not included in the swarm go about their business as usual, the foragers departing for the fields and returning, as if all this unusual activity is no affair of theirs and they are not concerned. There is no suggestion of sentimental farewells.

Often it is believed that the queen leads the swarm, but this is not true; she is, as usual, a follower, taking orders. Several days earlier the bees cut down on her food so she will lay fewer eggs, becoming lighter and better able to fly. By departure time she may be a third smaller than usual and harder than ever to distinguish among the massed workers, themselves larger than usual after gorging on honey in preparation for leaving.

The queen not only doesn't lead the exodus from the hive, but is likely to be in the middle or near the end. She may be fearful and have to be pushed along, hesitate, or even try to drop back and have to be forced out. One thing is sure: the bees will not depart without her.

Swarming must be a traumatic experience for the queen who has never left the comforting darkness of the hive since her mating flight. She may, in terror or confusion, topple over the landing board and have difficulty rejoining the swarm, an indignity that must detract from the sublimity of the occasion.

If the queen has suffered the further indignity and mutilation of having her wings clipped, a drastic measure taken by some beekeepers to prevent swarming, she may fall off the landing board, incapable either of flying or returning to the safety of the hive, in which case she will perish. The swarm will then return to the hive, its mission aborted, the great moment turned into catastrophe.

A swarm is made up primarily of older workers, along with some younger bees and possibly a few fledglings who have never flown before. Young bees are needed to form wax and act as nurses. A swarm can consist of up to about 35,000 bees, approximately nine pounds, or three times the usual bought package. Most swarms are smaller, usually no more than one-third of the parent colony. They tend to be smaller in cool weather, larger when it is hot. I read about one that consisted of an estimated 110,000 bees, but that could have been an entire colony that took off in desperation because its hive was honey-bound, leaving no room for the bees or new stores.

Swarming leaves unanswered many questions: Who decides to swarm and when? Who goes and who stays? How is the selection made? Are the emigrants like volunteers for the military, caught up in patriotic fervor or slogans? Who is in charge of logistics? Is there a formula or mechanism of selection to assure a suitable proportion of young to old, a blending of skills necessary to forge a new city?

Can we believe that the answers to the questions posed represent a consensus arrived at without any central authority? That the entire colony is so attuned to the silent voice of the distant past that each member acts spontaneously, each knowing instinctively her individual role, whether to go or stay without consultation or directive?

Efforts to resolve some of the mystery surrounding swarming have brought more questions than answers. In one experiment members of a departing swarm were dabbed with paint and then prevented from leaving. A few days later they were permitted to depart, but many bees from the original group dropped out the second time; and some that were not going initially went the next time.

Were the recruits, if such they are, first seduced by whim or fervor and then had sobering second thoughts? Was it a cooling of patriotic ardor, and some who lagged the first time were aflame with such fervor the second time? Was the selection process revised by the leaders, making it more or less attractive or enticing to differnt candidates? Did the time lag itself have an effect because of the aging of the members? Or did unknown and unsuspected factors change the swarm's makeup?

The only thing known for sure is that those departing risk all by sacrificing everything they hold dear, taking with them only enough provender to get started again, exchanging security and wealth for uncertainty and perhaps disaster. Such is the power of the swarming impulse.

FORTY-NINE

While instinct is the primary cause of swarming, it is believed to have several triggering causes, among them crowding, lack of ventilation, a failing queen (colonies with old queens are more likely to swarm), weather conditions, the supply of nectar, and the predisposition of the bees themselves; some races tend to swarm more than others, black bees being more prone to swarm than the yellows. Some colonies are also more inclined to swarm, suggesting a genetic influence that may be altered by changing queens.

Ironically, for a beekeeper, success can be its own worst enemy. The stronger a colony is, the more likely it is to swarm. If it has overwintered well, with minimal losses, and there are large stores of provender, the nursery full of brood, the odds of swarming are increased. They are increased further if the colony is fed sugar water in the spring to encourage it to raise more brood. The beekeeper is caught in a dilemma largely of his own making: prodding the bees to multiply their number, thus encouraging swarming, and at the same time trying to dissuade them from taking off. Ultimately he may help bring about the result he wants to avoid.

Beekeepers, understandably, do not see swarming from the bees' point of view and continually try to outmaneuver them, devising countless techniques and equipment in an effort to thwart swarming; these range from ingenious mechanical contraptions to the barbaric practice of clipping the queen's wings. I have never been convinced that clipping is painless, as claimed; at least I have heard no testimony from a clipped queen to that effect, and nerve endings in the wings suggest that the operation may be painful. Even if painless, the bees themelves must find it displeasing to have their queen mutilated; a bee born with a deformity is immediately done away with.

The most common method of trying to prevent swarming is to cut out queen cells and even to destroy drone cells before the bees take off, but this is an almost hopeless task. Swarm cells must be eliminated every few days, and as soon as they are removed the bees build new ones. This is a bludgeoning approach to force nature into submission.

Some beekeepers try to outmaneuver the bees by various other stratagems, attempting to deal with the primary urge rather than its symptoms. One involves a device with little gates that must be opened and closed on various schedules to change the hive dynamics and thus thwart the swarm impulse; it was invented by a British beekeeper name Snelgrove, who wrote a book ttled *The Control and Prevention of Swarming*. I built one of Snelgrove's contraptions but it was so complicated that I never installed it, fearing that the bees might become unbalanced trying to figure out which gate to use, and I was never quite sure of what Snelgrove had in mind.

Other stratagems are intended to deceive the bees into thinking they have swarmed when they have never really left home, or keep them so preoccupied that they forget or neglect what they had in mind. A bee must keep her wits about her every minute if she is not to be taken in by her wily keeper.

Modern technology is now asserting itself in beekeeping, as it is changing most facets of life. In Great Britain, according to my bee newsletter, beekeepers have taken to installing microphones in hives. When about to swarm, bees make a distinctive sound, alerting the keeper so he can stop them. Somehow this seems a bit sneaky, spyiny on the bees in this way, bugging them, as it were, unworthy of the British sense of fair play. I can't imagine bees giving into this sort of thing without making a fight of it.

Beekeeping, like most human endeavors affecting nature, has a primary law: tampering begets tampering. Nature, as we now recognize, is delicately balanced. When one change is made, others must follow to accommodate the first disruption. This often sets in motion a chain of unexpected events which ultimately bring about the very result the original tampering was intended to prevent, or worse.

My own feelings about swarm prevention are mixed. I see it from both points of view. It is not easy to reconcile "Stop them at any cost" and "Live and let live." I used to cut out swarm cells, divide colonies, manipulate frames, rearrange hive bodies, and engage in other skulduggeries in an effort to outwit the bees. Now I do nothing. They can take off if that is their desire.

This, I realize, is an attitude of luxury, an indulgence. Bees are a hobby and not my living. If I am fortunate enough to be around when they issue forth with that splendid roar and wild tumult, I merely sit under a tree and enjoy the show. Doing nothing may be my role in the grand design.

FIFTY

Generally, only one swarm issues from a hive, accompanied by the old queen, and this is known as the primary swarm. There should be only this one swarm. That is the rule. However, there may be a second swarm, and that is a perversion of the rule. In some colonies the swarming instinct is so powerful that a colony may develop "swarm fever," throwing off swarm after swarm, a kind of biological anarchy or madness. One hive actually sent forth thirty separate swarms, each accompanied by a virgin queen.

Each successive after-swarm is weaker than its predecessor, each having less chance of survival, until, finally, it is virtually a suicidal undertaking. Not only are the weakened after-swarms doomed, but the parent colony itself is so depleted that it too must die. It is as if some regulatory mechanism gets out of whack, or nature loses control over her own survival impulses, turning them into a terminal act of self-destruction.

Most after-swarms are small to begin with. If the virgin queen accompanying them fails in her mating flight or does not return, the colony will soon die out. Occasionally more than one virgin queen is found in an after-swarm, suggesting that the bees recognize their vulnerability and try to provide a reproductive fail-safe mechanism or backup. One beekeeper claimed that he found a swarm composed entirely of virgin queens; even nature would be hard pressed to top that.

Bee literature records an incident in which a drone mated with a virgin queen during a swarm flight, although I suspect this is based more on gossip than on scientific proof. If not unique, it is at least contrary to the rules, a kind of defiance of evolutionary principles. Was it some impromptu survival wisdom, or the act of an impetuous, sexually souped-up drone who saw his opportunity and took it? He seemed to be taking a good deal on himself, disrupting the institutionalized process of natural selection without having proved himself the fittest. What did the swarming workers think? Did they consider it a bit nervy or exhibitionistic?

These various oddities cannot be readily explained. Because they do not conform to usual patterns, we tend to dismiss them as aberrations or distortions of the natural order. But who is to say what the natural order is? There is no way of knowing whether the departures from the standards we call normal also play their own part in the scheme of life.

Those of us who look for order and consistency in the hive

as counterbalance to those qualities missing in our own lives and societies are usually doomed to disappointment. Order does exist, after a fashion, and there is consistency, of a kind, but both usually fall short of our expectations, just as he swarming impulse can take bizarre turns that prove more destructive than useful in helping colonies multiply and flourish.

FIFTY-ONE

*J*f swarming bees, upon charging forth from the hive with that unmistakable roar and commotion, behave reasonably and follow the rules, they will soon form a cluster on a nearby bush or in a tree. In cities they often pick the most unlikely place to alight, clinging to traffic signals, telephone booths, cars, power lines, and what have you. Given a choice they seem to prefer a more natural and sensible setting. The queen invariably is in the center of the cluster for protection. Wherever she lights, the swarm will gather around her; swarms are aptly described as looking like a bunch of grapes.

This respite has its logic. It is a kind of pit stop, or delay in route, providing the queen a chance to rest after her unaccustomed exertions and gather her strength, or wits, such as they are. More important, it gives the swarm a chance to regroup and take council. If the travelers have already decided upon a new home, they will likely remain only minutes or hours, overnight at the longest. Otherwise, they decide upon a new destination at this time. Nothing in bee literature is more fascinating than the way bees choose a new home, described by Karl von Frisch in *The Dancing Bees*.

Dozens of scouts are sent out in all directions, near and far, to look for something suitable, a hole in a wall, an abandoned beehive, a hollow tree, some recess not inhabited by other creatures. The returning scouts report their findings by "dancing" on the surface of the cluster, as foragers show the way to food sources, but more about that later.

Several scouts dance at the same time, some pointing in one direction, others in another; some indicate places nearby, others a considerable distance away. Some dances are more lively and cause greater excitement than others. The enthusiasm and intensity of the dance is in proportion to the suitability of the discovery and the dancer's enthusiasm. Among the things the scouts look for are the size of the entry hole, whether it is sheltered, if there are drafts, the smell (which must be pleasing), and who knows how many other things besides, states von Frisch:

> Within a few hours, or sometimes only during the course of days, something really extraordinary happens. The most vivacious of the dancers who have found a selected place gain more and more followers; these have taken a good look at it and show their approval by making propaganda for it by dancing themselves. Also other dancers, who until now have canvassed for less attractive dwelling places become converted by the swirl of the successful ones. They follow their advice and look at the other accommodation until they are convinced of its worth. Many of the bees which cannot show such enthusiasm as the lucky discoverers for their accommodation simply cease dancing altogether if things take this turn. Thus an agreement is reached; all dance the same measure and in the same direction. When everything is ready, the swarm dissolves, to fly off under the direction of hundreds of its members who already know the way to the objective which has been chosen as the best available.

Von Frisch also offers this comment: "There is much that man could learn from the bees, but he does not have the patience. Before the foregoing events have been brought to a conclusion, he interferes and draws the swarm into his hive—just as he so often destroys natural processes with his coarse hands for his own ends."

Left to themselves, swarms generally found their new city in a hollow tree or, more likely, some inaccessible place from which they cannot be evicted without considerable cost and destruction of property. They are especially fond of old houses, entering them through the eaves; they seem to like being near people, and there is the advantage of a warm nest and space between walls where ordinarily there would be insulation in newer houses. The damage done to a house by removing bees is usually greater than leaving them alone, but many people are uneasy about sharing quarters with them. I usually try to persuade those who want to poison or remove these visitors to leave them alone. Bees are not undesirable tenants; they "pay their rent" by pollinating flowers and gardens, mind their own business, and are cheerful, uncomplaining, and undemanding neighbors.

If lucky, a beekeeper can gather a swarm when it settles down near the parent hive. Bees are so gentle at this time that they can be taken with almost no danger of getting stung, even scooped up with bare hands or ladled out like so many beans. The trick is to get the queen, and the rest of the swarm will gather around her. By nipping off the branch they cling to, the entire cluster can be popped into a swarm box (a wooden frame with screened sides and a lid), or a perforated can or bag, and that's all there is to it.

Ingenious contraptions have been developed by beekeepers to collect swarms. The ultimate in sophisticated homemade gear is a gunnysack net tacked onto a barrel hoop which is attached to a long pole for overhead work. Some beekeepers specialize in gathering swarms. I read about one bee-hunter who caught 104 swarms in a single season. Others track swarms, which requires skill and stamina, as pursued and pursuer may travel several miles over rough terrain to a new home.

It has been my experience that swarms tend to alight high

in tall trees, and it takes a bit of daring, or perhaps insanity, to pursue them. But there is something about such a prize that makes the average sensible beekeeper come unhinged. He will climb tippy ladders to lethal heights, clinging to a tree with one leg wrapped around the trunk while trying to saw loose a branch with a few clinging bees. I have seen frustrated beekeepers saw down huge trees to collect a few bees. I am convinced that bees have a sense of humor, enjoying nothing so much as taking off the instant they are about to be captured.

It is a disservice to the average beekeeper to infer that he is motivated by frugality or greed alone. A free swarm is only part of the attraction. The beekeeper clings perilously to a branch, balancing on his fragile perch in a display of cunning and reckless courage, eye to eye with a pulsing, humming swarm of bees about to take wing; in that instant he captures not just a few transient insects intent on changing abodes, but a part of himself that he lost long, long ago.

FIFTY-TWO

It is probably not our successes that remain with us so much as our failures, those dark blotches of inadequacy that mar the canvases of our lives. One of mine occurred shortly after I began keeping bees. I had one hive and was hoping a swarm would come along so I could expand. I asked the local police to notify me if anyone reported a swarm. I similarly alerted friends and people I knew.

There were several calls, one from the police; a woman reported a swarm in a tree in her yard. I went immediately, carrying a ladder, homemade swarm box, saws, poles, and various paraphernalia. The woman said the bees had arrived the previous afternoon, remained overnight, and took off about fifteen minutes before I arrived. "They just left!" she cried, "What a shame!"

Another swarm had taken up quarters high in the eaves of an old house. The owner was determined to get rid of them at once. He was not dissuaded by my argument about what good neighbors bees are, but came around when I pointed out that bees were preferable to the cost and inconvenience of having the house dismantled to get to them, and someone possibly getting hurt and suing him; I have learned that economics carry weight where principles fail. I had two or three calls from strangers, and the "bees" turned out to be yellow jackets.

Finally I had a call from an acquaintance named Charlie. He formerly kept bees commercially but had sold them and was now in construction. "Are you still looking for a swarm?" he asked. I said I was. "I have one for you," he said, and told me where to meet him.

The swarm was near the center of town, conveniently on a low bush in a front yard. It was disappointingly small, apparently an after-swarm. Charlie must have noticed my disappointment. "There aren't enough to start a new hive," he said, "but you can unite them with the one you have."

I told him I didn't know that two strange colonies could be put together. "Oh sure," he replied. "You use the newspaper method."

"What's that?"

"Simple, I'll show you."

He professionally snipped off the branch the swarm clung to and popped them into the swarm box I had brought. As we drove to my hive, he explained that often when a colony is too weak to make it through the winter it is united with a second to make one strong colony.

The day was overcast, not at all suitable for working with bees, but Charlie assured me that the newspaper method was foolproof and there would be no problem with the weather.

"It'll only take a minute," he said.

We reached my place and went to the beeyard. The swarm was now clustered in a corner of the swarm box, protectively surrounding their queen. Charlie removed the cover and inner cover of my hive, took a single thickness of newspaper which he placed on top of the open hive body and then put an empty super on top of the newspaper. Cutting a few slits in the paper, he explained that the smell of the two colonies would mingle, and by the time the bees chewed their way through the paper they would be used to each other.

"You can spray both colonies with sugar water and they're too preoccupied with licking off the syrup to fight," he said. "You can also flavor it with anise to help disguise their smell. But I don't think that's necessary."

"What about the two queens?" I asked.

"The bees will work that out," he said. "But if you see the queen in the swarm and can remove her, it'll make things go easier."

Everything was ready. He dumped the swarm into the empty super onto the sheet of newspaper. Almost miraculously, it seemed to me, he spotted the queen, plucked her out, and asked if I had a queen cage. I got the one that my original queen had come in; he put the queen and three attendants in the case, inserting the cork in one end, imprisoning the four.

He covered the hive with the top. "There, you're all set," he said.

It seemed unbelievable to me. He had violated two of the fundamental rules I had been taught. He had worked the bees on a cloudy day, without protection of any kind, not even a net covering his face, and never once got stung. He was putting two strange colonies together. He had no apparent doubts that what he was doing would succeed. I envied both his confidence and his ease in handling the bees. I learned then how important a sure touch is. The bees themselves seem to recognize and respect it, as they sense fear and punish bumbling or rough handling. The "sure touch" is a rare talent some people are born with, others acquire, and most of us, unfortunately, never achieve.

"Maybe you'll find somebody who needs a queen," Charlie said.

I thanked him and he left.

The two strange colonies theoretically would chew holes in the paper, working from opposite sides, until they joined forces. Then if all went well, they would sensibly work together for the greater benefit of all. The problem was that it was people logic and not bee logic. Often they are irreconcilable, as commercial exploitation and nature are usually incompatible.

A couple of hours later I returned to the hive to make sure all had gone as Charlie predicted. But something was wrong. The bees, once more, had violated the rules. The new bees had been driven out of the hive and were huddled in a pitiful little cluster on the ground nearby. The earth was cluttered with dead bees, presumably the corpses of the weaker invaders who were kicked out or killed. Ranged across the front entrance of the hive was a row of sentries making sure the rejected swarm couldn't get back in.

I called Charlie. A long silence. "You're kidding," he said. "I can't believe it. That never happened to me before. I don't understand it."

He said that every colony he had ever given bees to had accepted the newcomers as added field hands, especially at the height of the honeyflow. "It just doesn't make sense," he mused. Since the swarm bees had lost their queen and home and had no place to go, they should be eager to join the existing colony. And the old bees could always use more workers. "It just doesn't make sense," he repeatd. "I'll tell you what to do. Try the newspaper method again, but this time first spray them with sugar water flavored with anise." He no longer sounded so confident.

By the time everything was ready, the clouds had become

more dense. A feel of rain was in the air. I carefully gathered the forlorn little clump of bees on a shovel and placed them on a newspaper inside the empty super. I sprayed both colonies with the anise-flavored syrup but did not cut slits in the paper, hoping to give the adversaries more time to get used to one another, or at least delay the debacle as long as possible.

I intended to stand by and see what happened. But drops of rain began to fall. Then the rain came in torrents and I ran to the house for cover. When it let up, I returned to see what had happened. Once more the swarm bees had been driven from the hive. Even more bodies were on the ground.

The few bees now left alive were gathered in a pitiful, sodden little cluster almost in front of the hive entrance. The resident bees were in a ferocious temper and trying to sting. I wore no protective gear and several succeeded. There seemed no point in returning the rejected bees to the hive for a third assault. By now there were too few left even to attempt to set them up in a separate hive. I did the only thing I could think of, putting a basket over the forlorn little creatures to protect them from the rain and leaving them to their unhappy fate. The next time I returned, all of the swarm bees had vanished. I had no idea what happened to them. Possibly they were eaten by some creature. I was depressed all evening.

For several days I kept the queen in the cage, pushing drops of honey and water through the screen, as if trying to make amends for what I considered, if not my bungling, at least my interference with natural processes, the "coarse hand" von Frisch spoke of. I wasn't even sure I wanted to continue keeping bees. I kept hoping I would hear of a beekeeper who needed a queen. I made several calls, but no luck. No one ever needs a queen when an extra one is at hand, but they are in urgent demand when not available. I have often called around, desperately seeking a queen in a crisis and found none. Then a few days later, after sending for one through the mail, I would get a call asking if I still wanted a queen.

I did not want to kill the queen, but knew that if she and her attendants were left in the cage indefinitely they would die. They are not like humans who can exist in solitary confinement for years.

I could have placed the queen in her cage in the hive and the bees would have fed the prisoners, even after killing all of the other strangers; queens have been maintained for long periods while caged and fed by a surrounding colony. But eventually the queen and her attendants would perish from being confined in such close quarters and the existing colony might become upset with a second queen in the hive and possibly kill their own queen. Bees will feed and care for a caged queen indefinitely, but release her and she will probably be killed at once, as if they can be compassionate only so long as they recognize no threat; compassion and threat rarely exist together. More likely, it is not compassion at all—the ever-practical bees may keep the extra queen alive in case she is needed.

I faced a dilemma common to people who try to manage nature, when human values conflict with nature's unsentimental imperatives. That is the part of beekeeping that I dislike and often it gets in my way. Is it more merciful to kill outright or to let creatures perish slowly and possibly painfully through want of their own kind and their own elementary biological needs? The manager becomes an arbiter of life and death. I was forced to confront a decision that was distasteful to me. Perhaps I showed a lack of character or resolution, flinching from the responsibility I had taken upon myself by keeping bees, but I decided against being either executioner or jailer. I let nature do the unpleasant job that was thrust upon me and that I flinched from.

On a late afternoon, I took the cage bearing the queen and her three attendants outside and removed the cork from the cage, placing it on the ground near the garden. A few minutes later the queen, now shrunken from imprisonment and not laying eggs, ventured out, followed by her three attendants.

She spread her wings, as if about to take off, and seemed to stretch her long, graceful legs. Then she began to walk, as if enjoying the luxury of being free to move after the long confinement. The queen strolled onto a blade of grass, followed by her retinue, the delicate blade of grass bending to the ground under her weight.

She walked on a twig and over a leaf. Was she experiencing a voluptuous pleasure in freedom, out of the wooden jail with metal bars that had held her, or was she confused, bewildered, terrified? Was she searching for cells in which to lay eggs and wondering what had happened to the familiar world she had left behind? Everywhere the queen went, her three loyal handmaidens followed, ready to serve if needed.

The little procession paraded back to the cage, over it, and then paused on a piece of bark lying on the ground. The queen stood quietly, as if in deep thought, trying to decide with her inadequate brain what to do next. The three attendants mimicked her every move. They stood as if they too were in deep thought.

The queen rubbed her antennae with a foreleg. Her attendants did the same, suggesting a general scratching of heads as if to stimulate imagination to resolve their dilemma. Perhaps they were discussing their plight, or each had her own thoughts about what should be done and none had the conviction to act or the information to act upon. It seemed curious that none of them seemed to consider taking wing. Had they been imprisoned so long that they had forgotten they had wings, or how to fly?

One of the attendants rubbed her antennae against the queen. The others did the same. Then they began licking and grooming her. Once more the procession walked over blades of grass and back across the cage, as if fearful of going too far from this familiar object in a new and strange world. Again they paused to rest on a dead leaf. There was something dignified, almost stately, about the queen's bearing; it seemed to say that she was bewildered but would not let her attendants see her discomfiture, and surely she would not demean herself by panicking.

I waited to see if the attendants would desert their queen. None did. Darkness fell. The little band remained quietly on the leaf. By then the night was turning chilly. I went into the house for dinner. Afterward, I returned with a flashlight. I hadn't enjoyed the meal. The gallant little procession I had condemned to death was on my mind.

By the time I returned, I had decided to put the queen and her royal attendants back in the cage. I would try again to find a home for them. But by then all had disappeared, vanished into the night, ending their unhappy little tableau, and I felt that I had failed not only the bees but also myself, not with my inexperience and bumbling, but my lack of resolution in a responsibility I had undertaken in trying to manage other lives.

FIFTY-THREE

Deception is, above all, the lot of the honeybee. As the art of beekeeping implies working with nature, its science is founded largely on hoodwinking the gullible little creatures. Some artifice or ruse is involved at almost every step, beguiling them into thinking the artificial and imposed are the real; they are provided with "company houses" (hives), foundation, sugar-water syrup, simulated pollen, and antibiotics; they are smoked, manipulated, moved about like migratory workers, and enticed to produce honey, pollen, and wax, which are stolen from them, until they drop dead from overwork. All of this is possible, undoubtedly, because they, like their wily keepers, have "a little larceny" in their hearts and go along with the schemes, scams, and subterfuges to save time and effort and to improve production and efficiency.

Consider further, if you will, the unconscionable deception inflicted on bees by nature herself: the worker dies in the act of stinging to protect her hive or when threatened. The drone loses his life in mating, fitness his undoing. The queen soon wears herself out laying so many eggs; each member of the colony has a built-in self-destruct mechanism, each is victim of her or his own inborn life-sustaining drives. Collectively they live and die for a future that is, for them, never attained, always somewhere ahead like a trembling mirage or dream.

Ironically, the greatest flimflam of all is one bees may inflict on themselves, an often-fatal self-delusion shared by entire colonies, a kind of self-imposed curse or biological fabrication, known to beekeepers as "the laying worker."

The stage is set for our scenario if the queen is killed or dies of natural causes and is not replaced at once. A queenless colony is a pitiful and melancholy community; there may be a mournful wail or lament from within, bees gather on the landing board, as if commiserating with one another at a wake, or discussing their plight. They are demoralized, have lost the will to work, and are just biding time.

Without intervention, the colony will die. But introduce a new queen and the most extravagant change takes place at once. There is purposeful activity. Loafing ends. The dead are dragged out. The hive is put in order. The colony resumes its business of preparing for the future. To bees, the queen represents continuity, a focus of life, a reason for existence and for answering the implacable call to work.

As we now know, the beekeeper may introduce a new queen, or if there are fresh eggs in the hive the bees can produce their own queen; any delay in replacing the queen will cause some weakening of the colony, but it will probably recover. But what if there are no eggs and the bees cannot make their own queen? Or what if the keeper is negligent or unaware that the bees have not the means to care for themselves?

An odd thing happens. Certain worker bees start laying eggs themselves. There may be one, two, or several laying workers, after the hive has been without a queen for two or three weeks. The laying worker is a phenomenon, a bit of presumption or effrontery, and the results must be unsatisfactory to all but the bogus queen herself. Her intentions may be good, but the result is usually disaster.

A laying worker is one of the most difficult situations a beekeeper must contend with, especially if he knows that it is due to his own negligence; the problem almost never occurs in a well-managed hive, and is most likely to occur in early spring when there are no eggs in the nursery for the bees to raise their own queen.

A bogus queen is easily recognized by her laying pattern. A normal queen, with her high sense of order, goes up and down the comb depositing eggs in distinctive concentric circles, or in a group of adjacent cells, depositing one egg per cell. But the laying worker, with no coherent plan or built-in sense of order, scatters eggs at random and commits errors that a bona-fide queen would never be guilty of; obviously this is the work of an amateur. Like most pretenders, the laying worker is only a mimic; she just hasn't got it on her own. Her fatal shortcoming is that she is the victim of her own duplicity and illusions, incapable of producing anything but unfertilized drone eggs; as the workers die off, unreplaced, the colony is doomed.

The laying worker represents a quirk of biology better understood by taking a second look at a worker's and queen's sexual status and instincts. A worker is not a neuter, as she is often called but, rather, has undeveloped female reproductive organs; this suggests that at one time she could lay life-sustaining eggs but either lost the ability or left it to the queen as specialization of labor (so to speak) became stylish in evolution. A similar error is made by referring to the queen as the only perfect female in the hive, because of her lack of any maternal instinct and inability to care for her young; worker and queen complement one another, each lost without the other.

Beekeepers long puzzled over how an ordinary worker bee, with her undeveloped reproductive organs, could suddenly start laying eggs. The accepted theory was that such females were probably raised in cribs near queen cells, exposing them to more royal jelly than regular brood, thus giving them a limited egg-laying ability. Now the cause is known to be more complex.

The answer is believed to lie in pheromones, those extraordinary chemical signals produced by certain glands and transmitted from bee to bee by direct bodily contact, in food, or even through the air. These signals probably affect almost every hive function, including clustering, danger alerts, attacking enemies, marking trails, comb building, the mating flight, and, perhaps most important of all, inhibiting egg laying in worker bees.

This may be the queen's real power, her only true hive clout. She produces a glandular secretion known as "queen substance" from glands in her head; the way it regulates order in the hive by keeping all her chaste daughters' ovaries inhibited may well be one of nature's more extraordinary inventions.

FIFTY-FOUR

How queen substance acts to prevent egg laying in worker bees is not known, but it appears to be closely related to a queen's fertility. As long as she is capable of laying fertilized eggs, she appears able to manufacture the secretion. But once her supply of stored sperm is exhausted, or she begins to fail, she seems to lose her ability to produce the substance.

How the queen produces the pheromone is unclear. But every member of the colony is exposed to it. The attendants get it by licking the queen's body, and they, in turn, pass it along to others. If deprived of the secretion, the bees know at once that their queen is failing, if not already over the hill. If there are new fertile eggs in the nest, they will immediately begin building supersedure queen cells.

This suggests that queen substance works like a kind of biological thermostat, automatically triggering certain responses by its presence or absence. While little is known about queen substance, it is believed not only to protect the queen from rivalry by her daughters who might presume to lay eggs themselves, but to act as a sex attractant during the mating flight.

The discovery that queen substance induces bees to supersede a failing queen resolves one mystery of the hive, but creates others: What is this incredible secretion and how is it produced? How does it affect worker bees and what are their receptors? Is the effect psychological, physiological, or both? What other hive functions or behavior might it also influence?

How many other secretions, or signals, do bees generate that also regulate or determine hive functions? We recognize that worker bees produce pheromones that enable them to communicate with one another, but how many others not yet identified may have equally profound effects? Research in the field of insect communication has barely been touched upon. We are still shaken by the realization that plants apparently can communicate with one another and even have emotional reactions. Are insects not capable of as much, or possibly more?

The idea of other species exchanging information, processing, and acting upon it is in its infancy. We still haven't fully absorbed it. We still find it disquieting to think of whales singing songs of love and seeking one another out in the vast reaches of oceans; woodpeckers thumping out a message on a dried branch like Morse code; the wolf urinating on bushes to establish his territory; turtles, birds, bees, woolly bears, bats, and woodchucks exchanging data; fish and other animals advising one another of new feeding grounds and perils; plants passing along word of weather aberrations and insects inviting friends and relatives to feast in a lush garden; climate changes, language expressed in scents, sounds, vibrations, touching, dances, and electric impulses; and God knows what else.

We still tend to reject that which we can't understand or prove in the laboratory. We still have not accepted the linkage among species or learned the common language of interdependence spoken by all life. We still do not know how many other worlds exist within ours, and outside, unknown and unsuspected by us. The enormity of the concept does take some getting used to. It must all be challenging and somewhat unnerving to the scientific mind that demands proof.

Laying workers are common enough in apiaries. Just as parthenogenesis is found throughout nature, females of some species produce only one sex, and others are capable of giving birth to both sexes. Is the laying worker a kind of spin-off of parthenogenesis? And does a female laying eggs without fertilization represent some well-thought-out alternate strategy of reproduction, an expedient solution to a shortage of males, or was nature herself tired and overwrought when she conceived the idea? Since parthenogenesis is so widespread it is believed to have developed independently among many species in many places, it could be an impromptu response to the mighty urge for life under any terms, an ingenious solution to an unmet need, fortunately one not copied by humans, who are having quite enough trouble with the standard way.

Parthenogenesis, outside the apiary, does seem to have its place, based on such wide acceptance and practice, but aphids have carried it to extremes. Only in the fall are both sexes produced; they mate and fertile eggs are laid by the female, those eggs alone surviving the winter. Females hatch in the spring and a dozen or more generations follow without further matings.

If bees were going in for partial parthenogenesis as an emergency measure, why didn't they go the next logical step and learn to produce both sexes, like the aphid? Bees probably rejected aphids as role models, deciding these simpletons had nothing of value to teach them. The prolific aphids are not only regarded as garden pests, bearers of disease viruses, but have not thrived in proportion to their astronomical numbers. Aphids are more or less controlled by the notorious aphis lions (lacewings), also called golden eyes; and who knows whether these deceptively exquisite predators evolved to devour aphids, if aphids appeared as food for aphis lions, or if they emerged in tandem or found each other by chance or design?

The answer is not important; it all works out to much the same thing, another of nature's precarious and protective balances. There is, in any case, no problem of overproduction by worker bees or need for further controls. Drones are produced only in modest numbers and are dispatched by a built-in self-destruct mechanism designed by pitiless but ever-efficient nature.

FIFTY-FIVE

The queenless hive, without queen substance to regulate it, assumes a new identity if a laying worker takes over. It must adapt to a terminal situation. The worker queen herself faces insurmountable handicaps. She is neither physically nor psychologically equipped for her new role. She can no more fulfill the queen's function than the queen could fill that of a worker. Both queen and worker have ovaries to produce eggs and an oviduct through which eggs can be released, but there is a crucial difference: the queen has a spermatheca in which she stores those millions of sperm that produce fertilized eggs.

A laying worker, with neither spermatheca nor sperm, can be no more than a parody of her fertile mother, a bogus imitator. Nor, so far as is known, can she produce queen substance to protect her from rival laying workers. This probably accounts for there often being more than one laying worker in a hive. But why does only one bee become a laying worker? A few, at most? Why don't all females have a go at motherhood? How does this ersatz queen establish her claim and protect her territory?

The laying worker has still another biological liability. She lacks the long ovipositor with which a queen deposits eggs in the bottom of each cell. Literally short-changed by birth in this respect, she has only an undeveloped ovipositor. She can, at best, usually manage to leave her eggs high up on the edge of the cells, a sure sign of an amateur guilty of inferior workmanship of the highest order.

Even this is not her overriding shortcoming. She has no sense of reality; arrogance without technique or proper equipment is not enough. With no instinct or a proper laying strategy to guide her, she is likely to deposit more than one egg in each cell, probably on the shaky theory that if one is good, two must be better and three better yet. She is prone to scatter her unmistakable drone eggs all over the combs, instead of going up and down the line purposefully, grouping them for easy care, like a true queen. Worse, with no nurse bees being produced to care for eggs laid by the bogus mother, the majority will never hatch. The hive is already demoralized by the loss of the queen. Now, with no worker brood emerging, it is dwindling in size. The end is inevitable.

Drones produced by laying workers tend to be smaller than those from regular queens, due more to mechanical rather than biological limitations: the worker tends to place her eggs in the smaller worker cells rather than in the larger drone cells, as unaware of her own limitations as she is of the demands of the job. These smaller drones can function sexually as well as normal drones; size and sexual prowess are rarely equated in any species.

Beekeepers usually can tell at once if there is a laying worker by the laying pattern and absence of anything but drone brood. But this can be deceiving. If a regular queen uses up her entire supply of stored sperm, she is no better off than a laying worker, producing only drones; she becomes a caricature of her former self, performing a ritual that is meaningless to the life of the hive, a queen in name only to the doomed colony, if it neglected to begin supersedure soon enough.

FIFTY-SIX

A laying worker seems a bizarre response by nature to a desperate situation, but desperate situations tend to bring bizarre responses. She is an aberration, and nature's preferred solution to error is ultimate death and starting afresh. This, almost inevitably, is the fate of the laying worker.

The laying worker is virtually impossible to get rid of. She looks like any other bee to human eyes, so cannot be told apart from others. She has, further, the human failing of enjoying the privileges and prestige of power, refusing to step down if a fertile queen is introduced; she may be so intoxicated by her assumed role that the rest of the colony is beguiled into sharing her delusion, a happenstance common enough in human societies where demented or psychopathic leaders with enough charisma and conviction attract followers of fanatical loyalty.

With bees, this allegiance is carried to such extremes that, if a real queen is introduced, the colony will usually kill her and retain the bogus queen, a bee cult of personality! Can bees not tell the difference between a laying worker and a genuine queen, or do they refuse to transfer their affection and attentions? Such fidelity is admirable, but does cast doubt on the good sense of bees; the inflexible course taken almost inevitably ends in death. Why does instinct, if not intelligence, not serve them better here?

Beekeepers have devised many methods of dealing with laying workers, but most don't work, at least not in my experience. The conventional technique is to take the hive a couple of hundred yards from its stand, dump the entire colony on the ground, and then return the empty hive to its original place. Theoretically, the laying worker, heavy with eggs and unused to being outside, can't fly back with the others, cut down by her own pretensions. This solution is tempting in its comforting implications and easy application. The flaw is that the laying worker, despite her bulk, usually hustles back to the hive with the others within minutes to resume her labors as a single parent, while other may die from the rough handling.

I have read many techniques guaranteed to introduce a queen to a colony with a laying worker, but do not personally know anyone who succeeded in reforming such deviant behavior. Occasionally a colony will accept a new queen and reject the laying worker, but this is rare. Many authorities believe that the only real solution is to kill off the entire colony, or unite it with a stronger one that is queenright; members of the latter we assume, are outraged by such corrupt behavior and kill the bogus queen to protect their own legitimate sovereign and conventional way of life. This represents a moral or political solution, the underlying theology supporting the quixotic notion that, given a chance, the erring bees will return to the path of virtue. Virtue, however, is helped along if the strong normal, or square, colony first kills the laying worker or reeducates her to her proper role.

The remaining workers must recognize that there is no salvation for them, and yet, in a final act of despairing self-deception they may build a queen cell around one of the drone eggs, suggesting that their need for normalcy has deprived them of their reason and they are trying to deny or wish away their troubles with a final heroic illusion, one last grand fatal fantasy.

The whole problem of the laying worker puzzles me. Usually bees are clever enough in resolving their difficulties, but here they seem fatalistic, stupid, or deprived of reason. I can find no excuse for them. Would it not be simple and sensible enough for a colony with no queen and no eggs to produce a queen simply by stealing a newly laid egg from another hive? Surely their scruples are not above it. They will steal honey from neighboring colonies quickly enough; they are not adverse to slaughtering their own kind, in robbing, to advance their personal fortunes. Why, then, this reluctance to take bold and imaginative action? Why this surrender to adversity and terminal virtue?

FIFTY-SEVEN

Despair is a quality usually associated only with man, and yet I have seen despair, or what passes for despair, in other creatures. Despair is not to be confused with sorrow, which is a sadness, usually over a loss—despair is an overwhelming black melancholy that comes with the certain knowledge or belief that all is lost, there is no hope, despair feeding upon despair. Because humans are volatile in their emotions, despair may be a temporary condition following a severe setback of some kind, and recovery will probably follow eventually with the healing balm of time.

In animals despair usually comes with a severe illness that precedes death. We have no way of knowing, of course, whether this is truly despair, as experienced by humans, or an exhaustion of energy or the life force; but possibly they come to much the same thing. Despair, wherever it strikes, saps the life juices so there is no will to continue striving.

Do bees despair? I think they do, which, if true, would argue for a certain level of intelligence, as well as instinct, to know that a situation is hopeless. I observed what I believed to be despair in bees early in my beekeeping days, and it gave me a new perspective to consider that bees, and possibly other creatures, are capable of emotions based on their ability to assess their position and prospects.

It was a sunny day in early spring when I checked the hives to see how the bees had fared during the winter. To my dismay I found evidence in one hive of a laying worker. The only brood was drone cells scattered over the combs. I had not encountered this before, and blamed myself because I was late looking in on the bees. The colony had been queenright the previous fall. The queen apparently had died during the winter when there were no eggs to produce a new queen. Except for the laying worker, or workers, the colony was not in bad shape. There were still a fair number of bees and a couple of combs of honey.

I did not attempt the heroic measure of dumping the bees away from the hive in hopes that the laying worker(s) would not make it back and the others would. I had heard too many times that it was futile. I did the only thing I knew at the time, sending to the south for a new queen. The bees promptly and predictably killed her. Later I learned various measures that can help acceptance of a new queen.

I could have united the bees and laying worker with a stronger colony but decided to let the drama play itself out on nature's terms. I did nothing except to look in on the hive occasionally when checking the others.

It followed the expected course. A few more drone cells appeared here and there on the combs. Each time I opened the hive there were fewer bees and less drone brood. The workers did not visit the fields but hung around the hive most of the time, as if demoralized. The colony seemed to sense that something was wrong. Often, as hot weather came and the other hives had hundreds of workers coming and going, as well as play flights of young bees winging nearby, the bees with the laying worker seemed to lurk inside the hive. I would see them inside the entrance, almost like bereaved people staring out at a world they had renounced, an indication that all is not well. A maxim in beekeeping holds that "when the bees look out, you look in." The bees seemed to know they were doomed and could do nothing except wait for the end.

By late summer the colony had dwindled to almost nothing. Only a handful of bees remained, hardly enough to form an effective cluster. There was no morale, no activity. Dead bees were not removed. Their corpses and wax cappings piled up on the bottom board. Then there was no more brood. The laying worker was dead or had ceased to function; even she, with her megalomania, must have recognized the futility of her pretense.

Then a strange thing happened. The remaining bees began to hang around the screen door of my house. A few flew around outside the hive but none went inside; they even avoided the landing board. I opened the hive. The inevitable had happened. A colony of ants had set up housekeeping on top of the inner cover, running wildly when exposed to the light. But there was much worse below.

Wax moths had invaded the hive in force, laying eggs that had hatched into wormlike larvae. The comb was a disaster area of webbing, tunnels, and mold, a dark sticky mass, as if the city had been sacked and burned by vandals. There was a stench of decay and death. Moth larvae ran in all directions; there were thousands of moth eggs. What a mess!

The greater wax moth is one of the major enemies of bees. When a hive weakens, wax moths invade to complete the destruction. A strong colony can generally repel moths, and most other invaders, but when the colony falls below a certain size it no longer can protect itself. After the moths take over, bees leave and will not return, probably because of the foul odor. I do not know why the bees came to the door; it was almost as if they were trying to tell me that something was wrong.

I dismantled the hive, seared the supers with a torch to get rid of moth eggs and smell, and threw the frames with rotting comb in a garbage can. The few bees left followed me and kept trying to crawl into the foul comb, reluctant to give up the only home they knew. I wore no protective clothing, but they were too demoralized to sting. They flew around my head and kept crawling over the comb until the metal lid went on.

Cleaning a moth-infested hive is a dirty job, one of the most unpleasant tasks in beekeeping. Some of the wood frames were badly chewed, as if the bees had taken out their frustration on them. When bees chew on the hive, there is usually a problem. The last step was to leave the empty supers outside to air. As evening fell I checked the garbage cans waiting to go to the dump. A dozen or so bees still circled about the covered cans. Just before darkness fell I made a final check. All of the bees were gone. I have no idea whether they joined another hive, or just gave up and died.

Later I decided to look at the old hive stand to see if any bees had returned there. It was completely dark by then so I used a flashlight. The beam pierced the darkness; there was only the two cement blocks on which the hive had rested; a daddy longlegs was perched on one. It seemed an odd place to find a daddy longlegs after dark. A soft humming came from the other hives. Bees were fanning at the entrance, processing the day's harvest of nectar into honey, as if no disaster had visited their little community that day.

I snapped off the flashlight ans stood savoring the night, the stars, the mist, the night sounds, the fragrance of the garden.

In that instant I had new respect and appreciation for the bees. They are among the more sensible creatures I have encountered. Their values are sound. They go about their business in a forthright no-nonsense way with a live-and-let-live attitude. Their objectives seem reasonable enough, all considered. They neither seek nor need deeper meanings. They live and die by the same defined sense of purpose; work alone is meaning enough, an end in itself.

I listened to the bees fanning for another minute or two and went inside to bed.

FIFTY-EIGHT

*W*hen the colony was young, the queen laid multitudes of eggs that became the workers who performed the hive's essential tasks, and it was only when the community became strong that she began to lay drone eggs. Eventually there were some two hundred of these huge, oval-shaped, bulky creatures, almost twice the size of the workers, arrogant and overbearing as they charged over the combs, knocking aside their sisters, to dip into vats of stored honey that they had no part in producing.

I have, until now, largely ignored the drone, that macho and maligned fellow, and he deserves better. He is generally taken for granted, written off as a buffoon or good-natured slob, lacking character as well as social achievements, but handy to have around when needed. The drone has variously been described as doltish, foolish, clumsy, gluttonous, dirty, coarse, and totally and scandalously idle. The German poet Wilhelm Busch referred to drones as "lazy, stupid, fat and greedy," which did not help their reputation. Even the term drone is uncomplimentary, more insult than description, representing a free-loader living off the labors of others.

Worker bees apparently feel that drones can be produced when needed and disposed of when no longer wanted. It is a cynical attitude, at best. I find it one of the most unattractive qualities about bees; nothing must get in the way of the advancement of the race, the "state" above all.

Drones seem to live more by sufferance than any value placed upon their services. They are, from the beginning, a book-keeping liability by measurable criteria. The larger drone cra-dles take more wax and time to build than normal worker cells, and then the dull-witted drone needs help chewing his way free. He eats three times as much as an ordinary worker and can't perform sexually for the first three weeks of his life. A sizable number of a hive's productive workers are kept busy just feeding and caring for their hulking, hungry, boorish brothers.

For the drone, summer must be a time of ecstasy. Long golden days beckon, hours spent languishing among the blossoms while his industrious sisters extract the flowers' juices to support him in his indolence. He is a voluptuary, living a self-indulgent existence, strutting across the combs, too lazy to feed himself, getting in the way of the workers, taking frequent naps, and leaving his droppings for others to clean up. He ventures out only on warm, sunny days, and then about noon, to sport among the flowers, or to join other fine fellows like himself, rakes and roues all, in the staging area where they await virgin queens to fertilize and their reward, instant death for the fleetest and fit-test.

Feasting ravenously, he is unaware of his shortcomings; he is defenseless, without domestic skills or social graces, obli-vious that he, too, like his queen mother, is a tool of the hive, to be tolerated while useful, sacrificed in the nuptual flight if proved worthy, otherwise superfluous, and, come fall, ruth-lessly dispatched.

FIFTY-NINE

*A*nd yet, are we not too harsh on the drone, assigning him such a limited role, such meanness of spirit? Is it not we who are at fault if we expect from others more than they are capable of being or giving? Is it not unfair to present him only as a spendthrift of time, a shiftless freeloader, a debauched roue duped by his own lust and appetites? Is he not, like his queen mother and worker sisters, indispensible to the colony's existence, a pawn of nature, given a job to do and fulfilling it the best he knows how?

The drone may play a more complex and subtle role than that of just procreator. Studies suggest that colonies with a larger drone population gather more honey than those with fewer drones. Why? Who knows? Could it be that drones, like certain individuals in the workplace, contribute more by their presence than any job description or time-motion study could indicate, raising morale and encouraging others to produce beyond their normal capacity, another of those mysterious forces that defy scientific proof?

While no fixed formula exists for the number of drones a colony maintains, if it is preparing to supersede the old queen or to swarm it will produce large numbers, timing their emergence so they will be at the peak of their sexual prowess at the same time the virgin princesses sleeping in their cradles are ready to mate.

If the bees change their minds about superseding the old queen or swarming is postponed or abandoned altogether, the drones are not kicked out or eliminated at once. The workers seem to take a charitable, almost philosophical, view, as if to say, "Well, now that they're here they might as well stay." Are the drones on standby status, if needed? Do we miss the point altogether thinking they are tolerated or suffered, while they remain to fulfill the undefined and unknown role or function referred to of which we have neither knowledge nor understanding? Does the drone, with his limited intelligence, "think" there is no price to be paid for this day in the sun, no fiddler to reckon with? Is he, like most freeloaders, an eternal optimist?

The drone, like other members of the colony, has been extensively studied, and while much is known about him more remains unknown. He does have an odd biological background, having a mother but no father, although he has a grandfather on his mother's side. The maximum life of those who survive the perils of sex is only about four months; most live only half that long. One investigator places a drone's maximum life at fifty-nine days, but this seems cutting it a bit fine; nature is usually negotiable in such matters and rarely so fixed in her timetables.

The drone's only defense is the raucous noise he makes while beating his wings; he is all bluff and bluster, feared only because of his size and fearsome sound, in truth, trading on his sisters' reputation for stinging. He is a swift and powerful flyer but is easily plucked from the air and eaten by a variety of birds and devoured by toads and other ground creatures who recognize him for the harmless, plump morsel he is.

It seems significant that nature provided him with such a tiny brain, only slightly larger than the queen's, as if nature considers procreation a mindless activity and the partners need only the minimum mental awareness necessary to perform their respective functions in the reproductive process. Nature, having slighted him in brain power and giving him no stinger shortchanged him on both ends, it would seem.

It could be argued that drone and queen, both specialists and with the limitations of specialists, gave all they had to their sexual development, in the same way that man sacrificed to the development of his great brain. The drone poses an overriding question: does nature in any way forewarn him of what awaits the victor in the nuptial chase?

I have a difficult time reconciling a drone's violent end in sex with Darwinian principles. Evolution is presented as representing an advanced or better method of survival through adaptive behavior or natural selection. How does the drone's built-in fatal misfortune square with Darwin's idea: "Natural selection will never produce in a being any structure more injurious than beneficial to that being, for natural selection acts solely by and for the good of each." Would a drone go along with that?

Who or what assigned the drone his lethal role? If not unique in nature, it is at least rare; the female spider and praying mantis eat their mates in copulation, but this form of dining out (or in), premeditated murder of sorts, does not compare to the drone's involuntary demise. While his abrupt end may have advanced the race it is hard to see it as a personal gain for him individually. Did he have no options? Was his role thrust upon him and, if so, by whom or what? What place do options and choices play in evolution? Where does the individual fit into emerging patterns that are only disadvantageous for him or her, as the drone's seem to be?

Did worker bees ever practice or attempt parthenogenesis as the queen does in giving birth to unfertilized drones? Laying workers would suggest as much. Why, otherwise, do they have ovaries? And is the stinger not believed to have once been an ovipositor? Are the worker's ovaries a vestigial organ that never developed, nature changing her mind or embarking on a new course? Were they once functional and abandoned? Are these ovaries neither rudiment nor vestige but somehow necessary to a worker's nurturing capabilities?

The role of parthenogenesis among bees is touchy and has been bitterly disputed among scientists. It is known that in rare cases fertile worker bees have been found in hives after the queen is dead or removed; workers have also been produced from virgin queens in experiments, and drones have developed from fertile eggs with only half the normal number of chromosomes, apparently some kind of error on the part of nature, one that bees recognize as soon as the egg hatches and take corrective steps by eating the larva. How are these oddities, rare as they are, explained?

The possibility of parthenogenesis having existed or been tried presents questions. Was the drone an expedient afterthought of evolution or an orderly part of the process, meeting an existing need? As the queen became an egg-laying specialist, was it necessary to devise a compatible sex partner for her, with the least fuss possible, thus freeing the workers for other hive tasks? Was the drone conceived and developed simply and wholly as a disposable stud? He is treated by nature and his worker sisters as such, almost with contempt, a satire of the macho male, mocked but needed by an almost wholly female society. I keep going back to the beginning and trying to figure out what went wrong for the drone, and why; somehow it all seems related to his lack of intelligence, his inability to see which way the wind is, or was, blowing, his failure to improve his lot over aeons, never making any discernible progress, the eternal victim of vanity, gluttony, and sex.

The drone intrigues me. Is he considered by evolution a finished product or in some intermediate stage of development, locked into a temporary but lethal limbo? Is he, possibly, a mutant or throwback? Evolution is supposed to proceed on a fairly straight course of improving the species, wiping out those that don't measure up, but I am not so sure. I recall a story I read about a flock of geese, and the ganders fought for the privilege of mating with the females. Theoretically the fittest would do the job of procreating, but, in fact, the weakest of the lot was the first knocked out, and while the more fit were mutilating one another to accommodate nature, the most unfit of all was off behind a highway billboard copulating with the females. How does evolution handle this sort of surreptitious remission? How common is it among the species? Are we all, in truth, not going forward as we think, but backward, unsuspectingly retreating toward the trees in a kind of reverse evolution? Evidence enough abounds to support such a conclusion.

Is this, then, the real story of evolution? That we go just so far forward and then decline or disappear as we become too specialized—rituals outweigh results and appearances are more important than content? Are we even now taking a new direction with the strong and fit losing out to guile, shrewdness, deceit, and image? Man, unlike timeless nature, abruptly changes the world and the conditions of survival. It wasn't nature that, overnight, introduced DDT, the bulldozer, and nuclear plants or positioned the highway billboard that shielded the gander and the impatient geese who were more intent on immediate self-gratification than improving the race. Fate may stalk us more insidiously than we suspect.

In any case, I never cease to marvel that queen and drone, the least brainy members of the colony, in their union produce offspring with more intelligence than either parent. I find equally remarkable that the drone, produced from an infertile egg himself, is the agent of fertilizing eggs that become workers who are born lacking the ability to reproduce themselves but possessing the physical equipment to gather nectar and pollen, the nurturing instinct to raise the queen's brood, and the intelligence that makes hive life possible. Did nature not outdo herself in this genetic chamber of mirrors that biologically interlocks the three members in their social unity and complex division of labor?

The drone's various shortcomings do not appear to be of great concern to him as he partakes of his pleasure while awaiting the sacrificial summons to duty, ignorant or indifferent to the price to be paid. In his innocence, the trembling ecstasy of summer must seem the perfect life while it lasts. But what of his long-suffering sisters who must tolerate his bullying and helplessness? Are we to believe there is no resentment on their part, that they do not look forward to autumn when he is no longer needed and the good life he enjoys will end in a blood-bath of their doing?

Only when the queen is failing and may have to be superseded are drones permitted to live beyond fall. If they are found in a hive during the winter months, it is a good bet that something is amiss. But for those drones in strong, queenright hives, those who have not fallen in line of duty or misadventures along the primrose path of pleasure, autumn is a time of reckoning, a balancing of the books.

Their hour in the sun ends abruptly. They die in a violence as macabre and unexpected as that which overtook the fittest of their kind who triumphed in the heedless pursuit of virgin queens. So perhaps it doesn't make so much difference after all. Life is short! Sex must be a more agreeable executioner than one's vengeful chauvinist sisters.

SIXTY

There is, at first, no sign of menace, although the drone's worker sisters have grown increasingly testy as the nectar supply tapered off with the end of summer. The drone is, as usual, swaggering across the combs, shoving aside workers who get in his way as he heads toward the capsules of honey. But this time something is wrong. A couple of females block his path. The big fellow is surprised by this unexpected resistance. "What's going on here?" his manner says. The workers do not yield before him. Then both females suddenly fall upon the startled drone, pummeling him, biting his fine wings, tearing at his antenna and legs, violating his macho male superiority. The carnage is under way.

The startled drone is at first too stunned to resist. Then he rallies and tries to defend himself, dodging and parrying the claws and jaws of his assailants as best he can. He beats his powerful wings, making a ferocious sound, but the workers are not taken in by this bluster; his superior size and boisterous protests are no match for their fury. The three of them thrash about on the hive floor. He is knocked over on his back, helpless, flailing his now-mangled legs and tattered wings, once his pride, in a desperate effort to regain his footing, freedom, and what remains of his dignity.

Other workers, excited by the struggle, pitch in, also beating on the helpless drone. His protests and resistance become fainter. The struggling little mass heaves this way and that until, finally, the battered drone is pushed and dragged into a corner and held prisoner in the hive where he once reigned as a prince. What must his thought be in this moment, if capable of thought he is?

This death rite of autumn, bearing the poetic if grisly name "the massacre of the drones," is often depicted with considerable dramatic license, much like the St. Valentine's Day Massacre or Guy Fawkes Day. It is claimed that the workers do not begin the slaughter until late one afternoon in the fall, as if letting their condemned brothers enjoy one last day, and it is over almost at once. I have read claims that these massacres occur almost simultaneously in every hive in an apiary not only on the same day but almost at the identical moment, as if at a signal agreed upon in some previous congress of the assailant worker bees.

This is a tempting explanation, more satisfying than the facts in its dramatic expression. But most authorities agree that the attacks do not take place at once on a grand scale, but unfold gradually, often beginning with the workers withholding food from the drones and gradually turning murderously violent after their brothers are weakened from not eating. The attacks can occur over a month or so, at any time toward the end of summer after the drones' usefulness is over, a Machiavellian tactic that is more effective than admirable; the timing, like the technique itself, varies from hive to hive.

While the ethics of the massacre are to be deplored, the logic behind it is unassailable from the worker's point of view, representing the best business-management thinking about personnel reduction during slack periods: why should the drones be allowed to linger through the winter consuming precious honey when their services are no longer needed? In the spring, before another swarm season rolls around, more of their kind can be produced easily enough, or so the thinking must go.

One thing bothers me about the killings that are stretched out over days or weeks. Doesn't a drone who sees his brothers being knocked off, one by one, have any idea of what is in store for him? Does he block out or deny that which he doesn't want to believe? Is it incomprehensible that such a monstrous thing could befall a fine fellow like him? Is he resigned? A fatalist? An optimist with scales over his eyes?

I tend toward the latter explanation. Reality does not play a large role in most lives; there is a kind of fatal optimism that rules the affairs of bees and men alike. Each species, in its own way, seems to expect that things will work out in the end, regardless of errors or misfortunes that intrude and, fortunately, it more or less usually turns out that way, or at least it has until now. This is optimism of the highest order. It is admirable, but does present certain liabilities if calculations prove wrong or circumstances go amiss, as happens in the case of the autumnal drone; he is one of nature's lesser optimisms gone awry.

Let us return to our scenario. The battered victim previously described cowers in a corner, held prisoner, more dead than alive. The other drones have, by now, almost all been killed. This is the grand finale, a kind of epic slaughter relished by poets and savages, which I describe with the same dramatic license that I previously deplored.

The few survivors are ruthlessly beaten into helplessness and driven into corners or dragged out of the hive, the tormented hulks making a great rattling noise that sounds like, "Burrrr. . . . burrr. . . ." Is this a cry of distress? A futile call for help? But rescue is not forthcoming. There is no freemasonry of assistance here, no "hot line" to help, no one to assist. Every remaining drone shares the same plight; size and strength are of no avail against this female onslaught, especially in the starved drones' weakened state.

The long-put-upon workers, feasting on their own anger and enraged like any mob justifying its violence and beastiality, step up the attack. They threaten the drones with drawn stingers but do not actually use their poisoned cutlasses against their defenseless brothers. Is it some notion of fair play? Compassion? A convention of the ritual slaughter?

Some of the ill-used drones let themselves be dragged or led, without resistance, out of the hive by a single worker bee. This could be a mutilated elder being helped along by a kindly passerby or good wayfarer, not one who has just beaten him senseless. Other drones, looking dazed or forlorn, huge, bulging, multifaceted eyes fairly popping out of their heads, resist slightly and are tugged or pushed out by two or more workers. There is comedy and pathos amidst the tragedy. The drones are a pitiful, bedraggled lot, some missing a leg or two; once-resplendent wings and antennae are torn, broken, or missing altogether. All over the hive individual struggles continue as the victims are dragged out, held prisoner, or tormented; this could be a pogrom, sexual genocide, a society slaughtering its own.

I ask the same question posed about the drones dying in copulation: are they really taken so completely by surprise? Have they no instinctive knowledge that this is their end? Why has evolution so misled and not enabled them to develop a defense or means of survival? I ask again, does it make sense?

How does a conspiracy of females continue for millions of years without having its cover blown? Why does nature signal the female oppressors but not the male oppressed?

This is more than your run-of-the-mill ritual slaughter. The workers obviously find glee in the carnival of death. Are they savoring revenge after the indignities inflicted upon them by their overbearing brothers? Is this the joy and excitement of all creatures in vanquishing their enemies? It must be doubly sweet for the workers, acting out of instinct; they cannot be burdened with guilt or remorse. They are "just doing their job, following orders from above," as it were.

The coup de grace is longer in the telling than in the doing. It is over almost as soon as it begins. The drones, cornered and held prisoner, are dragged or led outside, most of them now barely able to move. Workers pull the dead, mutilated, and maimed to the landing board, where they are shoved over the edge to die on the ground or be eaten by predators of misfortune. The dispatched could be pirate victims forced to walk the plank and perish in the sea.

The few drones left alive and more or less intact huddle pitifully on the landing board, trying to force their way back inside. The pull of home is powerful, even one turned treacherous. Perhaps the benumbed brains of the new homeless cannot absorb the enormity of this catastrophe. To lose one's home is to lose all. The ejected victims are prevented from returning by long rows of guards stationed at the entrance; each attempt to reenter is blocked. The drones' efforts become progressively feeble as evening falls and the air becomes chilly. Finally the exhausted creatures stop trying to force their way back, as if accepting their fate.

Night falls. The chilly air turns cold. The drones, unable to join the warming cluster inside, fall into a stupor and die on the landing board in front of the hive where they returned from so many happy summer revels. In the morning the workers pull or push the dead over the edge and go back inside without so much as a backward glance. And there is some justification in the workers' heartless bee logic: the drones who died in the massacre didn't have the right stuff, or they'd have perished in mating.

SIXTY-ONE

What is this strange silent voice that speaks to bees and no one else can hear? That commands the workers to dispatch their drones and when; that tells them to protect or kill their queen; to go to the fields and gather nectar and pollen and how to store it; to seal their city against coming winter that not one of them has ever seen or experienced; how to find new homes and found new colonies; to feed the queen or withhold food? The same silent voice tells them to build queen or swarm cells and how many and how to stagger the development of virgin queens and drones, which plants produce the best honey, how to cool the hive, when to cluster and how to search out flowers and return to the point of departure, when and how to protect the hive, and always to sacrifice self for community good.

I could go on and on. In almost every hive function the same mysterious voice commands the bees to act in concert. And yet, in some matters, it speaks to some members and not to others. It tells workers to kill their drones but does not warn the victims that execution will end their feasting and frolicking. It tells the queen to inspect each crib before depositing an egg but does not instruct her in caring for her young. It tells the drone to mate with a virgin queen on the wing but withholds the result, as if suspecting he would not perform so valiantly if he knew.

The worker progresses from nurse to scavenger, servant, undertaker, warrior, guard, and field hand. She is told that she can produce queens by feeding them only royal jelly, and that other brood requires less exotic fare; she knows how to produce wax and build comb, to seal honey in the hexagon-shaped cells she designs and builds, that drone cells must be larger than worker cells; she recognizes a duty to protect her queen at all costs, and in the end takes her own life, if necessary, rather than burden the community.

These things we call instinct, but this does little to explain or enlighten. Words and language itself carry us just far enough out of the darkness to blunt our reverence for the unknown by giving it a name or identity, carrying us further from our own origins. What is the great silent communication between the bee and the guiding life force? "Instinct transcends intelligence," observed William Morton Wheeler, who studied ants extensively, "and has its mainspring in the depths of the life process"; but we still do not know and probably never will know how it works; it is the great gap in the chain science forges out of verifiable fact.

Mysticism is all very well, but is there not some more direct and immediate chain of command or authority within the colony itself? The question is long overdue: what infinite mystery is it that we pursue and whose answer forever eludes us when we look beyond the logic of the hive to its source of intelligence? It is like looking at the night sky and seeking to fathom its beauty and poetry from a text diagram of the constellations. Our senses are blinded by the feeble light of the fragments of knowledge garnered from what we observe or think we observe.

Who rules the hive? Who is steward of its destiny? Who is responsible for the great decisions that order a colony's daily existence, and on what basis or by what warrant are such decisions made? Is it the tyranny of the majority? The elitism of the minority? Is there a power structure similar to that found in human societies? Is there delegation of authority? Accountability? Who or what is the technician and tactician for instinct?

Who or what force undergirds fate and provides a shape or form that gives each hive an individual character or personality, as each human and each society differs from all others?

Always we end up with the same puzzlement. We look at effect without understanding cause, often confusing the two. We study the colony and it looks like a society of equals, without rulers or ruled, an anarchy, perhaps, each individual contributing what she or he has to give out of an inscrutable sense of communal obligation, a perfect society existing in divine justice and harmony, cooperating instead of competing, obeying nature rather than trying to dominate her.

It is too much. How could such organization and order be possible without some hierarchy of command and imposed discipline? Without the enticement of reward or the goad of punishment? Can we believe in such goodness, godliness, such innocence and self-sacrifice in any order of life?

Despite all the research and study, the millions of words written, this remains the most abiding and perplexing secret of the hive. Who really does run things around here? Is there some consensus of the entire colony, arrived at by a secret or unknown democratic process or congress? Is it autocratic rule imposed by a domineering individual? By a small group of super bees, a kind of ruling committee or politburo? If so, how is the head bee on the executive committee appointed or elected? How does an individual or group gain control and assert its self-designated rule? What is the mechanism for the transfer of power?

The most curious aspect is the degree of consensus among colonies. Each has its own idiosyncrasies, foibles and quirks, style and methodology; there are differences in temperament, industry, and character, but individual variations are minor compared to the similarities. In every apiary within a given area almost the same events take place at practically the same time, as if all were tuned into the same central authority or broadcasting network.

Is it possible? Does there exist some kind of electromagnetic communication or transference of command? For want of an answer I again fall back on Maeterlinck's exquisite phrase "the spirit of the hive," which confers poetic beauty but no more answers our question than stating that God, fate, or destiny rules the universe, each less an explanation than a label for our ignorance, a symbol of that which eludes understanding or comprehension.

We know that temperature, hours of daylight, the amount of nectar available, the state of the colony, the fertility of the queen, and other factors largely determine various hive actions, or at least affect decisions, but this does not explain the individual differences from one hive to another. It does not account for the manner in which a colony changes its response to external conditions from generation to generation.

Aristotle took an elitist view, believing that the hive was run by rulers, there were always more than one in the hive, and the hive would go to ruin if there were too many or too few; he also thought that these rulers generated rulers to succeed them. A modern corollary to this comes from a researcher who holds that the key decisions within a colony are made by a small ruling clique of workers he calls "control bees." He contends that "these bees are not made up of the very young or the very old. They are probably between the ages of 14 and 21 days and are in the height of their prime. . . . These control bees are the ones that decide when the swarm shall issue, that defend the entrance and, when necessary, start the offensive. They are the stingers."

In the same way, he continues, the control bees will ball the queen when she fails, and they will carry out workers that are worn out and useless and the young who are crippled or feeble. "In fact, they will rule the whole colony," he states. "The young bees and the very old bees seem to accept it as a fact," and march to their tune. This is speculation, but it is as good as any other hypothesis or explanation offered.

If indeed there is such a thing as control bees, they presumably look and act more or less like all other bees. Their membership, however, would have to keep changing with the inflowing progression of generations. No one observing the hive, short of cracking its communication code, would know for sure who they were, how to identify them, or even if there is such a thing as a few special bees running the whole show.

We are not told how these so-called control bees are elected or assume power, how they assert or enforce their authority, whether there is privilege or abuse, if hive chores are delegated democratically by biological development and age or by authoritarian dictate, or if there is succession of rule.

What provision is made to transfer power every couple of weeks as age or infirmity disqualifies or disables those in office, and the once-mighty are reduced to the status of humble field workers, the rulers now ruled? Is the political process so different in the hive than in the statehouse and capital?

We ponder the major dilemma of the hive without coming any nearer to the truth. And beyond our unanswered questions lies an even more profound mystery: if indeed there are control bees, who or what controls the control bees? What universal wisdom and order rules every hive and all those who abide therein?

Just who does run things around here?

SIXTY-TWO

If there is a universal language in nature, it must be that of fear. There are those who inspire fear and those who react to fear, the feared and the fearing, and suddenly, with new encounters, roles change, the predator becomes prey and the prey predator. Almost every creature has some kind of weapon that makes it feared and respected, or it employs a protective strategy of defense triggered by fear; situations and protagonists change but fear is a constant.

The bee's primary weapon is her stinger, but compared to the weaponry found in many creatures, it is not terribly impressive; it does not measure up to the fatal sting of some spiders and scorpions. Bee venom is relatively mild, unless one is allergic to it, in which case it can cause severe reactions and possibly death, but this is rare.

A bee's stinger is more of a deterrent than an attacking instrument, a means of commanding respect and instilling fear rather than of obtaining food. While effective enough for the purpose intended, it does not seem especially well designed, from a bee's point of view; it is something like firing a gun in self-defense and while merely wounding or frightening the enemy the shooter is instantly killed in the act of firing. As the drone dies in the act of mating, so does the worker lose her life in stinging. It is a curious weapon indeed that, when used, is more deadly to its possessor than to the target.

A worker's stinger is located in the rear of her abdomen, at the tip of what once might have been her ovipositor, like a tiny sharp tail. When a bee decides to strike, her stinger protrudes through the sting chamber and a drop of venom appears on the tip. But in order to sting she must first get leverage by digging in her claws; if the victim is sufficiently quick, this brief warning is enough to swat the attacker before she can sting. It takes fast reflexes to beat a bee to the draw, but she loses in "winning."

Under a microscope, a worker's stinger is shown to be exquisitely shaped, delicately tapered, and polished. It is composed of twin daggers formed in a V shape, each spear lined with tiny barblike serrations. At the top of the V is a bulb, the poison sac, which holds a small amount of venom formed elsewhere in the bee's body. Venom is delivered from the sac through tubes in the lances.

When driven into flesh, the barbs catch like fishhooks, making the stinger difficult to withdraw, at the same time spurting venom into the wound. Given enough time, a bee probably could work her stinger free without damage to herself. But stinging is usually accompanied by considerable excitement, which probably caused the bee to sting in the first place. The terrified creature panics, and in trying to free herself, succeeds only in ripping out her stinger, rupturing her abdomen, and she dies, much as the drone succumbs in mating.

A California investigator let five bees sting him to find out how long they would live without stingers. As usual, the bees didn't respond as expected. Even with their intestines trailing behind them, they would eat honey, fly, and go about their business, even grooming themselves. They lived up to five days, but that was only when separated from the colony and protected. In the hive the healthy bees attacked the injured, making outcasts of them by driving them out of the hive. They made life so miserable for the stingless bees that the latter refused to reenter the hive and died of chilling and isolation rather than of their wounds. What is a bee to think of such treatment? What are we to make of it?

Once the stinger is completely detached from the bee, a strange thing happens: it continues to work its way deeper into the wound while venom keeps pumping from the poison sac, as if it has some independent intelligence or life of its own, the thrust so powerful that it can penetrate a felt hat and even leather, the pumping action continuing for twenty minutes after the stinger is detached.

One of the first lessons a neophyte beekeeper learns is never to remove a stinger by pinching it between thumb and forefinger, because squeezing the poison sac forces more venom into the wound, making it more painful. Stingers should be removed with a quick sideways flick of a fingernail or a sharp object such as a knife blade. The sooner the stinger is removed, the less discomfort suffered.

It is idle to speculate on the origin and development of a worker's stinger, but it is difficult not to wonder why nature designed it as she did. Why could it not have been formed without serrated barbs, like a queen's, so it could be withdrawn with no damage to the bee and used again and again? Why does the queen have an ovipositor and a stinger, which she will virtually never use on anything but another queen, and a worker has just a stinger in place of what is believed to have once been an ovipositor?

Darwin himself seemed to have trouble rationalizing this organ, dismissing it in almost a cavalier manner:

> If we look at the sting of the bee, as having existed in a remote progenitor, as a boring and serrated instrument, like that in so many members of the same great order, and that it has since been modified but not perfected for its present purpose, as to produce galls, since intensified, we can perhaps understand how it is that the use of the sting should so often cause the insect's own death: for if on the whole the power of stinging be useful to the social community, it may cause the death of some few members.

E. O. Essig, an entomologist, points out that "it is easier to describe the remarkable adaptations of insects than it is to explain the reasons for them. It is difficult to know whether the body structures and complicated life histories or the environmental factors were the most important. Many other factors may have entered into the long, slow process of change and adjustment."

Whatever her thinking, nature protects her secrets and evolution keeps its own counsel. There are so many false leads, twists and turns, odd byways, blind alleys, contradictions, and discrepancies, it is not possible to know whether the worker's stinger is some cruel jest played on her by nature, a happenstance of evolution with no explanation in logic or reason, or if there is a logic or meaning beyond our comprehension.

Bees seem to know instinctively that stinging has ill effects for them and they avoid confrontation if possible. They usually sting for only two reasons: to protect their hive or when personally threatened. I have often wondered if stinging is wholly an inbred reflex action or a considered individual response. Does a worker bee, unsheathing her stinger, know she is embarking on a suicidal act? Would it deter her if she did? Accordingly, I pose this question:

> Would the bee be
> So quick to sting
> If she knew it were
> Her final fling?

SIXTY-THREE

*B*ee venom is one of the more notorious but less exotic secretions produced by honeybees. Each worker is virtually a miniature chemical factory; from her small body come the toxic element in stings, glandular life-sustaining secretions to feed embryo bees, wax used in building comb, and enzymes that affect numerous hive activities; there also may be others not yet identified.

Bee venom is said to consist of eight components, including histamine, which is held responsible for causing pain and swelling when a bee stings. For most people the discomfort of a sting lasts only a day or so and can be eased by applying, as soon as possible, towels wrung out alternately in hot and cold water or a paste made of baking soda and water. I have also found the juice of aloe plants soothing. The wound should not be rubbed, as this disperses the poison and makes it more painful.

While bee venom is best known for its mild to severe effects in bee stings, it may turn out to have valuable medicinal properties in treating arthritis and other inflammatory diseases. A pioneer in promoting bee venom therapy is Charles Mraz, a professional beekeeper in Middlebury, Vermont, and an old friend of mine. He was pushing BVT more than fifty years ago, by his reckoning, and today points out that it is no longer considered a folk remedy but is under intense clinical investigation and has a scientific basis.

The strangest testimonial I ever heard for bee venom came from a woman in the beekeeping association I belonged to. Her daughter and son-in-law had a small farm with chickens, and the woman beekeeper and her husband kept a hive on the property. One of the chickens fell sick and was isolated in a small cage; the chicken had been viciously attacked by the flock and left with open wounds.

The woman beekeeper said that bees from her nearby hive, scenting the blood, attacked the sick chicken until it was covered with stinging workers. Her daughter saw the bees and shouted in panic to her father that his bees were killing her chicken. He was too far away to attempt a rescue, so the young woman covered her head with a blanket and rescued the chicken from the bees. It must have been a memorable sight: the young woman running with the chicken, a blanket over her head, pursued by bees infuriated by the taste of blood and wanting to complete the wounded fowl's destruction.

Incredibly, the young woman didn't get stung and somehow managed to hide her chicken from the bees. Her mother said that she and her husband removed some two hundred stingers from the chicken that night. "The funniest part," she added, "was that the chicken recovered almost immediately and since then has been laying an egg every day, which she never did before."

I am intrigued that some two hundred bees would give up their lives to sting a dying chicken. Is nature's command to dispatch a wounded creature greater than the bee's will to live?

There must be a moral to the story, but I am not sure what it is. I can't decide whether it is more revealing of people, chickens, bees, or bee venom.

SIXTY-FOUR

I stand beside my hives watching the industrious bees coming and going, stingers sheathed, pollen baskets full, bent on the most peaceful of missions—visiting the nearby meadow of blueberry blossoms and flowering locusts and returning with their bounty. It is early morning; the dew has not yet burned off the grass and hog cranberry (bearberry) in front of the hives. Night's mists rise from the valley as earth gathers the sun's warmth. A sweet fragrance clings to new growth. Dew glistens on green leaves. A rapture of new life is everywhere. The bees pay no attention to me, too concerned with their mission and the urgency of spring to be distracted by my presence.

But our truce, our mutual commitment to live and let live, is fragile. If I stand in the flight path of these couriers as they go to and from the fields, or if I jar their hive roughly, our accommodation is abruptly shattered. The peaceful colony suddenly turns into an enraged striking force. I never cease to be astonished at how angry these small emissaries of nature become when provoked or attacked.

Many a hero forced to take to his heels by outraged bees has pondered this transformation from peace to war. It is well established that an individual bee will attack if threatened or injured. But how is it that an entire colony will answer the call to arms when only one is affronted? How is the signal or command given? The answer lies in the pheromones previously mentioned. As human armies employ bugles, whistles, gestures, flags, and other signals, bees use chemicals.

These glandular secretions were long suspected but only in recent years identified and assayed in the laboratory. Fewer than a dozen have been isolated, differing among races of bees, but more are expected to be established. Known pheromones include the queen substance, already referred to, which inhibits workers from developing their ovaries and building queen cells, enabling the queen to protect her turf; other queen secretions are sex attractants for drones, aid in mating, and induce the colony to cluster; worker pheromones mark trails and alert the colony to danger; others yet to be identified undoubtedly will be found to regulate many additional hive activities. Gradually bees are being deprived of their secrets.

Pheromones are transmitted from one individual to another, throughout the entire colony, in a variety of ways—by direct bodily contact, in food, and even in the air. The various chemicals are as individualized, as mysteriously coded, as any cryptic message. Bees are tuned into these signals and respond to them at once.

While the discovery of pheromones provides insights into bee behavior, it also raises new and more perplexing questions: the deeper we probe the hive, the darker the glass through which we peer. Who gives or orders the alarm signal to be given and under what conditions? Can any member of the colony put the bees on a war alert or order an attack, or be authorized by them? What, if any, restraints or confirming authority exists? How much autonomy do individuals have? Is it the same for all hive members?

I was aware of the effects of pheromones long before I knew they existed. I have worked my hives in less than ideal weather and the bees tried to sting me through my clothing. Hours later, while in the garden, minding my own business, I would suddenly be stung. I had been marked with a chemical signifying "enemy." A passing worker picked up the signal and attacked. Was this an automatic response programmed into her so indelibly that she had no power to resist? Did she have a choice? Did she know or suspect that it was an irrational sacrifice, causing me only minor discomfort and costing her her life?

As usual, human logic cannot be applied to other creatures. The attack, which seemed unprovoked and senselessly suicidal to me, may have had some commanding logic to its victim, not unlike a son or daughter avenging a wronged parent to preserve an intangible valor or honor, or a blood feud among desert people. In the same way that bees respond to injury, real or imagined insult, and danger, men react to words and ideas that arouse passions and the mindless sacrifice of lives.

Bees show an altogether human response when angered or threatened. They need a target or scapegoat for their wrath or frustration. If the primary offender is not available for punishment, a surrogate will do, just as an angry person may turn upon a peacemaker in a quarrel or even an innocent passerby. Once I had to go into a hive that was queenless. The bees, already upset by this condition, were enraged by my meddling and turned their fury on me. Fortunately, I was protected by my bee suit. But soon afterward my wife, Peggy, took out the trash, far from the hives, and a bee stung her on the forehead for no apparent reason except that she was available and I wasn't.

Bees are not essentially ill tempered or uncharitable. They hold no grudge that I know of. As soon as the alarm pheromone disappears and the danger or threat is past, the incident is forgotten with no hard feelings, at least not on the part of the bees, by any measurable standard. Peggy was not so forgetful or forgiving. She claimed to bear no grudge or animosity toward the bees for gratuitously stinging her on the forehead, but afterward she refused to go outside when I was working the hives.

SIXTY-FIVE

*B*ees may be the most maligned of all creatures. People tend to call everything that flies and stings a bee. This, understandably, has given them an undeservedly bad reputation. I have frequently been called upon to get rid of a "swarm of bees" and almost always it turns out to be yellow jackets or hornets (both wasps), and once winged termites.

Yellow jackets are especially ill tempered and aggressive, usually making their nests in a hole in the ground and attacking at the slightest provocation; it is difficult to relate to yellow jackets or take a benign view of them as neighbors. Hornets are also generally unfriendly and not the least interested in coexistence, but I have had an agreeable association with wasps.

In the house we formerly lived in on Cape Cod, they had a nest in the wall. On sunny days, even in mid-winter, they would emerge and fly about in the dining room until we opened the glass slider and shooed them out. They promptly reentered the house through their private entrance, in the eaves above the kitchen door, and reappeared in the dining room; it was an endless procession of entrances and forced exits, a revolving-door arrangement that was for a long time mutually satisfactory.

Peggy was at first skittish about these visitors, but gradually accepted them as members of the family, more or less. Often they would be winging around our heads as we ate; I once counted sixty. We had a good relationship with the wasps: they didn't bother us and we didn't bother them. But it was disconcerting to visitors who seemed to have difficulty focusing on conversation with a score of wasps flying overhead; the guests usually perched on the edge of their chairs, eyes following the cruising wasps, ready to take off if one broke ranks.

Only once was anyone stung, and then by mischance. Peggy opened the kitchen door when a wasp was sunbathing on the knob. She did not blame the wasp, despite a painful swelling (more severe than a bee sting). Only after the wasps increased their numbers unreasonably did we decide that they had violated our tacit agreement and I reluctantly caulked their entrance into the house, terminating our relationship.

Although bees are not inclined to sting unless threatened or protecting their hive, certain things do tend to induce stinging. They are incensed by rough handling and any banging on the hive, jarring of the frames, or loud noises. If caught in hair or clothing fibers they tend to panic and sting; they are put off by the smell of sweat and abrupt or aggressive movements. Conversely, they are attracted by certain bright colors and perfume that must suggest flowers. Bees often drop in on garden parties, probably drawn by curiosity, tantalizing smells, and the prospect of finding sweets. If a party member gets excited and flails away at the unoffending visitor, this often leads to confrontation and discord, the innocent bee maligned as the aggressor. Many bees are needlessly killed because they are feared.

Bees traditionally have a strong sene of proprietary rights, maintaining protective zones around their hives; each colony has its own limit of tolerance, as nations vary in their territorial sensitivity and paranoia. Trespassers have been severely punished for violating these critical areas. Bees are especially irritated by anyone walking or standing in front of the hive entrance, blocking the flight path of foragers going to and coming from the fields.

The distance defended around a hive depends on several factors: whether there is brood, if a honeyflow is in progress, the size and condition of the colony, the weather, the time of day, the colony's general temper, and the guards on duty at any given time. How quick sentries are to challenge or sting interlopers varies from hive to hive, and possibly from bee to bee, although I have no documentation that one bee is more vigilant or stinger happy than another.

Each colony seems to have its own limits of tolerance, so spatial sensitivity seems to depend less on individual judgment, personal irascibility, or neuroses than on some kind of hive mandate or consensus. Some colonies attack when intruders venture within a few feet or yards from the hive; others are less aggressive. Horses and other domestic animals have been stung for grazing too close to hives. In one case a pony was nipped by a touchy bee, presumably offended by the animal's proximity or body heat. The startled pony lashed out and kicked over the hive. Enraged bees stormed out and stung the animal to death. I have no idea how many stings it takes to kill a horse, but about three hundred are said to be fatal to a human being.

Nature apparently decided that for bees to deliver a lethal jolt of venom they must, as in all other matters, act in concert. A bee acting alone, in almost any enterprise, is largely ineffectual, as nature probably intended. Only as part of the community does she become a powerful and even potentially deadly force. A honeybee can never forget her dependence on group action; alone she dies.

SIXTY-SIX

The honeybee, so bold and fearless in most matters, so ready to sting and sacrifice her life, also has her Achilles heel. While other creatures are controlled by a variety of means, including the giving or withholding of food, whips, clubs, spears, cages, habitat destruction, traps, poisons, chains, leashes, guns, longbows, quarantine, sterilization, tranquilizers, seduction, kindness, training, and breeding, bees recognize none of these restraints but are easily subdued by a few puffs of smoke from burning embers.

The fuel can be anything that burns and smolders, usually scraps of decaying wood, bark, chips, or strips of burlap soaked in saltpeter and dried; dried sumac is preferred by many beekeepers because it produces a "cool" smoke not considered injurious to bees. The chosen fuel is burned in a funny-shaped can with an attached bellows and a funnel-like opening for the smoke to pour out in a directed stream. The problem with smokers and their fuels is that they tend to go out when needed the most and it is disconcerting to try to relight a smoker with hundreds of agitated bees, stingers at the ready, flying around your head.

There are many theories about how smoke affects bees. The common belief is that it suggests fire, and as soon as bees are exposed to it they run to their combs to gorge on honey in case they have to make tracks and start over elsewhere.

Some claim that bees are not inclined to sting when full of honey because their stomachs are so extended that it is difficult for them to bend their abdomen for a good shot. Others dismiss this as nonsense, holding that when bees are full of honey they are in a good mood and not inclined to sting.

A third theory is that the smoke stupefies bees so their senses are temporarily numbed and normal responses blunted. Smoke does undoubtedly disorient bees; if given too much they are so placid that a day's production can be reduced or lost altogether. Beekeepers use the minimum amount of smoke necessary to control their bees. Smoke is used for the protection of the bees themselves, to clear combs or a super so they will not be smashed in working the hives. Extreme care must be taken not to damage the queen with too much smoke, or get the bees so upset that they ball her.

Smoke must have a traumatic effect on bees, psychologically as well as physiologically. Remember that bees live in perpetual darkness in the hive. Remove the cover and there is a sudden burst of brilliant sunlight that must be much like having the roof of your house abruptly ripped off at night with a powerful light beaming in.

Bees are especially upset if the hive is opened when the weather is cold or damp and their brood might chill; they respond in the only way they know, charging toward the source of danger, ready to sting the invader, their sole means of protest and protection. If intercepted by bursts of smoke, they turn tail and take refuge among the friendly, reassuring frames of comb and honey, standing by to protect their threatened home, ready to sacrifice their lives if necessary.

I do not pretend to know how smoke affects bees, but I have observed an odd reaction to it. If the smoker is left unattended, smoke barely curling out of the funnel, the bees show great curiosity about it, as they do about any unusual activity or new equipment near their hive, and hover over the plume of smoke. I have seen several suddenly dart into the mouth of the smoker to die in the flames. How is this fatal attraction for that which repels and kills to be explained?

The effect of smoke on bees may be more profound than we suspect: fire is considered one of the original elements of life, part of the heritage of all life, embedded in instinct. The sun, itself a mighty inferno pulsing deep in space, provides energy and largely controls the rhythms of life. When exposed to smoke, bees are responding not only to an immediate danger, but to events that go back millions of years in time and strike deep memories that have slipped beyond our reach, as we have fallen out of touch with most forces of nature.

While smoke is the most reliable means of subduing irate bees, there is a little-known defense that is an even more effective way to escape avenging bees. It is to take refuge in a dark place. Bees will not venture into darkness except within their own hive; like most other species, they fear the unknown and the darkness with the mysteries and threats that lurk within.

SIXTY-SEVEN

*W*ithin the great commonwealth of fear administered by nature, bees have their share of enemies. They are preyed upon by others but prey upon none themselves, prized for their flesh by some, for their honey by others, a few merely wanting to move into their hives for shelter and warmth. Their primary defense, as in all things, consists of acting in numbers, compared to the individual techniques of offense and defense that abound throughout the insect world, a world of hunters and hunted, kill or be killed, eat or be eaten, of strange symbiotic alliances, parasitism, indifference, and ingenious strategies but most of all ancient enmities in the unending and deadly struggle for existence.

E. O. Essig describes some of the armaments and defenses employed by insects, pointing out that "for some 250 million years insects have been able to flourish on land and water, in Arctic barrens and tropical jungles, in deserts and grassy prairies because they have developed special and wonderful adaptations to meet all the varied conditions of this earth. Not just a few but literally thousands of species, representing practically every order, live together in nearly every ecological niche.

"They have survived so long without being greatly altered in size and form or reduced in numbers. In direct competition with all other higher forms of life on land, they stand supreme in numbers of species and individuals. Only some lower microscopic forms like bacteria may outnumber them."

Their survival, he continues, is based on many qualities of insect fitness:

> . . . the hard, elastic, tough exoskeleton with its powers of renewal and its resistance to corrosive chemicals; the many pro-

190 · William Longgood

tective devices, such as rugosities, hairs, spines, and scales, as well as the folded wings; the many legs; the ability to lose and even to regenerate certain appendages without greatly interfering with life and reproductive processes; the protective waxes, resins, and offensive glandular materials; poisonous body fluids and gases; stinging hairs and other devices; the specially constructed living quarters in plant tissue, in water, soil, debris; the enveloping and protecting cases of wood, earth, waxes, paper; the webs, cocoons, spittle, nests, galls; the internal parasitic habits on other hosts; the innumerable other means of protection and of escaping natural enemies through the complicated processes of development; the methods of escape by protective coloration and mimicry, death feigning, jumping, snapping, and flight; the aggressiveness exemplified by ants, mosquitoes, bees, wasps; the ability to bite and sting; the ability to reproduce in such numbers as to overcome almost every opposing factor, even including larger animals and human beings. . . .

The list of bee enemies is long, and includes woodpeckers and some other birds, opossum, hedgehogs, shrews, moles, toads, frogs, spiders, wasps, ants, termites, rodents, squirrels, skunks, bears, and polecats. One of the more treacherous foes of bees is the crab spider, which crawls into a flower where it lurks in ambush; when a bee enters, the spider sinks its fangs into the bee, sucks out her life juices and casts out the dry husk.

The digger wasp is an even more imaginative and formidable predator, known in Germany as the *bienwolf*, or bee-wolf, according to von Frisch. She pounces on a honeybee about to enter a flower, sinking her stinger in the bee's soft throat, then "clasps that part of the bee's abdomen which contains the honeybag, squeezes out the nectar it contains through its mouth and consumes it." Having dined, the digger wasp carries the paralyzed bee to her underground nest where she parasitizes it; digger wasps are known to line up a half-dozen paralyzed bees and lay a single egg in just one of them. When the egg hatches into a maggot-like larva, it systematically eats up all of the bees placed at her disposal, their bodies preserved by the wasp's fatal venom, like so much fresh meat.

Kingbirds, martins, and swallows are notorious killers of bees, accounting for large numbers of victims taken on the wing. Toads lurk under hives waiting to devour the unwary, ill, or old who have been expelled, as well as workers who make navigational errors or arrive overloaded and miss the landing board. The greater wax moth, previously discussed, can devastate a weak hive. Skunks scratch on the front of a hive until bees come to investigate and are devoured in large numbers; these wily predators can be such a menace that wire fences are sometimes erected as protective barriers around hives.

Bears shot by hunters have been found with their mouths and throats matted with stingers after robbing bee nests. The invisible webs of spiders are a menace to bees and other flying insects; spiders leisurely wrap the snared victim in silk filaments, as if tying it up, then inject their own venom, dissolving the bee's flesh so the juices can be sucked out.

Ants and mice nest in hives, and in some cases are tolerated as tenants if they confine themselves to areas away from the combs and not in contact with the colony; in the south ants may viciously attack and ruin hives. Mice do great damage, chewing combs, stealing honey, and building a nest for the winter, a mouse equivalent of going to Florida for the cold months; a strong hive will sting an invading mouse to death, but the corpse is too big to move so the bees cover it with propolis, like a tomb, and go about their business as if it didn't exist.

Wasps and hornets bent on stealing honey occasionally tangle with bees, but a single wasp can usually defeat a single bee by stinging it to death with no ill effects to the wasp. Epic battles have been witnessed between marauder wasps and defending bees. As mentioned before, bees do not go to the aid of a comrade being mauled or slaughtered, but stand by as if uninterested, or like spectators at a sporting event. This is another contradiction of bees; usually they will attack anyone who injures one of their members.

Strangely enough, if the worker guard is killed, another takes her place. A wasp may slay a half-dozen valiant sentries before finally being worn down and killed, or fighting its way into the hive to help herself to the honey. How to interpret this? Why isn't the single wasp invader simply overpowered by several bees and dispatched at once?

I can't believe it represents some kind of sporting instinct or a sense of fair play among bees. Nor is it reasonable to think it is a bee equivalent of the Kitty Genovese syndrome, witnessing a tragedy without intervention or summoning help.

The only explanation I can offer, and I admit that it does not satisfy me, is that it represents another of those fatal optimisms on the part of the observer bees, that she won't be called to combat, or a type of fatalism often observed in nature and not understood by those of us who feel compelled to give meaning to that which may have no meaning in human terms.

Bees are also subject to many diseases, including the deadly bacterial infection foulbrood. As the name suggests, it kills brood, causing a violent stench; foulbrood spores can live on for years, reinfecting new colonies, but they do not affect the quality of honey for human consumption. Diseased colonies usually must be destroyed, their hives disinfected or burned. Foulbrood is prevalent and feared by beekeepers, so contagious that it can be passed from one colony to another by a beekeeper working his hives, and can wipe out whole apiaries. Many beekeepers are reluctant to gather swarms for fear they will introduce foulbrood in their own colonies, and routinely feed their bees antibiotics to prevent the disease.

Man also must take his place as an enemy of bees, the biggest honey thief of all. But his greater offense is the "progress" he unleashes, the most destructive force on earth, with its deadly blanket of pesticides that wipes out all forms of life, "pest" and ally alike, developments that cover the earth with a smothering carpet of concrete and asphalt, industry that degrades the environment and defiles all life. It is estimated that, of about ten million species of plants, animals, and microorganisms in the world, some two million will be wiped out by the year 2000, mostly because of man's interference with the environment. Each time a species goes under there is a break in the chain of life, some link that nature deemed necessary forever lost. Edward O. Wilson, a Harvard biologist, calls this "the folly our descendants are least likely to forgive us," one that will take millions of years to correct.

In this recital of bee enemies, I have saved for last the strangest of all, a whimsical relationship bees have with plant lice, which are not really lice but flies that gave up their wings to become parasites *(Braula coeca)*. These tiny spongers live among the fine hairs on a bee, roaming about at will; when hungry they migrate toward their host's head and, clinging to her mouth, tap her on the lips with their legs, the spot where bees tickle one another with their feelers when they wish to be fed. The host bee obligingly opens her mouth and exudes a drop of honey, apparently duped by nature and her louse guest. The louse takes her fill without so much as having to sing for her supper or a proper thank you and returns to gamboling about in the bee's bodily hairs until time for the next meal. It is disconcerting that a bee is so easily taken in, but I suppose a louse must eat too, although I can't figure out what nature had in mind with this odd arrangement; it seems to give the bee nothing and ruins the louse's character.

While the hijinks and skulduggery presented here are reprehensible, nature is full of deceit, treachery, and subterfuge. But can we be too harsh on this assemblage of scoundrels, kidnappers, assassins, vandals, parasites, scavengers, predators, degenerates, freeloaders, knaves, assorted villains, and other rascals when they are almost a mirror image of our own society?

SIXTY-EIGHT

*F*or the bee, honey is the ultimate reality. It represents the fulfillment of her life mission, the triumph
over her enemies, the continuity of the hive, the justification
for working herself to death. Honey is to bees what money in
the bank is to people—a measure of prosperity and well-being.
But there is nothing abstract or symbolic about honey, as there
is about money, which has no intrinsic value. There is more
real wealth in a pound of honey, or a load of manure for that
matter, than in all the currency in the world. We often destroy
the world's real wealth to create an illusion of wealth, confusing symbol and substance.

Honey, through the ages, has been used in some odd ways.
In ancient Burma corpses were steeped in honey until money
for the funeral could be raised and then the honey was scraped
off and reused, presumably eaten. The Assyrians smeared their
dead with beeswax and buried them in honey. Honey, as noted
previously, has been found in the tombs of the Egyptian pharaohs. It is mentioned frequently in the Bible.

Unfortunately for the bee, honey is also her pitfall, as wealth
often is for those who pursue it as a goal in itself. The lure
becomes greater than the reward. The bee is ultimately the
dupe not of her enemies or managers but of her own instinct.
She will continue to gather nectar as long as the last drop is
available, just as the avaricious person relentlessly and unceasingly accumulates wealth. The bee works unceasingly from
the time crocuses appear in the spring until the last goldenrod
is ravished by frost in the fall. This is what makes beekeeping
possible: the bees' appetites for honey and the security it represents. Bees are like people who make their living in tourist

areas. Both could have the same motto: "You have to make it in the season or you don't make it at all."

SIXTY-NINE

C apped honey must be one of nature's most noble expressions, representing the bee's true genius, one of earth's masterpieces of practical art. The supers are heavy with drawn-out comb, each surface a creamy white texture like fine linen, the capped hexagon-shaped cells exuding the fragrance of flowers, fields, and everlasting summer; honey is the essence of the bees, the sum of the work, dedication, lives, and deaths it represents.

By chemical analysis, honey consists of simple and complex sugars, which form up to 99 percent of its solids, along with traces of iron, salts, phosphorus, manganese, lime, sulfur, albumins, fats, waxes, formic and mallic acids, nitrogenous pollen, and some complex digestive enzymes capable of such useful feats as converting starch into malt; it is said to be the only food that requires no digestion and passes directly into the bloodstream.

Approximately 17 percent moisture (one-fourth of the original nectar from which it is derived), honey comes in a wide range of colors, flavors, and textures. It varies from white or nearly colorless to red-brown and almost black. Dark honeys generally are considered more nutritious, having a higher protein and mineral content. Flavor extends from mild to bitter, with intermediate stages of fragrant, aromatic, medicinal, and even objectionable. Most honey is sweet, requiring less of it than sugar in baking; the scent, like the flavor, varies with the flowers from which it was produced.

Honey varies in the proportion of sugars and other elements that compose it, chemical activity, and viscosity; it may be thin, light, or thick, depending on moisture content. Heather honey, produced in Scotland, is so thick that it will not run out of a bottle held upside down, or so I have read. Buckwheat honey, found extensively in the Midwest and considered a delicacy, is also thick and has a relatively high protein content.

Honey will keep almost indefinitely if stored properly, but the higher the temperature, the greater the loss in flavor; if not pasteurized (heated at a temperature of up to 160 degrees Fahrenheit) it tends to crystallize. I have no objection to crystallized honey and prefer it as a spread; the less tampering done, the better, in my opinion, but that is personal taste. Most commercial honey comes from clover, which is mild in flavor; clover is known as "the bee plant." Wildflower honey is darker than that made from clover and has a stronger flavor.

Most of the honey I get comes from shad, locust, and blueberry blossoms in the spring, wonderfully delicate in flavor and light in texture, but I rarely share in this early crop as the bees use it to raise brood. Any surplus that falls to me is generally produced in the fall, primarily from goldenrod and asters, which form a delicious full-bodied, strong-flavored honey.

Honey's unusual properties are believed to be due to the enzymes supplied by bees. These catalysts change the nature of sugar, producing some complex sugars not found in the nectar of flowers but formed in honey. Enzymes begin working on the nectar as soon as the foraging bee takes it into her mouthparts and honey sac. Upon returning to the hive with her load of honey, she transfers it to a house bee and takes off for another load.

The house bee, in turn, takes the nectar into her body, adding more enzymes and continuing the curing process, depositing it in a cell to ripen through evaporation. Bees have an uncanny knowledge of scientific principles, spreading a small amount of the nectar in several cells, rather than filling one, so there will be more exposed surface to speed evaporation. They are so wonderfully efficient and knowledgeable in their business that, if crowded for storage space, they will simply spread a small amount of honey on the upper portion or "roof" of a cell in which an egg or larva resides below, making the cradle do double duty. Bees will not cap honey until it reaches the proper limit of moisture; otherwise the honey is said to be unripe or green and tends to ferment. Beekeepers generally use no more than 10 percent "green" honey or they risk spoiling the entire lot.

Honey is acclaimed as a health food, consumed extensively by people interested in nutrition and athletes as a source of quick energy; it is used in infant formulas and fed to babies, old people, and those with digestive problems. It has about sixty-five calories per tablespoon, compared to forty-eight for sugar, and is widely used in cooking, to sweeten beverages, and as a spread.

Most bees are kept by backyard hobbyists. Of about 500,000 beekeepers, only 1,000 earn their full livelihood from bees, but 50,000 beekeepers own 80 percent of 5,600,000 colonies in the nation, according to the United States Department of Agriculture. More than 260 million pounds of honey are sold annually in the nation, representing an industry large and powerful enough to receive federal subsidies in the form of price supports. Professional beekeepers, usually a conservative lot, seem to have made their peace with this form of the dole. I do not know how the bees feel about it.

Honey has wide commercial application in facial lotions, skin conditioners, and other cosmetics. It was once believed to carry disease organisms but experiments proved that, instead, it has antiseptic effects; it now has many medicinal applications, including use on wounds and burns to promote healing, and is said to absorb moisture from bacteria so they die. It allegedly helps prevent anemia by increasing the hemoglobin content of blood; produces less growth of bacteria than sugar, reducing the number of dental caries; and aids in the retention of calcium—all claims that I take and present on faith.

Honey is often acclaimed as a miracle food. Several years ago it had a tremendous fad as a cure-all when taken with vinegar—the famous "Dr. Jarvis cocktail," named after its inventor, Dr. D. C. Jarvis. Millions of Americans began and ended their days downing millions of gallons of the Jarvis cocktail, swearing to its curative and euphoric qualities and to its power as a restorer of youth and virility, a fad that ultimately went the way of all fads.

The most unusual claim I have encountered for honey appeared in my bee newsletter, a correspondent reporting that a tablespoon taken before bedtime will stop bed wetting. I assume this is not a problem of bees and that they take honey for its life-giving qualities; certainly it seems to serve their needs well enough, providing the energy to work themselves to a premature death.

SEVENTY

If a colony is strong and there is a good honeyflow, a single hive may produce a surplus of 50 to 200 pounds of honey per season. Hives in a favorable location, in a good year, average about 150 pounds. The biggest surplus ever recorded for a single hive in one season, according to my *Guiness Book of World Records*, was 404 pounds.

These figures are more remarkable when it is considered that a single worker bee during her entire life collects only about one-tenth of a pound of honey, and then only if she keeps her nose to the old grindstone day and night and doesn't fall prey to all of the mishaps she is subject to. One pound of honey represents some fifty thousand miles of flying, enough to wear out the wings of the most staunch worker. A gallon of honey, I have read, will enable a single bee to fly one million miles, but I am not sure of the significance of this statistic, although it is impressive.

An average colony brings in four or five pounds of nectar a day during a honeyflow, but in an especially rich area of pasturage the figure may rise to twenty pounds; the record high is said to be a phenomenal sixty-six pounds, which suggests overachieving and possible nervous breakdowns among the overworked bees.

Some beekeepers keep their hives, or at least one, on oldfashioned spring scales, the type once used in corner grocery stores, to measure daily performance, a primitive type of timemotion study. I'm sure this is handy in helping to keep track of how the harvest is going—rather, coming—but I somehow find it depressing, another step in treating bees as a commodity rather than as a part of nature.

The most honey I ever harvested was about one hundred pounds, and that came from four hives. I never "push" the bees for production and I live in an area of poor pasturage shared by several beekeepers. In the fall each hive must have about sixty pounds of honey to carry it through the winter, or the bees will starve before new supplies can be made in the spring. After they put aside what they require, I take any surplus. If they do not accumulate enough honey for their own needs, they must be fed, a kind of bee welfare.

It is a wonder to me that bees never get discouraged by the repeated theft of their honey. What is it that keeps them working after their own needs are met? At no time do they seem to say, "That's enough to see us through the winter. Time now to knock off and take it easy. There's more to life than work!"

But no, they are like the corporate executive who works nights and weekends, refusing to take vacations or time off, long after he has acquired more wealth than he could ever use; the bee too is a compulsive worker, as driven as her human counter-part, well named a worker. She could have the same motto as the human overachiever: "Never rest, never be satisfied with what you have accomplished." It is, for both, the Protestant work ethic gone amok.

Wild bees, unlike their managed, domestic cousins, have built-in limits, the size of the nest or dwelling determining the amount of honey that can be stored, and production must cease when they run out of room to put nectar; nature seems to protect them from their own overdrive. But in the modern hive, with its movable supers and frames, avarice and industry go hand in hand. As long as bees are willing and able to work, their keepers remove full supers and replace them with empties to be filled, and the bees must start all over again.

There is no end to it. The bees keep producing honey until cold weather cuts down its source, and their bodies are worn out from overwork. They get no credit or admiration from me on this score. They are like their counterparts, the super-charged corporate executives, overworking not because they want to but because they must.

SEVENTY-ONE

A honeyflow is spoken of as if it were a single iso-lated event, but in truth, spring, summer, and even the lingering warm days of autumn in favored regions consti-tute a continuing honeyflow, as one type of bloom gives way to another. In good years this is a period of plenty and great euphoria among the bees. Fields of buckwheat, clover, or wild-flowers burst into bloom, acre upon acre of riotous blossoms nodding on delicate stems in the sensual winds of summer, perfuming the air and intoxicating the senses of bees, other insect foragers, and humans alike.

In a given area there may be but one floral outburst or several in succession as the season progresses. Nature staggers this sequence of birth and death, each succeeding wave of flowers sending the bees into renewed rapture and activity, but there is no suggestion of chaos or disorder in the hive as the scented liquid pours in, merely an intensification of the industry always present when nectar is abundant.

A colony's territorial demands during a honeyflow, as at all other times, are modest, not at all like the wolf who marks the perimeters of his domain by urinating on bushes and trees, or man with his fences, barriers, and signs to discourage trespassers and markers to delineate the amount of land surface he controls. Bees do not insist upon exclusive rights in the area, sharing any pasturage available with their neighbors. There is no competition among bees from different hives or the various species plying the fields; this is true whether there is a shortage or wild explosion of blossoms. All recognize the same law, that the bounty is to be shared by all.

The only limitation or advantage is individual willingness to work, each forager moving busily about her task, unmindful of others. Bees at this time are not inclined to sting, as if they haven't time for such distractions and can't afford any weakening of their efforts by the needless loss of workers. They are never so placid, even gentle, as they are during a honeyflow; it is possible to go into the hives with the use of little or no smoke or likelihood of getting stung. This is the golden hour, the moment of truth. Do they have revels or rites to celebrate the beginning and end of a honeyflow?

As the stream of nectar flows into the hive and is converted into honey, the comb is drawn out farther, if there is a shortage of storage space, until, finally, the swollen vats can be extended to hold no more. The bees, after working all day, fan all night until the honey is ripe. The final step is capping the cells with wax. If young bees can't produce wax fast enough, the colony takes comb from elsewhere, usually the unused outer frames, leaving huge holes that may or may not be repaired later, or they may chew up foundation to resolve the immediate crisis. Bees always have their priorities in order.

A honeyflow may last a day, several days, a week, or longer, depending on the nature of the blooming plant and on the weather. Here, bees take the pessimistic view, assuming that such prosperity can't last and they must make hay, or honey, while the sun shines. In this way they are philosophers, recognizing that good fortune is not to be trifled with but must be savored to the fullest while it lasts.

SEVENTY-TWO

*B*ees, in their passionate pursuit of honey, led scientists to pose a question that baffled them: How is it that the honeybee is able to find nectar in the field, return to her hive, and direct other bees to share her discovery? By what extraordinary power of communication are they able to accomplish this feat? The answer was long in coming, but the mystery finally yielded to two forces: the invention of the observation hive with its glass walls, enabling investigators to watch bees go about their normal pursuits, and the keen perception of Karl von Frisch, a German professor of zoology, who translated the language of the bees into what he called dances, winning for himself in the process the Nobel Prize.

For years it was known that bees had a method of communication, but it was not understood until von Frisch discovered that forager scouts report their finds to the colony through a series of movements which send others scurrying to collect the treasure. This is considered one of the most astonishing achievements in all of nature, speaking an intelligence independent of instinct. The information conveyed in the dances is so precise that foragers are able to fly directly to the food source by the shortest route, even if it involves a detour, as if they had a road map.

The food dances have the same intensity and form as the swarm dances previously described, but are somewhat different. Basically there are two movements. The first, called the round dance, consists of the scout running in a circle over the comb; this lasts about a minute, signifying that nectar is nearby, within a hundred yards of the hive, and foragers have only to look for it. The dancer could be saying, "You can't miss it!"

The second, known as the tail-wagging dance, is more complicated, the directions more involved, because the food source is farther away. Here we have not a single round circle, but two narrow semicircles, as if the two orbs were pushed together with a straight line connecting them in the middle. The dancer runs in a narrow semicircle, suddenly stops, and continues down the straight center line to the starting point; she then runs in the opposite direction (something like following a figure eight) to the starting point. This may continue several times, first right, then left, right, left. As the dancer heads down the straight line, she wags her abdomen, or tail, rapidly. Researchers recently found that the wagging movement is accompanied by a sound but its significance is not known.

The wagging dance signifies the presence of nectar from one hundred yards away up to the two-mile range in which bees usually forage; beyond this distance there are no known dances and the explorer is on her own, such flights involving considerable risk. The most remarkable aspect of the wagging dance is that it tells the bees how far they must go and the direction to travel; the dancer uses the sun as a reference point, traveling straight up the comb if the nectar lies in the direction of the sun, to right or left if it is to be found there.

The pace at which the dance is done also plays a role in the directions. Using a stopwatch, von Frisch determined that the number of times the dancer runs down the straight line of the semicircles to reach the starting point in a fifteen-second period signifies the distance to be traveled. Bees were found to possess such an acute sense of time that each could be carrying her own watch. At first it was thought this was based on sunlight or solar rhythms, but von Frisch concluded that timing relies on some kind of internal mechanism that is not understood.

By timing the dancers, investigators were able to plot mathematically the distance to the food supply. The directions were so exact that if there was a blockade or barrier the bees would detour around it, compensating for time lost, and go exactly to the point indicated on a "bee line," as it were, no mere idle figure of speech. Von Frisch, not generally given to extravagant statement, calls this "one of the most wonderful accomplishments in the life of the bee and indeed in all creation."

The experiments became increasingly complex, testing the bees under the most difficult conditions. Food dishes of differing substances and varying sweetnesses were set out at different places; investigators extended the distance and moved the feeding stations about, marking the bees to see who went where and with whom, and even tried to confuse them with stratagems never found in nature. One of the more unexpected revelations was that if food was placed at precisely graduated distances each day, eventually the bees were waiting for it to appear at the mathematically designated spot based on previous moves; the bees could have been a soup line waiting for the handout to appear. The bees had plotted the investigators in the same way that the investigators had plotted the bees. Who was studying whom?

The dancer does not go through her gyrations in the darkness of the hive alone, but is trailed by foragers getting directions, crowding behind her, touching her with their feelers. The bees get wildly excited: the more abundant the supply of nectar, the more energetic the dance and the more stimulated they become. Some get so charged up that they can't wait for the end of the dance and take off before the dancer finishes, reminding us of impetuous individuals we have all known.

Scouts reporting a nectar find do not depend on giving directions by their movements alone, but may bring with them the scent of the flowers which clings to tiny hairs on their bodies, especially adapted to retaining the fragrance. The trailing bees touch the dancer with their antennae, those wonderfully sensitive instruments made up of a dozen joints covered by a forest of tactile hairs and thousands and thousands of pore-like olfactory receptors, enabling them not only to receive scent but to perceive the shape of objects as well; researchers have no idea how scent enables a bee to help determine the shape of an unseen object. The scout may also bring back a sample of the nectar to help in locating it if there is more than one type of flower available in the area. The trailing bees demand a taste and, if denied, they may attack the dancer; the whole thing gets very emotional.

The sweetness of the sugar in the nectar is reflected in the intensity of the dance, some nectars being sweeter than others, superior in sugar; the sweeter the sugar, the more ardent the dance and the more persuasive its effect. A dancer bringing in weak nectar goes through motions without much spirit or enthusiasm, as if saying, "This stuff isn't much, but if you want to give it a try, go this way . . . and when you get to. . . ."

If the sugar level drops too low, regardless of how plentiful the blossoms, dancing ceases altogether, as it gains momentum if the level is high. By this simple device the number of foragers is increased or reduced in direct proportion to the yield, and always the amount and quality of the nectar coming in determine the amount of brood being raised; bees, unlike man, never have a population that exceeds the food supply.

Because scouts who discover superior nectar dance with more vigor, they are able to attract more foragers, which von Frisch calls "summons by degree." A bee, he says, is able to say accurately and firmly: "Today the richest crop is to be found where there is plum-blossom scent." This serves the double purpose of attracting the greater number of foragers and ensuring pollination of the largest number of flowers, consequently assuring the most abundant production of seed; once more bee and flower serve one another in their symbiotic bond.

The dancing bees have a second language, one of scent; each worker has a scent organ, sometimes called a "scent bottle," consisting of a small, almost invisible fold near the tail; it is described as a pocket-like organ that can be turned out at will "in the form of a damp, glistening pad," releasing a scent secreted by special glands lining the pocket. This is the same gland with which bees summon laggards into a new hive to which they are being introduced, turning tail and fanning toward the others.

Upon finding nectar, a bee can turn her scent pocket inside out, releasing the fragrance and thus attracting other bees to share in the discovery; the scent is so pervasive that it can bring bees from a great distance. If the scout decides that a food source isn't worth the bother, she keeps her scent pocket closed.

Bees also have a pollen dance, much like the nectar dances, but scent plays a lesser role, as pollen has little or no scent. The scout reporting a pollen find returns with a few grains as samples, but she also may bear a particle of the blossom from which the pollen came. Nectar foragers pay no attention to the pollen dances. Only those who gather pollen follow the dancer and share her excitement.

The language spoken by bees is universal, the dances much the same from one country to another, but the bees speak in different "dialects." The shape the dance takes represents different distances; in Australia, for example, the round dance indicates flowers 275 feet away, while in Italy it represents 120 feet, as if the form is the same for all but each "nationality" had to work out the details for itself.

While we marvel at the genius of the bee and her wonderful

dances, we are reminded once more that bees, like people, are not alike. Not all are attentive when the dances are performed. Some do not follow directions. They may search far afield after a round dance directs them to a nearby food source, stay nearby following a wagging dance, or go off in the wrong direction altogether. Von Frisch wonders if they might have misunderstood the language. Or are they stubborn nonconformists going their own way?

No, he replies, asserting that whatever the reason for this "wrong" action these eccentrics also have their own use. If a field of blossoms is located in the north, it is desirable to dispatch foragers there as quickly as possible, but at the same time there may be a similar or better yield elsewhere. "Thanks to the eccentrics who do not follow rules, all possible sources of food are quickly brought to the notice of the bees."

This is worth pondering. Does nature in her wisdom intentionally produce noncomformists, or find a use for them, enlisting their disparate talents in her service? Is there a place for everybody, a reason for everything, and we fail to understand some underlying cosmic logic? Do acts that appear the most senseless to us have a rationale that we fail to appreciate? Are what we consider errors and mistakes really part of the grand design? How encompassing and integrated is the mosaic of life? Just how big and complex is this world that we define so freely and understand so poorly?

SEVENTY-THREE

Bees, for all of their accomplishments and good works, have a shortcoming common to most life: they are only as virtuous as need be. Until now we have, for the most part, held bees up as models of rectitude, but they too have a moral flaw. A colony will often turn to stealing when there is no honeyflow, usually in the fall, and nearby hives that are weak have honey more or less for the taking. Such hives are, in effect, poorly secured vaults bursting with wealth begging to be heisted.

Beekeepers can contribute to corrupting their colonies if, through inexperience or carelessness, they leave honey exposed while working their hives, presenting a temptation seldom resisted even by the most upright colonies. The temptation is increased if there is no honeyflow or a poor harvest has left inadequate winter supplies.

The ever-practical bees recognize this lack of principle in their kind and most colonies take measures to protect against marauders. When honey stores are built up, the number of guards is increased and the troops are on a war alert to repel trespassers, in the same way that weak colonies with inadequate stores are ill tempered and inclined to sting; the strong and the weak are equally dangerous, but for different reasons.

Robber bees, sensibly, prefer defenseless and weak victims; nature does not burden most of her charges with scruples. She gives them an appetite and a means of appeasing it and sends them on their way to work things out among themselves. Compared to other creatures of the earth, bees get along together better than most. They do not try to monopolize the flowers in the fields, but recognize them as common property, available to all, first come, first served. Bees have enemies, as we have seen, but bees do not attack unless they are attacked or threatened. For the most part they do not prey upon one another, a common practice throughout nature; when this does happen, it is for a sound, practical reason: hive economics.

It implies a moral posture to use the term robbing. In nature, where force and guile dominate, stealing is a fact of life, enabling the sly and quick to live at the expense of the industrious and dull. It is probably less compensation for other shortcomings than part of the evolutionary process enabling the fit to dominate and live at the expense of the less fit. That which we call robbing is simply another survival strategy, a means of evening things up a bit between haves and have-nots, in the competition among unlimited applicants for limited resources.

Honeybees are not inherent thieves but usually turn to robbing by chance events, sudden opportunity for quick riches, necessity if their own survival is threatened, or the temptation of effortless gain. Most robbing is sporadic and impetuous, ending quickly, as the weak hive is wiped out or the invaders, usually from a neighboring hive, are driven off and peace restored. But some colonies, once exposed to the quick and easy rewards of theft, are likely to take to the primrose path as a career, looking for victims, like brigands living off their neighbors.

It is no more possible to explain why some colonies turn robber and others remain straight than to tell why some people succumb to temptation while others resist. But who can deny that it is easier to steal than to drudge unceasingly, that it must be more appealing to a bee to steal honey than to visit thousands of flowers and fly long distances for a smidgen of raw nectar that must be processed into honey, when the finished product is to be had for the taking.

It is undeniable that the rewards of theft are more effortlessly obtained than those procured by hard work. Honesty, for all its acclaim, does have its limitations and disadvantages. To the credit of bees, they do not resort to moral subterfuge when the strong plunder the weak, and expediency or need takes precedence over live and let live.

SEVENTY-FOUR

Robbing appears to be a mechanism to eliminate the unfit, but when bees turn to robbing as a way of life the mechanism itself seems to have gone awry. Robber bees, however, do not approach their task with the confidence of agents assigned a vital role in preserving or uplifting the species. Rather, the lone robber bee is diffident, suggesting more a guilty conscience than a swaggering freebooter after loot.

Picture a day in early fall. The hive was weakened by excessive swarming and never recovered sufficient strength to lay aside enough honey for winter. It is ripe for theft and destruction. Weakness of any kind, in nature, is a terminal affliction. On this day foragers are out looking desperately for additional supplies. A single sentry is posted at the hive entrance; there is little to guard. All available hands are needed for field duty to find whatever nectar exists.

A worker from a neighboring colony has been out searching for nectar, without success, and is returning to her hive. She notices the poorly secured fortress and decides to investigate. Conducting herself like a professional thief "casing" a job, she alights upon the landing board and tires to stroll past the guard, acting innocent, as if she is a member of the hive, perhaps has lost her way or is paying a visit to a friend. It is a poor performance; she is nervous and furtive. She bears no honey and has an unfamiliar smell. The sentry is not taken in by her subterfuge. She knows this visitor is an imposter, not bent on honorable enterprise or a victim of error but simply a cutthroat attempting to look respectable. This, we assume, is due more to lack of confidence than guilty conscience; honey is where you find it.

The guard rushes up to challenge the imposter. Instead of taking off, the robber bee casts subtlety and pretense aside to make a bold dash through the entrance, pursued by the frantic guard who is calling for reinforcements. But there are only young and inexperienced house bees around, a kind of home guard, without experience in worldly chicanery and possibly not yet full grown. The invader climbs the comb, engorging herself with honey, while the distraught victims pull and tug in an effort to dislodge her.

Eventually the interloper is wrenched free and escapes, the occupants too demoralized and weak to stop her. This is a fatal mistake, as the invader soon will return with her fellow brigands. But flight is not easy for her. She is so heavy with the stolen honey that, upon taking off, she dips dangerously low to the ground before gaining altitude for the homeward journey; her hive is only a short distance away.

There she spreads the good news. She does a round dance, passing out tastes of the loot. This is finished honey, not nectar that must be processed, to be had for the taking. The dancer says, in effect, "Follow me!" The bees are wildly excited.

Do the victims know the assault is coming? They must. Are they desperately preparing fortifications? Sending couriers to summon home the forager-warriors from the fields? Is there panic? Resignation? A foreknowledge of their fate? If they do know or suspect what is coming, what can they do about it? They are like a force under siege awaiting the fatal attack, powerless to prevent or blunt it; they can only wait.

The attack comes soon enough. The invaders are excited and bent on loot; murder is incidental to the mission. They are experienced fighters and far outnumber the defenders. Right may be on the side of the defenders, but right is no match for greed and strength; here, might is right, and nature is ever on the side of superior strength. The combatants circle and collide in aerial combat, defenders and invaders tearing at one another, claw to mandible, on the landing board, even on the ground. Reason is gone; there is only the battle.

If two strong colonies clash, there will be heavy casualties on both sides. But this is no equal struggle, despite the agitation and roar of battle. Robbing is sometimes mistaken by novice beekeepers for the play flights of young bees in front of a hive. If a beekeeper is drawn to the battlefield, he can cool the combatants down with a fine spray from a hose, or he can reduce the entrance of the hive under attack, leaving less area to be defended. But it behooves him to be careful. Anyone getting near the fracas will likely be stung.

The fighting is as ferocious as it is disorganized, an uproar of buzzing confusion, winged bodies darting, dipping, swooping. There are no ranks, lines, or recognizable maneuvers, no organized attack or counterattack. All wear the same uniform.

There can be only one ending here. The powerful raiders force their way to the combs. They fill themselves with the sweet booty, carrying it to their hive to return again and again for more. The departing robber bees are so heavy with honey that they must climb up the front of the hive to gain elevation so they can take wing, a telltale sign that robbing is under way.

Darkness falls. The ground is covered with fallen warriors, the slain and mutilated dying. Later, creatures of the night will feast on their remains, and all of the honey, so painstakingly gathered over the summer, is now in the hive of the feasting robber bees.

SEVENTY-FIVE

A danger in robbing is that a colony which does it successfully, now and then, may turn to theft as a way of life. Once bees turn robber, the only corrective measure is to introduce a new queen and hope the following generation is more virtuous and doesn't acquire the bad habits of their robber nannies. But it must be conceded that virtue doesn't add one bit to the taste of honey.

I search in vain for some home truth or moral homily to condemn the robbing incident previously described, but I confess that I am not able to come up with one. It is nature's way of working things out to her own advantage, if not that of both adversaries; in its simplicity, brevity, economy, and efficiency, it does seem to have certain advantages over the system nations have muddled upon to settle their more serious disputes. But bees also have their shortcomings, and can be as easily misunderstood and misinterpreted as any human society.

Once I had a colony that was particularly strong and inclined to rob its neighbors. I was forever out spraying water from the garden hose on those brigands and narrowing the entrance to the hive under attack, frequently getting stung for my impromptu interference. Possibly I could have reformed the culprits, or at least improved their character by requeening the colony, but I was as greedy as they. That colony alone produced four supers of surplus honey for me; the others produced none. I was sharing the loot, stealing from them, as it were, more co-conspirator than keeper; they could have been following my example, taking their character from me.

But there was a deeper truth that eluded me: why did this particular colony take to robbing while the others continued to work? What secret of nature lay in front of me that I was incapable of fathoming? Eventually the situation resolved itself: the queen died; she was replaced and the colony departed the primrose path for that of virtue, once more working the fields instead of its honest neighbors, so I guess that is a moral ending, of sorts.

SEVENTY-SIX

A robbed-out, or starved-out, hive is a pitiful sight. In a final, futile search for food, the bees stick their heads into empty cells and die there. The handful of survivors are demoralized, making no effort to remove their dead or clean up the hive; they huddle together, a forlorn little mass, waiting for death or deliverance. Deliverance rarely comes.

Almost inevitably a wax moth will invade the stricken hive

to wreak her mischief, at first surreptitiously, and when not attacked, she begins to lay eggs in the combs. The eggs hatch into caterpillars that tunnel through the wax, feeding on it and leaving trails of silk as they advance. The larvae spin webs among the damaged empty cells to prepare beds in which to pupate. Finally, the once-splendid combs bursting with brood and honey are defiled with moth larvae, festering and evil smelling, little more than tangled jungles of webs, pupating moths, and dead bees.

The amazing thing is that a package of new bees can be introduced into a hive that has been ravaged by moths or abandoned to its own despair. Dead bees will be dragged out, old wax clippings swept out, and the eggs and larvae from wax moths destroyed. Within a few days chaos has been transformed into order, and a new city is under way.

The predators and destroyers that we call enemies are as important to natural processes as the progenitors of life. In the natural world there are no ends. There are only intermediate stages along the way from one form or expression to another, the chain of life so tightly woven that there is no finality. The great wheel never ceases to revolve: birth, death, renewal. That which we call destruction and death is, to nature, not an ending but a new beginning. Thus it is with the bees, as with man and all creatures, their habitats and the complex support systems undergirding them, all interrelated and indivisible.

SEVENTY-SEVEN

In the great cycle of the season, winter is a time of rest for bees, a time of renewal, a time to prepare for spring and another summer of toil, a time to glean the honey that will enable generations of yet-unborn bees to subsist through the following winter.

The nights become progressively colder. Workers leave the hive later in the morning and work only during the warmest hours of the day. Only a few hardy flowers now remain, opening their petals later and folding them earlier. One night there is a killing frost and thereafter the fields are brown, with dead blossoms clinging to lifeless stalks.

The days become shorter. Fewer bees now remain to search for propolis to seal the hive against drafts and winter's chilling blasts, a practice inherited from their wild bee ancestors, now without much meaning in modern hives, but still printed indelibly in the memory of domestic colonies.

To have as many young bees as possible to resume the work of the hive come spring, the colony continues to raise a small amount of brood right up to the first killing frost; these autumnal bees will live until spring when new brood is started, providing a continuity of generations, and who knows what traditions and wisdom may be entrusted to them to pass along?

The bees born in late fall will live up to six months, unlike their sisters of summer who worked themselves to death in four to six weeks; then they too will die to be replaced by succeeding generations that carry on the work of the hive. Individual lives are brief, but the colony goes on and on, a flowing river of life.

SEVENTY-EIGHT

$\int$t is one of the imperatives of nature that nothing remains constant. Climates change. Mountains erode. Rivers embark on new courses. Deserts and forests march and retreat. Ice flows melt. Seas rise. Volcanoes alter the land-scape, their debris darkening the sky and dimming the sun. Tidal waves and storms chew relentlessly at the shores. Islands rise and vanish. The mighty plates undergirding the conti-nents are themselves ever in motion. The grain of sand was once a boulder. A new Atlantis may even now be impercepti-bly vanishing into the deep, or an old submerged and van-quished mountain may be preparing to reassert itself.

Many of these changes are initiated by nature, some subtle, others gross. Many are speeded up or impeded as natural pro-cesses are disrupted or destroyed by man; all of life must accommodate to these changes or vanish. Bees, too, have marched to the drum of change; they are now found in north-erly areas where they formerly could not survive, often main-tained artificially.

Winter is not an easy time for bees, especially in the cold northern climes where they normally would not migrate in large numbers, if at all; their more natural habitat is farther south where warmer weather prevails. Bees, so far as is known, do not require challenges, a need to expose themselves to physical hardship to prove themselves, or to show their mastery over natural forces. When introduced into extremely cold regions, nature's usual dynamics are disrupted and man takes over with his artifices, and the bees must make the best of it.

In far northerly latitudes, where bees are not yet acclimated, they must be prepared for winter, protected by blankets of insulation wrapped around hives, barricaded by stacked bales of hay to shelter them from freezing winds, or even moved into climate-controlled cellars, row after row of hives stacked up like city apartments.

In most areas where bees have been introduced or migrated, such heroic measures are not required. But beekeepers can never agree about the amount and type of winter protection neces-sary. Some contend that the more bees are protected, the more warmth and activity there will be and the more food con-sumed, thus increasing the risk of starvation; others hold with equal conviction and logic that the colder the environment, the more honey must be consumed to generate the heat necessary for survival, thus increasing the threat of starvation. I have no special insights into this issue. Colonies have lived and died under both conditions; the survival rate of the opposing theories, like most conflicting opinions, is higher than that of the subject of dispute.

It is an article of faith among beekeepers that cold alone, within reasonable limits, will not kill bees, but dampness and chilling will readily do them in. Proper ventilation is considered the most important aspect in winterizing, along with having enough food. Colonies have been known to survive even when hives have been overturned and the bees exposed to snow and storms; as long as there exists sufficient honey and adequate ventilation to remove excess moisture, most colonies will survive in climates where they have been introduced or recklessly migrated of their own free will.

Many beekeepers in the northeast, like myself, winterize their bees by protecting them with a few inches of fiberglass insulation in a super placed on top of the two deep hive bodies, raising the cover slightly (with thin strips of wood) to provide ventilation. The only other preparation is to reduce the entrance, more to keep out mice than to prevent cold winds from entering. Domestic bees, unfortunately for them, must live or die with the experience, skill, dedication, and prejudices of those who manage them.

SEVENTY-NINE

*W*inter begins officially for bees when the hive temperature dips to approximately fifty-seven degrees Fahrenheit. They cluster in the usual spherical mass, clinging to one another for warmth. By now the food chamber is filled with honey so there is no room for them there; the cluster forms in the top of the lower hive body, where the center combs have been left, free of honey for the winter nest.

Immediately above and all around the cluster is stored honey that will provide food during the cold days ahead. This is really quite remarkable. Consider that people experience winter, year after year, and draw on that experience to anticipate and prepare for the cold in advance, but no bee in the hive, with the possible exception of the queen, has lived through a winter; if the colony was requeened in the fall, or even the spring, none has ever been through a winter.

Despite this lack of knowledge or experience the entire colony has made a concerted effort since spring to prepare for winter. Even bees never born before the hot days of summer give themselves fully to the effort. How do they know how to prepare for a future that they have no way of anticipating? How is this knowledge, this dedication to a blind cause, transmitted? Is it imprinted in the genes? Is it the mysterious force called instinct? Is it, possibly, conveyed from one generation to another in some form of language, chemical signals, or symbols unknown to us? How little we really know about the life all around us. Would we be so cavalier and ruthless with it if we understood it better?

EIGHTY

Bees do not hibernate like many other creatures, sinking into a deathlike sleep, vital processes slowed until they almost cease. Nor are they like mammals who live off of fat accumulated in their bodies during the summer. They are also unlike most insect species that exist only as eggs during the winter; they differ from their cousins, the solitary bees and the female bumblebees, who snug into a winter shelter, usually some hole in the earth, slipping into a deep torpor, arousing themselves occasionally to dip into the tiny honey pot prepared in advance, then sinking back into a slumber-like state until beckoned by the gathering warmth of spring.

Bees have developed a unique and ingenious system of climate control that enables them to adjust to the outside temperature; in this way they are the opposite of people, who must alter their immediate environment to make the surrounding air conform to their bodily needs.

In cold weather, bees fall into a semi-torpid state, more dopey than dormant, arousing themselves or becoming more sluggish as the ambient air temperature rises or falls. Being cold-blooded, their body temperature tends to be the same as that of the surrounding air. They adapt to wide temperature variations; this enables them to survive northern winters, but they will die if exposed individually for any length of time to a shade temperature much below forty-two degrees. In this, as in all other aspects of life, they are interdependent; their highly developed social organization alone makes it possible for them to survive winters. By huddling together in a mass, they are able to generate enough heat collectively to remain alive, even to raise small amounts of brood while the weather is still cold.

The secret of this self-regulating temperature mechanism is the size of the cluster. It responds almost like a thermostat; the colder the weather, the tighter or smaller the mass in order to hold the heat inside, as people huddle together tightly to conserve body heat, a or sleeping cat curls into a tight ball to keep warm. The smaller the cluster, the less surface is exposed to the surrounding cold; consequently there is less heat loss and less energy is required to maintain a constant temperature.

The cluster automatically contracts as the weather gets colder, and expands as it becomes warmer. In the coldest weather, bees mass so tightly that their cluster is only about the size of a small coconut; it seems inconceivable that so many bees can squeeze into so compact a ball.

Before winter strikes, bees empty honeycombs in the center of the hive, enabling them to form a nest there, surrounded by the vital honey. By then the colony is reduced in number; if it were at full summer strength, there would be neither room nor food for all. And yet, if the colony becomes too small it cannot generate enough heat to survive.

In preparing for winter, the bees must carefully balance their number so it does not exceed the food supply, but they also seem to know whether winters will be long or short and to adjust to that. When they do not have enough food to carry them through an extended winter, the fault generally is that of a greedy beekeeper, rather than bad judgment or mismanagement on the part of the colony.

EIGHTY-ONE

Nature has evolved fairly precise temperature ranges in which bees can survive; they can tolerate and adapt to outer limits of about 42 to 120 degrees Fahrenheit in the shade, becoming stiff and immobile at a temperature of 50 degrees. When the hive temperature drops to approximately 57 degrees, the colony clusters and begins to generate heat. It has a built-in biological thermostat almost as fine-tuned as any mechanical device made; sensibly, bees make no effort to warm unoccupied parts of the hive, which would be as wasteful as heating unused rooms in a house.

Experiments have shown that air surrounding the cluster is about the same temperature as the air outdoors. The only energy crisis bees recognize is a lack of food, which is to them as oil, coal, or other fuels are to man; the primary reason for insulating hives is not to keep out the cold, but to prevent sudden chilling of the colony, especially the vulnerable brood, when the weather changes abruptly.

The temperature at the center of the cluster is never less than about 75 degrees. The outer shell, regardless of outdoor temperature, remains about 44 to 46 degrees; bees at the surface of the cluster could not remain alive long at a temperature much below the critical 42 degrees, so those on the outside of the cluster keep working their way in toward the center.

This inner migration of bodies forces the bees in the warm interior out toward the cool surface in the usual communal spirit of equal treatment for all, another manifestation of interdependence and that the welfare of one is the welfare of all, in sharp contrast to competitive human societies that refuse to recognize the universal need for mutual reliance; in this way bees have it all over us.

A bee with a full sac of honey can live up to sixteen days, about the time it takes to make her way from the chilling perimeter of the cluster to the warm center. Is this coincidence or calculated logistics? Is the food supply geared to the length of the journey, or the length of the journey geared to the food supply?

If bees on the outside surface of the cluster run out of food and are not able to reach the center for a prompt refill, the inside bees relay emergency stores of honey to those in need, passing it along from "hand to hand." This is not a form of hive welfare or kindness, but in the self-interest of all; each individual must have enough food to help provide heat for the collective warmth of the colony, to remain alive as part of the protective heat source and the nucleus that will survive until spring.

The queen is always kept warm and protected at the center of the cluster, where the temperature may be sixty degrees warmer than the ambient air in the hive. If the temperature at the surface of the cluster dips to twenty-seven degrees, bees exposed to it for any length of time will die. But that, fortunately, is rare in the areas where bees have colonized or been recruited without their agreement.

EIGHTY-TWO

Winter deepens. Snow falls and drifts, providing an insulating blanket of its own, deep yet fluffy and porous enough for air to penetrate the covered hive entrance. Icicles form on the edges of the hive cover, aided by the sun and warmth from within; they melt and form again in bizarre and artistic shapes. But the constant activity of the bees clustered between combs of honey inside generates enough heat to withstand the wintry blasts.

When additional heat is needed, the bees tug and pull at each other to stoke up the temperature, as any exercise raises body temperature. If the weather turns extremely cold and extra energy is required, bees at the center of the cluster fan their wings to generate additional heat, as their now dead sisters had fanned in the summer to stir up air currents to cool and ventilate the hive. This is less paradox than similar means being used in different seasons for different ends, as a fan can move and refresh the air in the summer and distribute heat in the winter.

The top of the cluster always remains in direct contact with the combs of honey above. As the overhead food supply is consumed, the colony keeps moving upward, never breaking ranks; when the bees reach the top of the hive and no more honey remains above, they must wait for a warm spell to recluster under full combs and start the upward march again.

At times, however, the weather refuses to cooperate and this can lead to disaster. The bees reach the top of the hive with no more food above them; rather than break the cluster and risk chilling the queen at its center, the entire colony may starve to death with honey on all sides, now victims of the same instinct, rigidity, and wisdom that have preserved the species through the ages. Instinct can betray in the same way as can intelligence. The tragic death of a colony under such circumstances is reminiscent of the recluse who starves to death in a miserable hovel with a fortune hidden under the mattress he dies on.

A colony that is wiped out by winterkill, or suffers severe losses, is a pathetic sight, especially if starvation is the cause. Dead bees are found with their heads poked into empty cells in a final desperate search for a last drop of honey. On the bottom board are hundreds or thousands of dried corpses mixed with wax cappings. Only a few bees may remain alive, and they are disoriented and doomed, living their time out while surrounded by the mounds of their dead comrades. There is no queen, and therefore no brood or young bees in the hive, so there can be no rebirth or hope.

It would seem logical by human standards for the few survivors to flee this city of death and throw their lot in with a nearby thriving colony, but that is not the way with bees. They stick to their own hive until the end, clinging to the sinking ship, as it were.

The remaining bees make no effort to remove the dead or restore order, a task that must seem monumental and futile; in this respect the bees are realists. The few survivors huddle together for such warmth and protection as they can give one another until it is no longer possible to sustain life.

I had a colony decimated in this way. In the spring I cleaned out the dead and put the hive in order as best I could, and fed the survivors sugar water, turning the hive into a kind of bee hospice. But, oddly enough, each morning the few remaining bees would dash out as if they were living a normal purposeful existence, going to the fields, and at night they would vanish into their ghost city of empty combs. One day I checked the hive and found no more bees. On the bottom board were a half-dozen shriveled bodies. I brushed them out and the hive was ready for the new tenants who were already on their way to take over.

Bees not only have a need for food and warmth during the winter, but must get out of the hive periodically for a "cleansing flight" to eliminate accumulated bodily wastes. Without such relief they may develop a form of dysentery, caused by the infectious parasitic organism *Nosema apis*. The dreaded nosema, as it is known by beekeepers, can wipe out an entire colony or devastate whole apiaries. It was with one of these cleansing flights that our story began.

When the temperature reaches forty-five to fifty degrees in the shade, bees may break their cluster to take brief cleansing flights, particularly if they have been confined for a long period. A few venture out when the temperature is below forty-two degrees, but they fly only when the sun is shining brightly and then at great peril. Bees risk death by chilling rather than soil their hive; if the weather turns abruptly colder, or if the chill penetrates a flying bee's body, she may plunge to the ground and perish, another sacrifice to the hive's welfare.

EIGHTY-THREE

Winter continues. Storms come and go. The cold intensifies and abates. More bees die. Eventually the corpses form a mound on the hive floor. Conscientious beekeepers periodically poke a thin stick or wire through the narrow entrance to make sure there is a free flow of air for ventilation and the reduced entrance is not clogged with dead bees or the accumulation of frozen wax cappings from opened honey cells. The number of dead bees is an indication of how the colony is faring.

Living in man-made movable hives, bees are deprived of the natural protective mechanisms that serve them in the wild. Living in hollow trees and other quarters of their own choosing, they usually get along quite nicely without help. Once installed in hives, however, they are like people living in condominiums; they may be comfortable, largely oblivious of the weather and external conditions, but at the mercy of those who service and care for them.

If, in checking or "sweeping" his hives, a beekeeper makes too much commotion, a few vigilant guard bees from the surface of the cluster may charge forth to see what is going on. They encounter the frigid air outside and plummet into the snow, a final fidelity to duty that costs them their lives.

The winter cluster is the bee's true genius. Most other insects die off in the fall, new life emerging in the spring from eggs or chrysalis. Did nature devise this unique method for bees to overwinter so, with no loss of time to develop, they could immediately begin their essential task as pollinators of the first blossoms? For the bees it must represent a chance to get a leg up on the competition, while at the same time serving nature; in this, as in all things, with all creatures, bees are nature's servants.

EIGHTY-FOUR

Relief finally comes with the January thaw. The temperature suddenly soars to sixty degrees. The sun shines brightly, giving the snow a dazzling glare; bees fairly burst from the hive, flying in great wheeling arcs, joyful as young bees on their first play flight, rejoicing in their liberation after long confinement.

Soon the pristine snow is soiled with brown splotches of excreta around the hive. Other bees, already relieved and returned to quarters, are busy with housekeeping chores, dragging out corpses to drop them over the edge of the landing board, sweeping aside wax cappings, and restoring order. The wonderful organization is once more apparent. There is no bickering over who does what, whether status and jobs are matched; all join in doing what needs to be done.

The sun suddenly slips behind a cloud; the temperature drops almost as abruptly as it rose. When it reaches fifty-seven degrees, the bees again resume their winter cluster, but now something new occurs: already brood is appearing in a small patch of comb in the protected center of the nest. These bees, remember, have not experienced spring, and yet they are preparing for it. Are we to believe that some deep, inherent optimism is one of nature's legacies? Not really. A more mechanical, more extraordinary explanation is offered. Once more we have the principle of the thermostat regulating a life process.

Researchers formerly believed that additional hours of daylight induced the queen to start laying eggs in mid-winter, but now a more complex reason is suspected: when bees are unable to get out and relieve themselves, feces build up in their intestines, making them restless so that they move about more. This added activity raises the temperature of the cluster; when it reaches the range of ninety-two to ninety-six degrees; the queen automatically starts laying, only a few eggs at first, no more than the cluster can cover and keep warm. The massed bees can maintain a temperature of ninety-two degrees in the center of the cluster, even when the outside air is below freezing.

The days turn warmer. Now the cluster is able to expand, making it possible to enlarge the brood area; the queen lays her eggs in an ever-enlarging concentric circle, the form retained throughout the season. Beekeepers take advantage of this mid-winter egg laying by feeding their colonies as early as January or February, depending on location and climate, providing them with a thin mixture of sugar water that resembles the consistency of nectar.

Once more the gullible bees are deceived. Thinking it is a premature honeyflow, they start feeding the queen the sweet mixture, stimulating her to start laying more eggs in the frames of honeycomb now empty of honey. Young larvae are fed royal jelly by older bees whose shriveled glands must be reactivated to provide the vital secretion. By what new miracle does nature make possible this biological adjustment?

Older larvae are fed bee bread, composed of the pollen stored in combs the previous summer mixed with honey and the mysterious elements in saliva; if there is not enough pollen put aside to raise brood from this artificial stimulant, the beekeeper may seduce the bees by feeding them a pollen substitute, primarily composed of a mixture of powdered milk, brewer's yeast, and soy flour, for protein, mixed with honey and served in the form of flat cakes placed on top of frames above the cluster. As soon as real pollen is available to foragers, this artificial offering is rejected for the real thing.

By the time spring arrives, the hive is already full of young bees ready to carry on the work of the hive. Older workers that survived the winter rapidly die off, and the new generations take over in the universal rhythm dictated by forces that know neither beginnings nor ends.

EIGHTY-FIVE

*B*ees are one of our few remaining links with unspoiled nature. They have not changed fundamentally, so we are told, in millions of years. They are still harbingers of spring and couriers of summer, as they have always been. In our increasingly mechanized and sterile world they remind us of sunshine and flowers, of gentle winds, of the soft rustling of grass and leaves. They move with exquisite grace among the petals of flowers and, while watching them, we briefly experience a sense of harmony and unity with our own forgotten beginnings.

The world itself has changed while the bee has remained constant. Many of earth's natural contours have been moved this way and that, gradually by natural forces, and abruptly, often violently, by man's powerful machines, like a child's sandbox and its ever-changing form. Many species of plants and animals have been wiped out or are endangered. We have degraded the earth and defiled the air, destroyed habitats, and disrupted delicate and irreplaceable ecosystems, imperiling the base on which life rests. We are at war with nature, although we call it by euphemistic names: development, growth, progress, and that overused phrase "the bottom line," which places profits above all else

Wildlife, once abundant, now exists primarily on game preserves, in cages, and in zoos, prisoners of war, as it were; we are doing to wild creatures what we once did to the Indians, confining, squeezing, exterminating. It is said that the first settlers fell upon their knees and then upon the Indians and the trees; in attacking wildlife and nature, we are, in effect, "falling" upon ourselves.

The loss goes deeper than decimating wildlife and degrading the environment; we have forgotten our own origins in the artificial world we have created. We have traveled far from the country people of Europe, peasants mostly, who had a personal relationship with their animals. Bees were considered members of the family; if a beekeeper died, a black ribbon was attached to his hives, an ancient custom known as "telling the bees."

A few years ago British papers published a picture of a young country bride, dressed in her wedding finery, standing beside a beehive, whispering, "Little brownies, I am getting married." Country people had many superstitions about bees. Not to tell them what was going on in the family was believed to bring bad luck; if a swarm landed on a dead plant, a member of the family would die. Such beliefs seem quaint to us, but represented the bond between people and nature.

I compare these notions and way of life with an incident involving a New York couple I knew, both professionals, middle-aged and successful in their fields. They visited friends in the country, and a summer storm at night—brief, violent, and beautiful in its intense fury—terrified them; the cry of a loon on a nearby lake was further unnerving. The unbroken and unaccustomed darkness was as frightening as the terrors that came out of it, and the couple lay awake all night, the lamp burning beside them; at first light of dawn they headed back to the safety of the city, with its high-rise apartments, crowded streets, tangles of automobiles, lights that obliterate night, and the predictable urban threats and dangers.

Do such people represent a new direction in our lives? A new dimension? Are they a new breed embarking on a new evolutionary path that eventually will be incorporated in our genes, further estranging us from our origins? Will our only link with the natural world be a geranium on the windowsill, a canary or parakeet in a cage, subservient dog or cat (declawed and neutered), both creatures as removed from nature as their masters, an apartment in a condominium warren with artificial climate controlled by thermostat, superinsulated walls with sealed windows and air exchangers, a television screen to sense the world, and a computer to manipulate the unseen forces they live by? Are we so far from that now?

We have become increasingly dependent upon machines. Does the ubiquitous computer represent a response to a newly created need in our technological revolution, a mechanical equivalent of biological progression on our part? Have we become so confused and alienated by the distortions, complexities, and fragmentation of the world we have created that we have an almost mystical attachment to the computer and lesser machines under the illusion that by controlling external elements we will bring more order into our lives and have some control over our uncertain fate? Already we, as a people, relate better to the computer than to nature, which we have so largely forsaken.

The bee represents a sanctuary, a constancy lost from our lives. Even in the island of asphalt and tall buildings, to city parks, roof gardens, and exposed house plants comes the bee, one of nature's last emissaries, perhaps stirring some neglected part of our being, or, more likely, being swatted and killed in panic as a reminder of terrors that lie buried in the human unconscious.

The bee is domesticated but not tamed. She has not recognized man as her master; he subdues, manipulates, and beguiles her into working for him, but the bee remains what she has always been, part of nature, a part of ourselves forever lost, part of the joy and sadness in the long march from an unknown beginning toward an unknown ending, like man himself, part of the great inconclusive experiment called life.

EIGHTY-SIX

This, then, is the end of my story. Whatever errors or omissions I am guilty of, I plead no want of diligence or lack of dedication to truth. Perhaps bees, in their diversity and perversity, perform the same tasks or functions differently at different times and places and under different conditions for different observers; they are not so easily tricked into surrendering their secrets and revealing their innermost thoughts and intimate relationships. If I am guilty of presenting facts or figures at variance with those stated in other studies, by other writers, or based on different observations or wisdom, I blame it squarely on the treacherous bees.

Those who seek absolute truth or universal order and consistency in beehives, as in all things, are almost sure to be disappointed, as those who look beyond life's capabilities will find their undoing in dreams. Life is not made up of absolutes, but of half-truths, compromises, falsehoods, misconceptions, misrepresentations, the semblance of truth masquerading as truth itself, the shifting sands of change and differing perspectives, of imposed reality tempered with illusions and tinged with sorrows.

A book, like a person, must be measured as much for what it attempts as the degree to which it succeeds or that which is dismissed as beyond its limits or reach. I have made no effort or pretense here to explain the how-to of beekeeping; there are already many excellent texts available and no want of experts better qualified than I to write more, if needed.

In the beginning of this work I noted that it was primarily about the honeybee, but its greater ambition was an appreciation of her role in nature. If the next time you, reader, see a bee going about her business, and you pause to ponder the complexity and importance of her mission and life, the universal miracle and mysteries she represents, I will have succeeded in the task I set myself.

DEBTS AND THANKS

Many unseen hands and unidentified voices contributed to this book. Hundreds, possibly thousands, of people have written about bees, and their observations and thoughts have largely composed the base of factual information that I drew from and built upon. I acknowledge and express my thanks to those anonymous contributors. Others were named and quoted in the text; their observations and insights were invaluable.

I have a special obligation to several individuals who played more immediate roles: Pam Johnson, an old and cherished friend, did an exquisite job with the cover and illustrations; she was a logical choice for the artwork because of her talent, her love of nature, and her sensitive portrayal of it. Jim Mairs, vice-president and editor with W. W. Norton & Company, and his associates, made this book possible. I am especially grateful to him for his excellent suggestions without ever attempting to dictate the direction or content of the work. I am similarly grateful to others at W. W. Norton who did the design, read copy, corrected proofs, and performed the numerous other unsung tasks woven into processing typewritten manuscript into book. My wife Peggy read copy for me, made helpful suggestions, and was steadfast, as always, in giving encouragement and support. Winnie Lubell, a fellow writer, put me in contact with Jim Mairs. My son Bret, as noted, inadvertently got me started with bees. Dr. Charles Davidson, a friend and neighbor, made his nature library available to me and took time to chase down obscure leads in unlikely volumes. Finally, there are the bees themselves, the real authors of this book, who provided their enduring and hopeful message of life.